Bound by Fire and Fuel

Nora Kensington

Published by Nora Kensington, 2024.

Copyright © 2024 by Nora Kensington
All rights reserved.

No part of this book may be reproduced, distributed, or transmitted in any form or by any means, including photocopying, recording, or other electronic or mechanical methods, without the prior written permission of the publisher, except in the case of brief quotations embodied in critical reviews and certain other noncommercial uses permitted by copyright law.

This is a work of fiction. Names, characters, places, and incidents are either the product of the author's imagination or used fictitiously. Any resemblance to actual persons, living or dead, events, or locales is entirely coincidental.

For permission requests, please contact the publisher at: nora.kensington.author@gmail.com

PROLOGUE

Isabel

What a bastard! — I screamed internally, cursing that vile bastard.

I didn't get this far to hear that. He couldn't be serious, could he? I was confused and did the only thing I could think of at that moment. I tore his check into pieces and threw it in his smug face. My blood is Spanish, I act impulsively and on the heat of the moment in all areas of my life. I know I might regret some of my actions, but I will never regret this one. I know "never" is a strong word, but as long as I breathe, I don't want a single penny from the man standing in front of me.

"You can swallow that check of yours, Lorenzo River Nolan!" I yelled, my blood boiling with rage.

"I knew you'd make this difficult for me, you're so proud that you can't see beyond the tip of your nose." I grabbed my purse and, indignant, left that place before I couldn't answer for myself.

He was terribly mistaken to think he could buy me like that; I never needed that, not even from my own father, let alone from the man who got me pregnant. Deep down, I knew he would do something like this, a check, and that was it. I know I was reckless to stay with Enzo, he's a first-rate womanizer who can't take anyone seriously. But damn, the man is handsome, charming, and sexy; I fell for his charm.

Despite everything, I want to have this child, and I won't give that up, not even my studies and the dream of being a traveling doctor. I don't regret the decision to raise my child alone and make do just as I saw my mother do all her life. I knew she would support me, she wouldn't leave me alone like this; despite thinking I was impulsive, she wouldn't judge me because she knew I would give my best to everything I pursued in life. I would never give up on my dreams for anything in the world. I would make it happen, even carrying a baby in my belly. There was nothing that could make me give up once I set my mind to something. I wouldn't stop until I got where I wanted to be.

I knew it wouldn't be easy, especially being pregnant, single, and so young. I would have to work hard, but my mother wouldn't let me down, and that's exactly what happened. That was the last day I saw Lorenzo River Nolan's smug face, as I avoided even bumping into him, moved to Barcelona, and focused on taking care of myself, my child, and my mother.

I passed the medical entrance exam at the Autonomous University of Barcelona. Since my grades were very good, I was thrilled to receive a full scholarship. Since the classes were all day, I didn't work while attending university. My mother got a fantastic job as a sous chef at a renowned restaurant, which really helped us pay for our modest apartment. She promised she would hold the fort so I could study and graduate just as I had always dreamed. In the beginning, it was tough, but over time, my mother advanced and was promoted to chef at the restaurant, and we started living better. Dona Inês always loved cooking, and she has a gift; she cooks with love, and everything she makes is delicious, modesty aside. So, I knew it was only a matter of time before she earned a promotion at the restaurant.

Months flew by, and my pregnancy progressed well. I managed to follow the prenatal care, though by the end of the day, I couldn't bear how swollen my feet were, but I kept going. My family needed me, and I needed to pursue my dreams. Despite the tough days, we managed, and that damn check never became an issue. I'm proud of who I am today.

After a tough natural childbirth, because I had never felt so much pain in my life, those contractions are pure torture. But it was worth it to see my little one crying at the top of his lungs, showing what he was made of. My son, Guilhermo García, strong and determined like his mother, over time I noticed his features resembled his father's, but his upbringing would be to have integrity and responsibility.

I graduated in Medicine with honors and started the fight to become one of the most sought-after doctors. It was then, after leaving my mother with Gui, once he was eight years old, that I began traveling from country to country to attend to rare emergencies in both large and small hospitals, just as I had always dreamed. When I saw that it was working, I returned and brought my son with me because I couldn't stand being away from him anymore. I missed him terribly. Every night I cried when I heard his voice on the phone, as well as my mother's, who had never abandoned me.

I faced many challenges during all this time—prejudices and judgments, everything bad you can imagine. But I learned a lot from my work, and the ability to help people when possible is a gift to my life. Leaving my mother in Barcelona broke my heart, when I went to bring my son, I tried to convince her to come with us, but as a true hard-headed Spaniard, she refused and told me to live my dream fully. In the first few years, Guilhermo missed his grandmother, his home, and his friends a lot, but over time, he adapted, and we spent two to three years in each country before moving to another. During this time, we got to know many cultures and languages, and I have to highlight that my son adapted very well to all the changes.

Until we went to Brazil, and my son was already a young man, eighteen years old. We lived in São Paulo and Rio de Janeiro for four years. I always tried to maintain a good dialogue with Guilhermo; we talked about everything, and I didn't hide anything about his father. He knew everything that happened. When he was a child, he understood little and was still very curious about him, missing a father figure, but after he grew up, in our last conversation, he told me he didn't want to meet him. I wouldn't interfere in that; the decision had to be his. I know his father wasn't right in what he did to me, but in the end, he's his biological father.

When I had to leave Rio de Janeiro, I had to leave Guilhermo behind, as he had started university in Automotive Engineering and had formed some bonds. Besides friends, he met a girl he was dating and seemed quite in love. My departure this time was for South Africa, and it involved many years of dedication. With great regret, I left my son in Brazil, promising to visit him.

After some time, I scheduled his visit, and when we met in Africa, we hugged so tightly, he was different, his look was empty and lost.

"Madre!" his choked voice hit me, and my eyes filled with tears. I had missed him so much. It had always been the three of us against the world.

"Mi amor!!!" When I smelled him, I felt at home again. He's my home, and then I heard him cry harder and pulled him closer into my arms. "Gui, what happened?"

"I lost her, madre, and I couldn't stop it" he said desperately, and I gently stroked his hair, furrowing my brow as I tried to make sense of what he was trying to say.

"Lost who? You need to calm down first." I let go of him while keeping him close. I looked into his eyes, and there was so much sadness in them that it made me feel bad to see him like that.

"Mari, she's gone, but I don't want to talk about it, at least not right now. I can't even talk about it" he murmured, his voice still strained, as if he were holding himself back.

"It's okay, mi amor!" I added, kissing his forehead with all my love.

"I'm sorry, breaking down like this, I didn't want to see you like this after so many months."

"I know, don't worry about it. Just come in and make yourself comfortable. Let's talk more while sitting on the couch, and if you want, I can still offer you my lap. You know I'll always be here for you, no matter your age."

"I know that, madre. I'm so emotional, and adding that to the exhaustion from the trip, the homesickness, and everything I've been through these past few months..."

"It's been too much, I understand, mi amor." I quieted him, and he smiled faintly, nothing like the Guilhermo I left in Rio. "You haven't called me much in these months, and I was really worried. I know you have your life, and I respect that a lot, but you can't go without contacting me. No matter what, I need you to call me always."

"Sorry, but these months have been the worst of my life. Can we talk about something else?" he asked with a pleading look. I respected it, and we changed the subject. We talked about my work with the African children, and soon his demeanor changed, and I felt better, although I could still see the shadow of sadness in his eyes. When we are mothers, we know exactly when our children are feeling sad or going through pain; it's a mother's instinct, strong as a rock.

After a few days in Africa, he helped me with some activities, and the children loved meeting him. My son started talking to them about cars and motorcycles, explaining that he was a MotoGP rider, and they got excited about everything he shared. A few more days passed, and he received a call. Even though I didn't know much about what it was about, I felt relieved seeing Gui smiling and excited.

"Madre, you won't believe this!" His joy was contagious, and I felt genuinely eager to know what had made my son so happy.

"What, mi amor?"

"I'm in the MotoGP World Championship!" he shouted, emotional and overjoyed.

"How wonderful and how proud I am, Guilhermo!" I said, and we embraced. That night, we celebrated together as if we were in Spain, dancing and enjoying the news. It had been my son's dream to participate, and he had been trying for some time to get in. Since he was a child, he had been interested in cars, but always loved motorcycles and wanted to understand everything about how they worked. That's why he decided to pursue Automotive Engineering. He opened a shop in Brazil, made some connections, and assembled a team to enter the world of motorcycling. He succeeded and inherited the determination of the Garcías.

I felt so proud of my son, my heart leapt every time I knew he was on the track. After all, it's something with enormous risks, but I pray a lot to the Virgen del Pilar, the patron saint of Spain, to watch over him whenever he went to those competitions, and now I would be even more at her feet.

A few days later, he left me, as he had meetings and many trainings ahead. Guilhermo didn't tell me what had happened with Mari, his girlfriend, but Anita Ortiz, his assistant and best friend, called me to ask how he was doing. She spoke very vaguely about the loss of the girl, which had occurred during one of those illegal competitions, and my heart broke.

Worry took over me, but she promised she would take good care of him, and this is something common in a mother's life: always worrying, especially when your son loves racing on dangerous motorcycle tracks.

Despite all of this, I feel like this story is just beginning, and I will still see my son's name everywhere as the best rider. I will be even prouder of having raised him so well. I never gave up on him or my dreams, and I raised him with these thoughts and values. I knew that Guilhermo García would never disappoint me.

CHAPTER ONE

Guilhermo

"Could you at least leave the curtains closed?" I asked, my voice still sleepy and with no desire to open my eyes; I just wanted to sleep a little more.

"Of course, darling! I'll keep them closed since you don't need to get up for any important appointments." Her sharp voice, laced with sarcasm, was enough to snap me out of my calm state in an instant.

"I can't believe I forgot!" I said, frantic, knowing I was running late.

"Your luck, Casanova, is that I anticipated this and came as quickly as I could after several missed calls."

"Anita Ortiz, you have my heart and all my soul, you know that, right?"

"Stop talking nonsense and get to the bathroom, I'll pick out an outfit for you." She never cares about my declarations, but she knows she's my rock, the one I trust most, the person who manages and supports my career as a MotoGP rider like no one else. The best part is that Anita doesn't back down from anyone who tries to humiliate her, and that makes me admire her even more every day.

I stepped into the cold shower to help wake me up and because I needed to clear my head. The nightmares wouldn't stop and had become more frequent at night. I almost couldn't fall back asleep; it was always the same since she left. I pushed the bad memories away, stepped out of the shower, dried myself off, and when I left the bathroom, I saw that Anita had already laid out my clothes on the bed, perfectly arranged. She's obsessed with organization, a true Virgo who loves everything in its place.

"Guilhermo García, stop thinking about my organization, put that outfit on and move your ass right now." She even seemed to know everything, as she knew exactly what I was thinking. I was always startled by her ability to read my thoughts. I quickly dressed, grabbed my phone, and checked the time—exactly ten minutes to go. I left the hallway and saw her sitting at the table, her computer on, everything ready.

"I've left a glass of juice and toast here for you to eat in ten minutes. You know I don't accept anything going wrong. We've fought for years to get here, and this team is everything to us. Alex and Tenner will also be there. They'll handle the mechanical issues with your bike since they developed it. By the way, they did an excellent job."

"Yes, I agree with you, and I apologize for the delay. The nights haven't been easy to deal with. It's good that Alex and Tenner will also be there." I said, grabbing the juice and toast, eating quickly while she logged into the virtual meeting room.

From then on, we spoke with our new sponsors and the new team. I returned from Africa a week after receiving Anita's call telling me we made it—I couldn't believe it. Before I left, at the airport, my mother told me something that gave me so much hope. She looked at me, holding my face, and said, "Sometimes all we need is to start over, and now you have a new chance to rebuild yourself. No matter what you've been through, it only makes you stronger, mi amor."

That was exactly what I needed to move forward with my life. It had been some time since everything, and the only thing that made me a little happy was being in my workshop or on the track, racing at high speed, feeling the adrenaline seep through my veins, giving me the perfect dose of dopamine.

I couldn't live without riding. It's the air I breathe, where I can truly find myself. That's why I love what I do, and Anita, along with Alex, helped us reach the top. I participated in many dangerous races around the world, and that gave me visibility. I made my name seen, heard, and sought after. The result couldn't have been better. We joined the Wacco Racing Team. I went from 125cc to Moto2, and now to MotoGP. In other words, I advanced and reached where I had always dreamed.

In a few more days, we'll have to travel to Spain, where everything will start again. Getting into a team like this is already a victory, but we want more. The bike for this year will arrive in Spain in a week for testing, and I'll be able to give my input on everything, which is important since I have knowledge of mechanics. Pointing out improvements helps a lot with the bike's potential and consequently improves performance on the track.

After the meeting, Anita and I focused on finalizing the details for our trip and stay in Spain. She got the tickets, and she also arranged for the team to take my bike, as I really wanted to land in Seville and drive to Jerez de la Frontera.

FEELING THE BREEZE at high speed, that powerful feeling of freedom took over me. I'm arriving in Spain in the best possible way. Many would say I'm crazy for leaving a plane just to hit the road, but for me, it's something unique. My mother and I never stayed in one place for more than two or three years. Only in Brazil did we stay for six years because she saw an opportunity to help more people, always following her instincts and the needs of the place.

Returning to Spanish soil felt like coming home, though there was a mix of anxiety and apprehension about facing part of a past I didn't even know on this journey. I only know what my mother told me, and honestly, I don't know if I want to unearth everything, but that's a possibility I'm not considering. Enjoying the road, already approaching Andalusia, on the long highway, a Ducati 1209 passed me by, moving at incredible speed. It slowed down and popped a wheelie, balancing on just one wheel.

I slowed down, very amazed, and then saw that it wasn't a man riding, but a woman. I saw the curls of her brown hair flying even with the helmet on, and the people in the pickup truck next to the left lane shouted and filmed the entire stunt. She took one foot off the bike and placed it on the asphalt, and I can't even explain what I felt at that moment—a mix of adrenaline and fear, something I only experience when I'm on the track. Then she returned to normal riding position and sped up even more in front of me, disappearing from view, leaving me speechless and really curious to know the identity of the woman who was riding so boldly. I was impressed, but I know how dangerous it can be, and the outcome... I'd rather not even think about it.

When I arrived in Jerez, it felt like the first time I passed through there for a race, but this time it was only for three days, and I couldn't stay to enjoy the city. This is the life of a motorcycle rider; we never really enjoy the countries we pass through—it's from the circuit to the airport and then on to the next. Jerez de La Frontera is a municipality in the province of Cádiz, in the autonomous community of Andalusia, Spain. The town is famous specifically for sherry, a type of fortified wine typical of the country, horses, flamenco, and motorcycling.

The city has its traditional charming squares and cobblestone streets, as well as enriching museums. It's a city with a beautiful historical culture, with origins dating back to prehistory. Very charming and pleasant to live in, I would spend the next few days there until the start of the Championship, and then we would move on to the next locations for the races.

When I arrived in the city center, I was waiting for Anita and Alex to arrive with the rest of the team. That's when I spotted a bar across from the main square with red letters that read "NAVARRO, the most traditional and modern bar in Jerez." While I waited, I decided to have some water or juice since it was pretty hot. I knew that the summers here are very intense.

As soon as I entered the bar, I could hear Spanish music filling the air and noticed how cool and complete the place was. It wasn't just a bar; it had a counter with wooden shelves stacked with various bottles of liquor, a dance floor, and a beautiful, well-lit stage with colorful LEDs. It seemed like the perfect place to visit at night. Then I realized that this was the bar of Juan Sanz Navarro's family, a well-known person who had accompanied me in some races.

That's when I saw him enter, taking off his sunglasses and loosening the collar of his white shirt. Juan is tall and very strong, and as soon as he entered, he grabbed a cigar from the counter. When he turned to me, his eyes widened in surprise at seeing me there.

"Guilhermo García, long time no see!"

"You know, it was only after I made the connection between your last name and the bar." We shook hands and exchanged a few pats on the back. I remember how much fun we had in Ireland after the madness that was the Isle of Man TT race, an autonomous community located in the sea between Ireland and Great Britain, one of the most dangerous races in the world.

"Man, you remember our last celebration, right? That race was incredible, the best I've ever watched, actually. But how about you, how are you?"

"It was incredible indeed. I stayed in Brazil for a while after that race, and now I'm here in Spain for the World Championship."

"Ah, there's no way I'm missing that. So, what do you want to drink?"

"No alcohol, it's still early. I just need a cold water. It's so hot here in Jerez."

"It's summer, my friend." He served me water with ice and lemon, and we kept chatting until I heard her voice.

"You already found a bar, didn't you, Guilhermo?" Juan stopped organizing the glasses and fixed his gaze on my agent, Anita, in an intense way. Despite being my friend, my agent, and almost like a sister, she has a unique beauty. Her dark skin and full hair are truly striking, and when she smiles, men can't help but sigh. I've seen her break many hearts; she's a woman who loves to live freely, but I know she yearns for a passionate love story, and she deserves that and much more. Even though she always says otherwise, we can see in her eyes that she longs for someone who can conquer her in an intense and special way.

"I just came for some water, didn't you feel how hot it is here?" I had to cut through the tension between them. "Alex, look who I found here!" I said, turning to my friend who smiled.

"Well, look if it isn't Navarro in the flesh."

"And lots of muscle, darling." Anita added, smiling slightly in a way I knew well, she liked him, surprisingly.

"That's right, pleasure to meet you, I'm Juan Sanz, owner of the bar and buddy of these two who have disappeared on us." he said, pointing to me and Alex. Anita approached him, and they shook hands, locking eyes, until she whispered.

"Anita Ortiz, the pleasure is all mine."

"Okay, okay. We disappeared, but for a good cause. Look, we're here for the World Championship again."

"That deserves a good drink, don't you think?" Juan asked suggestively.

"We'll come back tonight to see the crowd, but right now, I need these two to get some sleep for the meeting we have later."

"Got it, I'll see you both tonight then." He winked at Anita, and we shook hands, smiling. We left the bar and followed the car to the hotel where we would stay until the rented house was ready, as my efficient agent had arranged for us to stay.

As soon as we finished checking in at the reception, we headed upstairs to rest. The trip had been long, and we were tired. And at night, I really wanted to go to Navarro's bar to see the place in action and watch the Spaniards having fun.

CHAPTER TWO

Dolores

"One, two, three, and let's go." They followed my lead, moving to the right, then to the left, flipping our hair forward, ending with a sensual Latin rhythm. "Wonderful, everyone! Thanks for the rehearsal, and that's it for today. The night is already promising. The makeup has already been sent in the group, and we'll be wearing the golden outfits."

"You know how much I love it when you perform in golden outfits, right?" I heard the deep, husky voice of my boss, Juan Sanz Navarro, owner of the bar and my best friend.

"Sí, we'll have flamenco too." He smiled even more and moved closer.

"Is everything okay?" He could always tell when something was off. We've known each other for many years, since childhood, and nothing escapes Juan.

"I can never fool you, huh?" He raised an eyebrow, a look he always gave when he wanted to show he was right.

"Lola, you know that I understand everything about you, and I'll always be here for whatever you need. That will never change; I consider you my sister."

"I know that, it's mutual. It's just that my mother came home after me last night, and I'm worried she's drinking again."

"If you want, I can check with Barbosa. We know that if she started drinking again, she'd go there, to the place she used to frequent."

"You know I'm not the type to be afraid of anything. I've faced everything life has thrown at me, but I thought about checking, and I just couldn't bring myself to do it."

"I completely understand you. I've lived through that, and I know the fear we feel when things might suddenly go back like that."

"I hope it's just a misunderstanding and an overreaction on my part. I thank you for always helping me. Now, changing the subject, I heard the girls saying that we'll have a ball this weekend."

"I'm not even going to respond to the help comment." He furrowed his brow, looking at me seriously, almost hurt. Juan's way is too much; I love him like a brother. "Now, as for the ball, it's something special to welcome a friend."

"What friend? Do I know him?" I was immediately curious.

"You don't know him personally." He said, walking out and heading to the counter. After rounding it, he started organizing the glasses and bottles left from the previous night. "Although he was born on Spanish soil, he hasn't lived here. He's traveled the world, so maybe you've seen him in tabloids."

"You're only going to tell me that, Juan? Are you really going to leave me curious for the rest of the day?"

"How many questions? The only thing is, you'll meet him tonight. I hope River Nolan doesn't show up here, though, because things could get ugly."

"What does Jacob have to do with your special guest?"

"Everything!" That was all he said, leaving me even more curious.

"My God, help us then! I hope he doesn't come; I can't stand his seductive talk with that blonde on his arm. If he only knew how ridiculous he is, he wouldn't keep bothering me, especially after I said no."

"That's like a determination bomb for River Nolan." Juan added, smiling to the side. "He doesn't tire, and the blonde lets him be with whoever he wants. They both preach freedom to each other."

"I have nothing against their open relationship, but for me, it wouldn't work. I hate sharing."

"I'm with you, despite everything I've done in my life." We smiled at each other, conspiratorial.

"Well, this conversation is great, but I need to get to the restaurant. The double workday is just like this."

"Go ahead, good luck and good work." He said goodbye, and as I turned to leave, he called out to me. "And Lola, you'll get where you want, sooner or later." I smiled at my friend, grabbed my things and helmet, and said goodbye to everyone, waving at Juan.

I put on my backpack and helmet. There are three things in this life I love deeply. The first is my family, the second is dancing, and the third is riding motorcycles. It might not make sense to you, but for me, there's nothing better than feeling the wind and that sense of freedom and adrenaline. I mounted my Ducati 1209, which I won in a local dance contest, and started it up. Hearing its engine roar is music to my ears. I backed up and took the road to the restaurant, still wondering who Juan's special guest was and why he had everything to do with Jacob River Nolan.

AFTER SERVING SO MANY tourists at the restaurant and being friendly with everyone, I finished my shift, exhausted, and bumped into a tall, muscular man. His delicious scent hit me. But I couldn't even hear his apology because he quickly walked away before I could say anything. Handsome men are always a danger. I try to stay away from them, I don't stop having fun, but I'm very careful with my heart, and these good-looking guys are walking dangers. They always break hearts wherever they go, and honestly, I don't need that in my life.

I arrived home, and the chaos was evident as I could hear the loud voices of my sisters. Luna was laughing, probably having done something to Olívia, who was retaliating loudly. I wonder where the house owner is, who hasn't put order in with these two, but Mrs. Dulce came home later than I did last night.

"You knew this sandal is mine, why are you taking it? It doesn't even fit you." Olívia scolded her, but Luna didn't flinch under her sister's angry gaze. Luna is bold and faces everyone here at home. Sometimes, I'm the only one who can control her, but I'm not always around since I work during the day, and at night, I can't keep up with everything. Still, I try to help and manage all my responsibilities.

"Let's stop this silly fight. Luna, give your sister her sandal back, you can't wear something like that yet, and you might hurt yourself, my dear." She looked at me with wide eyes, dropped the sandal where it was, and ran to me. I received her with a hug.

"You took too long today, Lola, and it's almost time to leave again. You know I miss you." My younger sister is very attached to me, and honestly, I'm attached to her too. It's as if she were my daughter.

"The restaurant was crowded as always with tourists, but don't worry, my day off is coming up, and we'll go out together. I'll take you to dance with me at the Navarro rehearsals. What do you think?"

"I think that's more than amazing, my Lola!" I caressed her face affectionately and kissed her forehead, then looked at her seriously.

"Now, go clean up the mess you made in the living room. As I've already explained, this is not the place for that. Go play in your room." She agreed and left, picking up each of her toys one by one.

"Oli, how are things going?" I asked my other sister. Yes, I have two sisters. Luna is the youngest, she's ten, and Olívia is fifteen.

"As you can see, I'm managing everything today because our mother hasn't left her room."

"What? Did you check if she's okay?"

"Of course, but she was sleeping every time I went in there, and she refused to get out of bed. Don't tell me she's relapsed?"

"I can't believe this." I fumed, what I feared must have happened, and I didn't know what could become of us.

"Okay." I took a deep breath and exhaled, which helped me think more clearly about what I'd do since I still had to work tonight. "Don't worry, I'll check on her and see what happened." Oli agreed and left, stomping off. I closed my eyes and shook my head, refusing to believe that after so long sober, my mother would let herself fall into drinking again. There's nothing more heartbreaking for me than this. I try to stay happy and strong for my sisters and even for her. Will this ever end, when I finally thought we might have a little peace?

Summoning courage, I approached my mother's bedroom door, put my hand on the doorknob, and tried to listen for any sound from inside, but the silence was total. So, I opened the door and went in. Dona Dulce was lying on her back with her eyes closed.

"Madre" I called out, approaching and gently poking her with my hand. She flinched and stared at me with wide eyes, quickly sitting up too fast.

"What's going on?" she asked, trying to understand, but I was the one wanting to know something since she had spent the whole day locked in her room, sleeping.

"It's me, Dolores, mother!" I said, my voice tired, showing all my exhaustion from the situation.

"What do you want here?"

"Is everything okay? The girls said you've been asleep all day and didn't eat or do anything."

"Today marks twenty-five years, my daughter." She didn't look at me, her eyes remained empty and sad, fixed in front of her, glazed over and filled with tears.

"Twenty-five years?"

"If your father were here, we would have celebrated, and we would not be living like this." She said, and then I remembered it was their silver wedding anniversary. My father was taken by cancer that started in his lungs, and there was nothing more to be done. He was a smoker, and everything we went through wasn't easy. Before I went to Barcelona to study dance, we lost him, and I had to put my studies on hold for the time being. I spent some months with my family and took on the responsibility of helping raise my sisters and taking care of my mother.

"Ah, mi madre!" I whispered and took her in my arms, holding her until she surrendered to the embrace and cried as much as she needed to.

"I know you're worried, but yesterday I went to the restaurant your father took me to. I remember we had a delicious wine, the famous 'sherry.' But I sat at the table, ordered a glass, and stared at it for two long hours, remembering your father's charming smile, our fun conversation. He used to think I was cheerful and full of life. But..."

"Madre, you can still be that woman. He would want to see you like that. You can't let your life go this way. It's been over..."

"I know how many years it's been since he left. I don't want to remember, but today I spent the day counting all the time we couldn't spend in his presence."

"I can imagine what you're feeling, because I miss him every day too, but I keep trying to stay strong and cheerful for you, because I know that's what he would want from us. So, let's get up and make dinner for your sisters. I still have to go to the bar to perform, and they miss you."

"Okay, mi amor! You know that without you, I'd be lost. I don't know what I'd do with my life."

"You know we're in this together until the end. It's the four of us against the world."

"He must be so proud of his girl, wherever he is." My eyes filled with tears, and I felt my chest tighten and my throat burn. But I smiled at my mother, it was what she needed at that moment.

After that, she got up, and I quickly organized the room, opening the curtains and windows so some fresh air could come in. Despite the hot weather in Jerez, the afternoon was getting better with a nice breeze.

My mother hugged my sisters, and they called her to the kitchen. She always liked everyone's help. I did what I could and went to take a shower since my night would still be long. It's flamenco and Latin choreography night, and Saturday nights at Navarro are always busier. On Sunday, I still had to get up early for a rehearsal for the MotoGP World Championship selection. At events with sponsors, they want Spanish dancers for the general performances, and I knew this was a unique opportunity for me.

After having dinner with my beautiful sisters, I kissed my mother affectionately and sent a message to my fellow dancers. I forwarded an audio message to my friends to inform them about the flamenco night at the bar, which always attracts many tourists who want to experience it, and they loved it. I grabbed my backpack and helmet, and left the house. I've always liked arriving early to prepare myself calmly and still go over the steps with the girls.

As soon as I arrived, I parked in front of the bar, in my usual spot. I got off the bike, and a tall man was staring at me. I didn't notice his face, just the scent that, if I'm not mistaken, was the same as the one I smelled earlier when I bumped into the handsome man at the restaurant. But that must have been a coincidence, right? I took off my helmet, shook my hair out, and fixed it with my other hand. I entered through the side door since I didn't want to run into that River Nolan right away. The night hadn't even started, and I needed a little peace to do my two performances.

CHAPTER THREE

Guilhermo

We arrived at the hotel, and I went straight to take a shower since I was tired from the long trip. When I lay down on the soft, fragrant bed, I relaxed a bit with my eyes closed and remembered her. Mariana would have loved to visit Spain, especially Jerez. I could almost hear her laugh because I didn't know anyone more joyful than Mari. She lit up everything around her with an incredible, contagious energy.

I ended up falling asleep, thankfully, because whenever I thought about her, I couldn't sleep. I woke up to my phone ringing and vibrating on the nightstand next to the bed, and of course, it was Anita. I answered while rubbing one of my eyes and putting the phone to my ear.

"Did I wake you up?" her question sounded more like a statement. She knew me too well.

"Yes, how did you know I could sleep here?"

"Of course, you were exhausted. It's good that it helped you sleep."

"At least that's something, right?"

"You need to move on. I know it's not easy, but you have to keep going, at least try."

"I know that, but it's not that simple."

"Just allow yourself to relax a bit. I know you can only do that when you're on your bike, but take advantage of this Championship for that too."

"Okay, okay, I'll try!"

"Great, and count on me and Alex. Speaking of him, are we going to Bar Navarro?"

"I knew you wouldn't take long to ask about that. For your happiness, yes, we're going. Juan told me tonight is flamenco night, and I love watching it."

"I'm excited to see the performance, but I won't lie, I'm really looking forward to seeing the owner of the bar."

"Ah!" I couldn't help but laugh into the phone when I realized how they stared at each other earlier. "I already knew that, you don't hide it when you're interested in someone."

"I don't hide anything at all, so how many minutes until you're ready?"

"In fifteen minutes, I'll take a shower and get dressed."

"Don't forget the perfume, just in case you run into..."

"Stop right there!" I interrupted Anita quickly. "It's still too early for me to get involved with anyone."

"You might think you're not ready, but fate could prove you wrong, so at least be smelling good just in case the right time has arrived."

"I'm always smelling good, Anita!" I heard her laugh on the other side, and it made me smile.

"I know, I was just messing with you, Gui! Now, go get ready quickly. Alex and I will be waiting for you downstairs in the hotel lobby. Don't take too long because I can't take it anymore, you need your dose of Alex for today."

"Okay, okay." I hung up, threw the phone aside on the bed, and jumped up. Despite everything, I wanted to distract my mind from the memories of the past. I knew there was also a risk of running into Jacob River Nolan at that bar since Navarro is one of the most popular bars in Jerez. He's my brother, only by my father's side, but I don't know him, we've never spoken. I know our meeting will be inevitable because I know he's also competing in this year's MotoGP and was at the penultimate Moto2 race I missed. Anyway, I just hope this night helps me relax a little and doesn't bring me more problems.

I took a quick shower, opened my suitcase, and chose a simple black shirt. I put on dark jeans and sneakers. I combed my hair with my hand, sprayed on some perfume, smiling as I remembered what Anita had said. I stared at myself in the large hotel bathroom mirror. Despite everything, I wished I could see a happier version of myself, but the reflection only reminded me that I still hadn't gotten over her being gone forever.

The phone beeped loudly, pulling me out of that strange moment. I shook my head, grabbed my wallet from my pocket, and left the room. As soon as I reached the lobby, I saw Anita pacing back and forth and Alex sitting, talking. Sometimes, he could be tiring with his daily doses of long, meaningless conversations. But he's the best in our team and a friend for all occasions.

"Finally, I'm here for my daily dose of Alex."

"About time." Anita looked at me, half smiling and half annoyed. I threw my arm over her shoulder, pulling her into a hug.

"You can't live without your Gui, can you?"

"The two handsome guys over there forgot I'm here too, what daily dose?"

"We like to tease you a bit, Alex!" He smiled, showing his white teeth, and slapped me on the back. "Ready to meet the Spanish girls?"

"You know I already know them. I love their charm and how they make an entrance."

"I know well, the expert on women speaks. I don't even need to remind you of the trouble you got us into back in Rio, right?"

"Unnecessary, Guilhermo!" He frowned, expressing himself in his usual way. I have to remind myself that my friend and coach is a man who attracts women, with his brown-greenish eyes, light black skin, and a toned body from all the hours he spends at the gym and his morning runs. But Alex always ends up with women who are a real mess, it's like he has a magnet for it. It's incredible how he gets into these traps and troubles. Most of the women are married or have boyfriends, and it always causes fights, leaving me and Anita to get him out of it.

"I was just warning you to keep an eye on the hands of the women who approach and see if they're accompanied. For the love of your dear friends."

"Don't worry, I'll keep an eye out." I raised an eyebrow and stared at him. He smiled and then grew serious.

"I promise."

"I can't wait to see, because right now I'm just thinking about drowning myself in drinks at Navarro."

"But seriously, what's going on with her?" Alex asked, and she just winked at him. "Did she fall for him?"

"A man like that, we don't let him slip away, my dear. Now, get in the car, your bike arrives tomorrow, and we can enjoy the streets of Jerez with a lot of wind in our hair and adrenaline." I smiled, put on my helmet, and got on my bike. There's nothing better than hearing the purr of my baby, the Bonneville Bobber T120. It's music to my ears.

We weren't too far from Bar Navarro, but a quick ride on the bike never hurts. Later, we could make up for it at the hotel gym or take a little run through the streets of Jerez. I don't know anything that could give me as much pleasure and make me feel so good as riding—whether on the track, through the streets, or on the road. The feeling of freedom is simply indescribable, and I feel complete.

When I arrived, I managed to find a parking spot by some miracle, but I think it's because we arrived early. Anita couldn't contain herself to see the bar owner. I remember well when she got so excited like this—it was at the Moto3 final, right after we did well in the race at one of the most challenging circuits, in Austin. She met one of the big sponsors of the race, and they exchanged some sharp words before things got heated. Alex and I quietly slipped away, smiling. My friend loves a challenge, and that man was betting with her that I would lose, that I wouldn't place well. She knew she wasn't here to play, Alex prepared me with the team, and I trained well to make perfect pendulums on the curves. It was a great improvement during the race, and we were very pleased with the result.

The roar of a Ducati pulled me out of those memories. I immediately turned around and then recognized the bike and the rider. Could it be the same woman I saw on the road earlier, leaning on one wheel with such mastery that it left me intrigued?

Her floral perfume hit me as she shook her full, wavy hair. Then Dolores grabbed her bag from the backseat and walked away without looking back, leaving me stunned. I immediately remembered what Anita had said earlier and was stirred, but I took a deep breath and headed toward the bar entrance because I needed to find out who that woman was. It almost felt unreal, but I had to be quick, before she disappeared inside. Before I could even look for her, I was yanked, and when I turned around, I came face to face with an angry Anita.

"Where were you going?" My friend seems to sense things, but I'll keep this from her for now. I don't want to hear the famous "I told you so."

"I thought you'd take longer, so I went in. What happened?"

"We got a slow driver, you know how Alex gets impatient."

"I can imagine, but tomorrow your bike arrives, be patient, let's go in."

"Wow, what's gotten into you on the way?"

"Nothing, I just want to grab a drink and find us a spot while it's still empty." She frowned, and we entered the bar. It wasn't as empty as I thought, but I knew it would get even more crowded as the night went on. Most of the patrons there are tourists, so we passed the tables and went straight to the bar. Alex whistled for Juan, who smiled and raised his hand, signaling us to come over.

"My God!" I heard Anita say, clearly impressed to see Navarro dressed as the bartender. I knew he got his hands dirty, making most of the drinks, and they were always a hit. The Latin music, "Que Calor" by Major Lazer feat J Balvin, played in the background with a catchy beat, making the atmosphere even hotter, and people couldn't stop swaying their bodies. You could say it was both a bar and a nightclub. Juan truly deserves credit for expanding the business since he started managing it after his father retired.

I looked around, searching for the woman I had seen earlier, but I couldn't find her anywhere in the bar. As soon as we reached the counter, Juan smiled at Anita and winked at me. Alex was already excited about the chemistry between them.

"Welcome to Navarro!" He said, staring at my friend and agent. I had no choice but to sit on the bar stool and watch the scene, maybe I'd spot her now.

"I'll order my ice-cold beer, you know I love the craft beer. The last time I came, it was unforgettable."

"Guay, can't go without it," he replied. "And you, Anita?"

"I'll take your recommendation since you know the best drinks. Surprise me."

"You two, I won't say anything, Anita. But I'll be up front, since you can't stop flirting..."

"Shut up, Alex." She glared at him and put her purse aside.

"Well, you arrived early. Tonight is flamenco night at the bar, and it gets crowded. Tourists love to see that performance. So, does Anita like fruit?" He asked, already preparing a red drink in a glass with ice.

"I love fruit."

"Great, I think you'll like one of Spain's most popular drinks."

"Sangria?"

"You know it, it's also the most popular and the most ordered here after beer."

"I won't pass up a cold beer. Brazil introduced me to beer, and nothing beats it after that." Alex said while ordering his glass. Juan finished preparing Anita's sangria and handed it to her, while I drank my beer, observing the bar's movement from a different angle, still looking for the woman, but nothing.

I looked at the stage, and the curtains were closed, with just a white spotlight on it. I turned to my friends, and I already saw Alex talking to a blonde who had come to the bar. He never wasted time, I just hoped the woman was single, I wasn't in the mood to break up any fights. A few more minutes passed, and still no sign of Lola. I actually gave up; she probably hadn't stayed in the bar.

When I thought that woman wouldn't surprise me anymore, the bar went dark, the music stopped, and the spotlight on the stage grew stronger. The guitar strummed loudly with blues in the background, perfectly blending. The lights turned colorful and moved. That's when I spotted her on the Navarro stage, wearing a red frilly dress, her light brown skin glowing, her full red lips, and her bright, sensual gaze.

She moved her body to the rhythm of the music in such an intense way that my eyes were glued to the scene. I had to admit that Dolores managed to leave me even more stunned; not only could she ride on one wheel, but she also danced like a professional. She started tap dancing and moving her arms so lightly and strikingly. My eyes couldn't look away, her dance followed the lively and vibrant rhythm of the song, then she began clapping and swaying her hips. The rhythm changed to something more Latin, I didn't know much about music, but I could tell by the beat. Everyone was completely involved and captivated by the performance. She drew attention with sensual and powerful steps until she expressed pain and suffering in her movements and expressions. Something truly amazing and fascinating, swinging from one extreme to another, bringing the audience a myriad of emotions.

The lights followed her movements, and she swung the train of her long dress forward and back, revealing her beautiful and sensual legs. Her sinful gaze truly hypnotized me. Then she turned her back, and the rhythm changed, returning to the Latin style. She swayed her hips and moved in a way that really activated all my hormones. Watching her dance made me forget where I was, I only realized the music had ended when I felt some taps on my back. I turned around, angry, and came face to face with Juan Navarro, the bar owner himself, who looked at me with a serious expression.

I choked up in nervousness, my whole body alert, like when I'm riding. I had never felt that way before. The curtains closed, and at the back of the stage, only the man in black remained, playing the guitar. Suddenly, the spotlight turned toward the curtains, and her shadow appeared perfectly, marking her wide hips and narrow waist. She raised her arms, moving and swaying her whole body. I could spend my whole life sitting there, watching her, burning with desire.

CHAPTER FOUR

Guilhermo

"You drooled over Lola the whole presentation," Juan commented, staring at me while opening a *long neck* with no difficulty.

"I couldn't resist, is she your sister?" I don't usually get this curious, but that woman made me want to know every detail about her.

"She's not my sister, but I consider her one. Dolores is my best friend, the person who has always been by my side, and we've known each other since childhood."

"I get it, it's like me and Anita. She's the sister I never had."

"I already noticed how close you two are and how you work together, just like Lola and I. It's good to know she's special and amazing." "You know, I would even approve of you and my sister together," he asked, smiling sideways.

"Hold on, Navarro. Damn! You're just like Anita, already predicting the future. I only admired her dance performance, it was spectacular."

"Lola is a professional dancer, but she's still looking for the big break to be recognized by one of those professional dance academies. I hope it comes soon, and besides that, she's a strong and hardworking woman. She practically supports her household alone and helps her mother, who needs much more than just financial help."

"She deserves the best, I understand now, and you do well to protect her, you're absolutely right," I added, and he nodded.

"But I know you a little, and I saw the spark in your eyes when you watched her dance."

"Don't fantasize too much, Juan. I'm still trying to get over Mari's loss, and it's consuming me."

"I can imagine, but life goes on, and it needs to move forward."

"My God! You sounded just like Anita. You two make the perfect pair. You've got my support, just don't make her suffer." He burst out laughing, then suddenly became serious. I turned to see what had wiped the smile off his face and came face to face with him. I knew I ran the risk of meeting him, but not so soon.

My gaze fell upon Jacob River Nolan. I knew him from magazines since his mother is a famous chef with a chain of restaurants throughout Europe. I stared at him, furrowing my brow. We had never met before, but from his intense look, he knew who I was. Of course, he knew.

He raised an eyebrow and smiled with an unmistakable smirk. Then, he stared at me, and acting on the impulse that his gaze had triggered, I stood up and moved closer. Our eyes were inches apart, and the uncomfortable silence spoke for itself.

"Welcome to Spain, Guilhermo García!" he said with mockery, and the blonde woman next to him scanned my entire body before finally looking at me with an interest that made me feel disgusted. Jacob extended his right hand to me, and I hesitated, wondering if it was a genuine gesture, given his mocking expression. He seemed to be enjoying the situation, and the blonde too, smiling provocatively.

"Thanks." I decided to shake his hand, and he came closer, becoming serious as he stared at me more intently. The tension spread through all my nerve endings. Who did this spoiled brat think he was, playing around with my arrival like that? There was nothing I could say to him.

"Here, we welcome our brothers well, didn't know that?" Then he released my hand, turned around with a smile, and shouted, "Navarro, get drinks for everyone on my tab, let's celebrate! My brother's back at his place, and we'll be adversaries!" He raised his glass, putting on a show. Everyone cheered, and I approached him, smiling through gritted teeth.

"Don't worry, I know where it all ends, on the MotoGP track, where only one River Nolan will come out as the winner."

"I'm not really worried, because I know who the winner will be. And guess what? It won't be you." I clenched my fists, the rage building inside me with an uncontrollable heat. I've always been calm and stayed out of fights or trouble, but this kid made me want to punch his face. What audacity for him to think he'll beat me, really. But then, I smelled the strong floral perfume that filled the room, and I turned around. For the first time, I locked eyes with her. I stared at her intense green eyes and her full, red lips.

"Well, well, this just got even more interesting. The one I wanted to see has arrived," Jacob said, moving closer to Dolores. She never once lowered her head, keeping it up and staring at him with a boldness that really impressed me.

"Save me from your advances, so the other River Nolan finally showed up? Another one to keep us on edge. We already noticed how much you two resemble each other, with those inflated egos," she put her finger to her chin, pondering her theory. "Interesting!" she said, staring at us.

"Oh, Lola! You don't know him yet, I forgot that detail," I continued staring at her. Up close, she was even more beautiful, with a unique beauty that radiated joy. The sparkle in her eyes and the courage she showed in responding to a guy like that made me much more intrigued.

"Let me introduce her to you, Jacob," Juan said, moving around the counter.

"Guilhermo, this is my friend Dolores López," she came closer, smiling sideways, while I extended my hand for a handshake. I saw her consider whether to accept it or not, and she finally did. When I felt the warmth of her hand, an electric current shot through my arm and my whole body. I stared into her eyes, which stayed locked on mine with an intense glow, and a sideways smile that seemed to be her greatest charm.

"No, I'm not immune to a woman like that, because it's not just her beauty that attracts me, but her joy and that firm handshake that already shows how strong she is. Also, from what Juan said, she's very determined and a fighter, I like women like that. Despite everything I've been through, I'd like to be alone for a bit, but this beautiful woman with hypnotizing green eyes has me enchanted. It's impossible not to want to go after her, too crazy, isn't it?"

"Even so, I feel like I should keep admiring her from a distance, because I need time to think better before acting. Especially because I noticed how Jacob stared at her, his eyes sparkled. I noticed his interest in her right away, even though he has a blonde who never leaves his side."

"Take another drink, my friend," Juan said, placing a drink in front of me. The music that started playing mixed rhythms, and then another show began at Navarro's bar.

The place darkened, and the colorful lights focused on the lady in red, dancing alone in the center of the bar, among the chairs. I've traveled the world and seen many different and interesting places, but nothing like the energy of this bar. I don't know if it's that beautiful dancer that made it more interesting, I just know I turned to the bar and leaned on it, all I could do was admire Dolores dancing to the song *3 to tango* by Pitbull. The catchy beat brought an energy that ran through my entire body, and a few more dancers joined her, following her synchronized steps, shaking their shoulders from side to side.

I couldn't keep up; one of the dancers grabbed a chair, and Dolores sat on it, moving her hips provocatively. Then she lifted her leg and dropped down with impressive speed and balance, all while smiling and making sensual expressions. I noticed she was coming closer to where I was, and suddenly, she stood in front of me, shook her shoulders, and smiled, offering me her hand. I helped her, and without much hesitation, she climbed onto the bar and began to dance sensually while everyone followed her steps in awe. The entire bar started dancing, following her tango and Latin beat.

When I turned, I saw Alex dancing with a curvy red-haired woman. I silently prayed to God that she was single because I couldn't handle breaking up a fight that night. Next to them were Juan and Anita, dancing tango in a very beautiful way. My friend loves to dance, and she learned everything from me and Alex. There was nothing better to pass the time between races and training with the team. We always had a great time together, my friends are the best.

I turned to leave the group that was dancing when I felt warm hands pull me. I couldn't do anything but give in. When I looked at her, I saw the challenge in her fiery eyes, and I decided to show her that even though I just wanted to watch her performance, I could be quite the partner. So I spun her around me, admiring her flawless and firm steps. I held her and locked eyes with her, my face much closer. I could feel her perfume and warm skin, as well as her body turning. She slid down provocatively, going to the floor. I barely had time to catch her and pull her back to me, finishing her show, watching her disappear into the crowd that quickly gathered around us.

I continued drinking at the bar next to Anita, who wouldn't stop chatting with Juan, who kept making drinks, until another bartender arrived and they made me leave because I was getting more and more lost in the conversation. That's when the blonde came near, offering her hand to me, introducing herself as Jacob River Nolan's girlfriend.

That didn't interest me much. From them, I just wanted distance and nothing more. So without saying a word, I looked for Dolores again around the bar. Not finding her, I left the bar and got on my bike. I noticed hers was no longer there. That woman captured my interest so quickly and intensely, I was impressed to learn she was the same woman I saw riding like that on the road when I was coming into Jerez.

    I got on my bike and took to the streets, feeling the cool breeze across my body. It cleanses the soul and calms the heart, at least for me, being able to ride was everything in my life. In that moment, when everything inside me was boiling for that woman, nothing could be better.

CHAPTER FIVE

Dolores

I had never felt that way when seeing a man, I mean, he wasn't just any man, but Guilhermo García, one of the best MotoGP riders of the moment. Oh yes! As a fan of the sport, I love staying up to date on all the news about motocross. Juan hadn't mentioned that he was his acquaintance, though they seemed like good friends.

The only thing I could think of was the electric shock that ran through my body when he shook my hand. Something so unusual, since I live far from men as handsome as him. They're a danger, but not satisfied with just being introduced to him, still not understanding why, I provoked him into dancing with me, pressing my body against his and grinding like crazy.

Then, I left right after the most intense performance of my life. All that closeness when we danced left me on fire, more than I've ever felt before. On my way home, I decided to extend my route to calm my body and heart, that's why I love riding my bike—the sense of freedom and peace it brings me is something I'll never give up on in my life.

On the streets of Jerez, I found my control and returned home, but I was still thinking about him. That's what I'm telling you, it seems like these handsome men cast a spell on us, how could it be? I entered the house, and my sister was waiting for me, as always. Olivia always worried about me; she wouldn't go to bed until I got home.

"Hello, Lola! You took a bit longer today." I forgot to mention how controlling my sister is. Even though she's younger than me, she gets worried. My mom would wait for her with me, but recently she had a relapse and was probably already sleeping due to the medication.

"The show ran long, two mixed rhythms that required a lot more time. Still, it was surprising to dance at Navarro's tonight."

"Can I know what surprised you on an ordinary work night?"

"You can't imagine who I met tonight, and as incredible as it sounds, thinking about it now calmly, there was another coincidence related to this person."

"But *por Dios*! Come sit here right now and tell me everything. I'm seeing a different sparkle in your eyes." We sat in the living room, I was in the armchair, and she was on the sofa, staring at me excitedly.

"You're going to love hearing who I met. Since you know all the biggest names in any field, you know who the current big name in MotoGP is."

"No way! You met Guilhermo García? What an amazing news!" I nodded, and she jumped off the sofa, excited and shouting. I smiled at her enthusiasm.

"In the flesh. Actually, I was face to face with him, we shook hands, and I even danced with him," I said, putting my hand over my mouth, still in disbelief about myself for reacting this way. I need to calm down.

"I'm shocked, the newest famous MotoGP rider, but it makes total sense that he's here since the championship is starting in a few days."

"I knew you'd react like this, Oli."

"But tell me, how was it seeing that walking temptation in person? You even shook his hand. How lucky you are, sister! But I'm sure by the look in your eyes, you liked Guilhermo more than you thought, and was he nice to you?"

"He was, even though there was some tension with River Nolan at the time."

"What? How's that?"

"You know they're competing and are brothers, right?"

"Oh my God, I didn't know they were brothers, that never came out in the media."

"It seems that's well hidden, but based on yesterday's interaction, it might be revealed soon in the tabloids."

"Wow, this is going to cause a stir. You know the media is curious about Guilhermo's personal life? They only know that he was raised by his grandmother and mother, with no father around."

"His father is Lorenzo River Nolan, but there must be something really bad behind that, since it seems like they had never met before."

"What a scandal! This is definitely going to cause a lot of talk, just imagine!"

"It's going to, but Guilhermo probably doesn't like exposure. I don't even know him, but by the way he is, he seems pretty private. He's different from Jacob, who's in MotoGP more for the show."

"He was at Navarro's too, I saw it in Eve's *Instagram stories*, that woman is so full of herself."

"I don't like her, she always looks at me with an air of superiority and mockery. But since I'm not stupid, I always smile at her, and Jacob melts."

"Is he still hitting on you?"

"Unfortunately, yes. Their relationship is open, and Eve knows he's crazy about me. I think that's why she looks at me mockingly."

"If she's bothered by how he hits on you and they live in this relationship, why don't you talk to him? What do the other women have to do with it?"

"You don't understand, she has a problem with me, with the others, it's not like that. I've seen bizarre and very bold scenes of him at Navarro's."

"Look, I have nothing against their open relationship, but for me, that would never work. Can you imagine seeing your boyfriend kissing someone else and just accepting it?"

"Oli, even I wouldn't have the nerve for that, honestly. Now, changing the subject, how's mom today?"

"She had a good day, cooked for us, we talked, took her medicine, and it was peaceful."

"Thank God. You know you can call me anytime, and I'll come running."

"You don't need to worry, Lola! Focus a little on Guilhermo, see if you live a bit more. You only think about us and work. You deserve to enjoy your life more."

"I know, but I can't even do that, you know. The only time I have fun is when I'm on stage dancing, it's what I love."

"One day, you'll get where you've always dreamed of. It won't take long, and you definitely deserve the world, Lola!" she said, coming to hug me. Then we went to the bedroom together, I took a shower, and we got a few things done in the kitchen. We went to bed very late after talking a lot. Olivia is so mature for her age, I've always been so proud of the person she is, and how intelligent, studious, and hardworking she is. I don't say this because she's my sister, but because it's truly who she is, in addition to helping a lot with Luna, our little treasure.

As soon as I laid my head on the pillow, I began to remember those intense eyes staring at me. At that moment, it felt like it was just the two of us in that bar. My heart jumped, and all the blood in my body boiled with the restlessness and electricity that coursed through it, something I had never felt before. As I said, these are symptoms of imminent danger approaching, and how could I get away from this unscathed? I felt an intensity emanating from him mixed with a sadness deep in those beautiful, impetuous blue eyes. I'm literally *screwed*.

I need to find a way to stop thinking about his body pressed against mine, the woody scent that came from him and wrapped me in an endless cloud of desire. The red lights in my brain have never blinked so much, even though my body says other things, very indecent and inappropriate things.

I couldn't get involved with Guilhermo García, who, even if he didn't want to, is a River Nolan. Just imagine how that would hit Jacob, being with the one he hates the most because that show of his was a way of showing how much he disliked seeing his brother back and ready for the MotoGP Championship. But, in reality, the reason I can't get involved with Guilhermo is something else, nothing to do with Jacob, but that last name and everything they represent, I couldn't allow it with myself.

Thinking about it, he's not losing anything by waiting, Guilhermo won the Isle of Man, one of the most dangerous races in the world in Ireland, and I'm sure he'll win the world championship and become the official MotoGP reference. In fact, he's already famous, all anyone talks about is the fast and daring way he rides. I root for that, because I couldn't stand Jacob's arrogance if he ever won something that big. I need to recognize that the guy is also a good rider, but not like Guilhermo. I've always loved this world and started to understand the riding techniques well, watching many races on TV and reading everything about it.

When I saw Guilhermo at the Isle of Man, the videos of him on that track are some of the best performances in the history of motocross. Adrenaline, daring, and emotion from start to finish. I remember my heart racing, and my whole body shivering from how beautiful and crazy it was to watch him ride on such a dangerous and magnificent track. Because yes, it must be crazy to ride there, dangerous curves with the most beautiful view. You flirt with danger in an exuberant way.

The sensation is indescribable, I imagine, because just watching it drives you crazy. I keep thinking that Guilhermo must feel that chill in his stomach before, and when he's on the track, the sense of freedom and that he loves what he does. That's why I admire him, because he manages to transcribe that into every turn and victory he wins. Jacob still needs to bring that fire and love for motocross in a natural way because that's the difference between the two brothers who are riders.

With my mind boiling but overcome by a body tired from a day full of work and also from the emotions I experienced, I fell asleep and dreamed of Guilhermo riding with me on his back. Insane and delicious. Despite everything, deep down, the desire and curiosity to get to know that rider better will end up winning over all my rational side.

CHAPTER SIX

Guilhermo

The days were passing quickly. After that meeting with Dolores at the bar, I haven't seen her again, and honestly, it's probably for the best. It became clear that if we spend some more time together, we'll just add fuel to the fire, as my grandmother would say. Right now, I need to maintain control and focus on the upcoming championship, and then there's Jacob River Nolan—my brother is going to give me trouble. I know he's no ordinary rider; he's been slowly making a name for himself, so I can't afford to relax. I'm at my peak now, and I need to stay secure.

In MotoGP, it's all or nothing. You have to give it your all and do your best, but despite that, I feel a love for being on the track on two wheels. It's the greatest pleasure I have in life, my moment of peace and freedom. Riding brings clarity to everything in my life. To this day, I haven't found anything that brings me as much happiness, and it's been good to focus on the championship. Since Mari passed away, it's been difficult to find my way back. I want to be the Guilhermo I was before, although I know I can never be the same, but I need to at least try to rediscover myself.

My mom always warned me when I started getting involved with her, that being with her all the time wouldn't be good in the future. It's amazing how mothers know everything about your life, I never doubted that. But back then, I didn't really listen, I thought she was just jealous because I had found the woman of my life. Just like

Mari entered my life, she was taken away, too quickly. That's why I want to take things slow next time, I've closed myself off to future relationships, but I can't deny everything I felt when I first saw her on that bike and then on the Navarro stage.

"Gui!" I felt a slap on my back from my friend Anita, followed by her snapping her fingers in front of my face.

"What's up?" I asked, lost in thought again.

"I've been calling you for a while, and you haven't noticed, you're way too far away."

"Sorry, I was just thinking..." she cut me off with her usual impatient tone. Anita sometimes has no patience to let us finish speaking.

"I know exactly what you were thinking, Guilhermo García." She stared at me with a very serious expression.

"You know I can't control..."

"I know, but could you pay attention for a minute, please?"

"Yes, sorry."

"Stop apologizing, you're starting to annoy me today. Where's Alex?" she asked louder so he could hear. It didn't take long before my friend arrived running, holding a beer in his hand.

"Well, now that I have your attention, I got the house key so we can check it out tomorrow morning. If we like it, we can start moving our stuff in and get everything organized."

"The house is furnished, right?" Alex asked, and since she had already told us that she got it just how we wanted, I closed my eyes, already predicting the scene that would unfold before me.

"You know you drive me crazy sometimes, Alex?" He made a face like he didn't know anything, pretending to be clueless.

"I just asked a question, calm down An..."

"I've already explained this. Remember, I told you that I got the house furnished the way we wanted? We just needed the key to check it out before finalizing everything."

"Ah, that's right!" He put his hand on his head, frowning in his typical way of acting like he forgot. "I'm such a slowpoke, sorry, my dear." Alex walked over to her and started hugging our friend, something she didn't like when he irritated her like this.

"You have no limits, good thing you have us," she said, breaking free from Alex's hug.

"You know I can't live without you guys, MotoGP, and women."

"Alex is a lost cause. What do we do with him, Gui?"

"Honestly, I don't know. Like you said, a lost cause."

"Hey, hey, I'm right here, you're talking like I'm not here, but I am," Alex said, acting like he was upset.

"You know how we love to tease you, but don't worry, there's no way we're letting a coach and team leader as good as you slip away."

"No chance of you all stopping messing with me."

"No way, but back to the house topic, it's already furnished, which makes it way more practical for us. Guilhermo, after the championship, do you plan to stay in Spain?"

"I'll call my mom, I know she'd like to settle somewhere, and she mentioned here, in her country of origin."

"She knows that the River Nolans are settled here in Spain, right?"

"Of course, she knows about them. Don't you know Miss García?"

"I know her well and I love how strong and smart your mother is, no one can pull the wool over her eyes, she's simply impressive."

"I'm so proud of her, my hero, and of her health too!"

"True, well, I'm off now. Tomorrow we have a lot to do, don't forget the team meeting. I've already marked the training sessions, as Alex sent me in the schedule."

"Great, I set a reminder on my phone. Since it's still too early to sleep, I'm going for a ride on my bike."

"Guilhermo García, please don't overdo it, though you probably need it."

"Ah, woman, let him have some fun," Alex said, looking at Anita seriously.

"Alright, it's just a bike ride around the streets of Jerez," they don't know how I really feel. I said my goodbyes and left. I got on my bike and felt the cool night breeze. There's nothing better to clear my mind and make me think about life. I love being a rider, I just don't like the spotlight that comes with fame. But to make your name known, that's part of the deal and much more. Most people think it's simple, just get on the bike and go, but it's much more than that. Tomorrow, we have the meeting about the bike presentations coming soon, to kick off the MotoGP season. Our team this year is Wacco Racing, one of the best. We secured incredible sponsors, all thanks to Anita, she knows how to negotiate and no one can fool my agent."

I rode through the little streets of Jerez and ended up stopping at Navarro's bar. I got off the bike after spending a good amount of time looking for parking, as the place was crowded at this hour. Obviously, I shouldn't have come here, but what could I do? The whole ride had led me here. I entered, and indeed, the place was packed, with many tourists mixing with the locals. I went straight to the bar and spotted Juan serving drinks to a group of women who looked at me with smiles. I feel like I've moved past that phase of getting excited about picking up random women at a bar. After everything I've been through, it's still hard for me to get interested, which is why I still didn't understand my sudden and strong interest in the dancer. While I waited for my friend to serve the girls, I turned to face the stage, looking for her. But I couldn't find her anywhere, I searched all around, but nothing.

"Guilhermo, looking for someone?" I felt Juan's hand slap my back, and I turned around speechless.

"Navarro, you were busy, so I decided to watch the crowd."

BOUND BY FIRE AND FUEL

"Yes, but I know who you're looking for, and she's not performing today. It's her day off, but for your luck, Lola is in the pool area, on the other side, towards the back."

"Who said I was looking for your friend?"

"No one needs to say it, Guilhermo, I can tell by the way I caught you walking in and already looking for her." There was no way to hide it from him.

"Is it that obvious?"

"Written all over your face. But look, Jacob is here today too, and he's crazy about Lola. Just asking you not to put on any shows."

"What do you mean? Doesn't he date the blonde?"

"Yes, but they're in an open relationship that no one really understands, because Jacob gets insanely jealous of Eve, depending on who she chooses to be with. Don't ask me anything, I only know what people talk about here."

"My God, why am I not shocked by what you're telling me? I don't know him that well, but I know he's impulsive and daring on the track and in his personal life too, it seems."

"Yes, no one understands how his mind works, but he's in an open relationship and has never hidden how much he's interested in Lola. But my friend never gave him a chance to get close to her."

"Good to know she doesn't care about him." I felt more relieved to know that Dolores wasn't interested in Jacob, but the problem was him.

"Yeah, but don't think he'll leave you alone if he knows you're interested in her. It'll complicate things even more with him, especially on the track."

"I know that, don't worry, I'm taking it slow. Honestly, I can't get involved with any woman right now. But Dolores left me impressed. I saw her popping a wheelie on the highway, and that fascinated me while also bringing back memories."

"It's better to take it slow. Dolores is different from any woman you've met. She's determined, and I've never seen her shaken by any man since her last troubled relationship."

"I understand. We all have a past. Now, bring me a nice cold beer." He held my arm on the counter and stared at me seriously.

"You can be sure you don't understand. Dolores has been through a lot and supports the household on her own without hesitation. So if you can't handle getting involved, don't even try to get close. She deserves the best and nothing less." His look told me Dolores had suffered a lot, and yet she kept going for her family. I got a lump in my throat, agreeing with him with a nod of my head, and he went to get my drink, leaving me with my head spinning.

After that, Navarro handed me the drink and had to attend to more people at the illuminated bar. Even though I was there, my mind was far away. I began to think about Lola and her not-so-easy life and how she doesn't show any suffering in her eyes; on the contrary, there's only a special glow. With that in mind, I left the bar and went to the other side, towards the back, where there was a pool table. I knew I shouldn't be doing this, but it felt like I'd completely lost my mind. As soon as I saw her, standing with a cue in her hand, preparing for a shot, my whole body lit up. Beside her was a blonde woman with long hair. They seemed to be the same age, and she was cheering for Lola, very excited.

"Make the shot, Lola!" she said loudly, so her friend could hear.

"Calm down, I'm seeing if it'll work," Dolores said, focused, and my eyes were glued to the beauty of that green-eyed woman. Lola was wearing light, tight jeans that hugged her curvy body, a red cropped top with polka dots that matched her golden skin, her curly hair loose and pulled back with a floral scarf in front, and her full lips in a beautiful red. How could I resist a woman like Dolores?

She sunk all the balls and smiled at the woman beside her. The two of them celebrated, and then the two men on the other side went to congratulate the girls. I watched the whole scene as they insisted on the girls going with them, but Dolores and the woman next to her, who must be her friend, chose to stay. I stayed a bit longer watching until she was alone, and then I decided to step into her line of sight.

"You..." she said in a soft voice, looking at me with that irresistible sparkle in her eyes.

"I was watching you, you're really good at pool."

"Yes, I like to distract myself with the game. If you want, we can..." I didn't let her finish, too intrigued to play with her.

"You'd dare..." She moved closer, making my whole body shiver. The energy flowing between us was too intense.

"Dare to challenge you?" Dolores smiled sideways with those tempting full lips, leaving me even more intrigued. Finally, she stared at me boldly and seriously. Her mysterious green eyes would've made me stay there for hours just watching her.

"I'd like to know, but by the look on your face..."

"You already know, but first, I need to put on my show, and it involves this pool table, so watch and learn how it's done."

CHAPTER SEVEN

Dolores

I was clearly challenging him in pool. My God, the idea of staying away from him evaporates every time I see him. He thinks he can face me, but he doesn't know my boldness yet. I knew staying away was best, but that was out of the question since my whole body was telling me the opposite of what my mind wanted. Besides, that fire in Guilhermo's eyes was too much to ignore. I wanted to take the risk. I only felt an urgency to know what's behind those sensations that awakened something inside me—crazy, right?

I associate this feeling with when I'm riding. Danger is an aphrodisiac for humans. It doesn't matter what it is, whenever we're at risk, everything becomes more intense, the blood rushing through our veins, and your whole body craving to live it without thinking about the consequences we might face. Adrenaline is powerful, a hormone that consumes us with the same intensity as fire.

In a silence full of words, I arranged the balls in a triangle pointing towards the other table, leaving the white ball at the other end. Without holding back, I took the first shot to spread the balls, never breaking eye contact with Guilhermo. I managed to sink two balls, giving me another turn, but by mere millimeters, I failed to sink the others. He smiled sideways but said nothing, as it wasn't necessary. Our gazes said it all, and even more than that, they screamed for what our bodies desired at that moment.

One touch and I knew we were going to set Navarro on fire on that table. There's no way to misunderstand this; it's a language we only understand when the other allows it, and that man wanted it. It was as clear as crystal in his gestures and gaze. Of course, I didn't want to get involved with a River Nolan. I know he wasn't raised with his brother and father, nor does he use their last name, but they share the same blood, and I feared for my heart. Despite that, there was still the blind and fearless interest Jacob had in me, and nothing in the world would stop these two.

He positioned himself and sank three balls without breaking eye contact with me. The music that flowed through the bar's sound system wrapped us up in its captivating beat. Until it was my turn, I stayed silent and positioned myself for the shot when he approached.

"Excuse me, but if you stay like that, you'll have a better chance of sinking all those balls." He got too close to my body and spoke in my ear.

"And why are you helping me?" I turned and looked at him with curiosity, what I saw was his gaze darken when I let him see my not-so-generous neckline. Guilhermo swallowed hard, took a deep breath, and closed his eyes, as though fighting with himself. Just like I was there, because I didn't want to do anything I might regret.

"I just gave a tip, nothing more," he said, stepping away from my body. At that moment, I just nodded and took my shot, sinking all the balls. With my heart still racing from his closeness, I celebrated and acted on the impulse of the moment, hugging him tightly. When I realized what I had done, I tried to pull away from his arms, fearing he could hear how fast my heart was beating, and my entire body was trembling. That's when Guilhermo began to run the tip of his nose across my neck, his lips leaving a hot trail. My legs froze, and I couldn't move, I was limp and completely affected by that unexpected touch that set a wild heat coursing through my body.

I closed my eyes, surrendering to all those new and tempting sensations.

Suddenly, I forgot where we were and gave myself to everything I was feeling, and my body craved more. My hands came alive, and I started to run them across his defined back, imagining him without that shirt. Then, unable to resist, I bit the lobe of his ear and kissed his neck, completely hypnotized by the spell he cast. We managed to make eye contact, and his blue eyes were filled with a fire I had never seen before. He alternated between my eyes and lips. Then I heard someone clapping, snapping me out of that trance.

"Well done, congratulations on the show!" I heard Jacob River Nolan's voice, and instinctively, I rolled my eyes and saw Guilhermo furrow his brow, pulling in a deep breath, trying to control himself.

"There was no show today, my dear," I replied, but with a more contained tone, as I was trying to keep my patience in a situation where my heart was still pounding like crazy in my chest, and my legs couldn't move, so I stayed still and Guilhermo positioned himself beside me.

"Who do you think you are, interrupting people at the bar like this?" Guilhermo unloaded on him impatiently but still holding himself back.

"I'm more than you can imagine, but that's not the point right now. But I was surprised to see the beautiful, reserved, and tough Dolores López surrendering so easily to a man who barely just arrived in Jerez," he mocked, smiling with disdain, making me feel disgusted. He really is an idiot who doesn't back off, even with the blonde in tow.

"How dare you?" Guilhermo lunged at Jacob with impressive speed, and I thought quickly, stepping in front of him, standing between him and his brother. At that moment, I felt all the eyes on us, people really are just a bunch of curious onlookers. I approached

Jacob, not breaking his gaze, glaring at him furiously for insinuating something like that about me.

"You don't need to defend me, Guilhermo. I can handle this nuisance that is your brother."

"The brave one speaks..." Jacob started to speak, but I didn't let him finish.

"Shut your mouth, I didn't give you permission to say anything, and listen well to what I'm about to say: Never again dare to refer to me in that way," I moved closer to him, and fueled by anger and disgust from his comment, I spat in his face. "You're no one to come here and judge me the way you did. Don't think for one second that you'll humiliate me. You didn't earn that right. I'm not even your acquaintance, just keep your distance from me."

"But from him..." I pointed my finger at him.

"Oh, what did I just say? You're nothing and never will be a match for me, Jacob River Nolan. Just stick with your girlfriend and leave me alone. And that includes you having no right to judge me. I'm a woman who makes her own decisions and does whatever she wants with her life, I owe you nothing. So just get out of my face and stay away," he closed his eyes, not believing what he heard. He stared at Guilhermo with eyes burning with rage, and his little girlfriend held him back as his hands were turning red from clenching into tight fists.

"Come on, Jac, let's go. It's not worth it!" I heard Eve say, and I had to hold myself back from flying at her as well. I swear I don't understand these two, I respect people who live in open relationships, but Jacob and Eve clearly live in a toxic relationship where he controls who she can be with outside their relationship while the pretty boy gets with whoever he wants. It's absurd how openly and shamelessly he does this.

Guilhermo pulled me, and when his hand touched my arm, I looked at him with regret. I didn't want to get involved with someone who had River Nolan blood in them. This wouldn't be good for me, especially since they're rivals and will compete against each other like no one else, both on and off the track. I couldn't imagine myself in their world. I needed to return to my reality and focus on becoming a famous and accomplished dancer. That's why I quickly pulled away and swallowed hard before speaking.

"I need to leave, I'm sorry, but I can't stay in the middle of this," he didn't seem to agree, and when I turned my back, he pulled me again, this time pressing me against him. My God, I don't have the strength to fight everything that Guilhermo makes me feel when he gets close like this.

"I'm not like him, and I don't want you in the middle of anything, but it's not fair that..."

"Please, don't finish that. I just want to go home. I can't with this, you guys are rivals, and apparently, I'm just another challenge in the life of the River Nolans."

"You misunderstood all of that, but I'll respect your decision and let you go. But this isn't over," then he did something that left me ecstatic, he kissed my forehead with those hot lips. I closed my eyes tightly and ran away from him. I didn't even say goodbye to Juan and Nina because they would have a million questions I wasn't ready to answer. I left home today after so long without letting myself stop because my friend Nina insisted so much, and I couldn't refuse her invitation to have some fun.

It's not easy when everything is solely on your shoulders. I'm the one responsible for keeping my home and my sisters. I never complain; I do it with my head held high and a smile on my face. But the burden is heavy. I try so hard to keep my sanity intact. I don't get involved in any trouble and with any man. I'm not a saint or reserved, like Jacob said, I just prefer to focus on my career and family at this point in my life. That's why I left Navarro, my heart still racing, without saying goodbye to my friends. I got on my bike and rode around Jerez, trying to understand the whirlwind of sensations that Guilhermo's touch awakened in me. It felt like he had plugged my body into an outlet because honestly, I've never felt so out of control as I did when I hugged him. I'm lost, completely *screwed* if this keeps up and I can't control myself anymore.

CHAPTER EIGHT

Guilhermo

The truth is, I've always liked playing with fire, being on the edge of danger, or rather, living it. It's insane how much it drives me crazy. And no, I've never felt this with any woman. Until I felt what her gaze does to me. The same feeling I get when I'm riding, combined with an overwhelming desire to feel her mouth on mine and her body against mine.

That fateful night, we went from heaven to hell in a matter of minutes because Jacob River Nolan showed up with all his arrogance and boldness, interrupting a moment between Dolores and me. I had to hold myself back from exploding and fighting with that guy. He thinks he can affect me and mess with my life. Who does he think he is? The king of Spain?

In his mocking expression, I noticed how much he truly resembles his father, Lorenzo River Nolan. The man who let my mother leave with a child in her belly without giving her any support, not even calling her over all these years. Honestly, I didn't want to feel this anger bubbling inside me, but since I ran into Jacob, it took on another dimension. When I was far from them, I didn't feel this way, but being so close is a whole different thing.

I need to learn to deal with these feelings, they're too new to me, I've never felt like this before. When my mom told me everything about my dad, how it all happened, it hit me hard. I had hoped to know my father figure, I imagined him many times since I was a child, idealized him in my young mind. But after hearing everything, I came to the conclusion that it was nothing more than an illusion. Something I created to soothe my sadness about the absence of a father.

I think I was even more upset when I researched his life and started seeing news about the River Nolans in magazines and newspapers. His current wife, Jacob's mother, is a famous *chef* with well-known restaurants all over Europe. They're always in the tabloids, and Jacob is Daddy's little darling. Lorenzo encourages him and is part of his motocross team. This bothers me to some extent because I always imagined a father who would've been by my side before stepping onto a track. But I never lived that, only in my imagination.

Despite all of this, my mom has always been there for me, even with all her traveling and work, I could always count on her unconditional support. She would go crazy whenever she knew I was on the track, racing over 300 km/h and making dangerous turns.

"Guilhermo, have you seen the news today?" Anita caught my attention, so I left those thoughts behind.

"Not yet, what are they saying?" I asked her, knowing she was already noticing my lack of attention.

"'Guilhermo García will begin his participation in the official MotoGP World Championship practices this Monday, with the eyes of major teams and riders focused on his performance: after winning the last races in 2019 in Valencia, the young rider confirmed his status as a title contender. Last year, Guilhermo finished the competition in third place in Moto E, the best result by a rider in World Championships.'"

"Wow, after this we're even more excited for the official practices," Alex smiled, clearly excited about our entry into MotoGP.

"For sure, we're going to win. We didn't fight to get here for nothing. Actually, you're already a champion." Anita encouraged me with her chin raised, her eyes sparkling with excitement. They are my strength, they've been part of my team from the start. Without them, I'm nothing, especially Alex. He's my coach, the one who knows everything about bikes, tires, and riding techniques, and also helps with the mechanical side.

"It will all work out," Alex encouraged me and then frowned. "You know your half-brother Jacob River Nolan is going to compete for the *Aspire Factory* team?"

"I know that, but that's not the main reason I want to win this World Championship. I want to be the best rider, it's a personal achievement. I love being on the track on two wheels."

"Good to know that, because you know I don't agree with conflict. This is a competition that should be healthy. Don't fall for Jacob's mind games, I know his reputation in the motocross world, he's a provocateur and loves to generate competitiveness among riders, in the worst possible way."

"You're right, Alex. I don't want to and I won't get into that. It will be tough because he's very arrogant."

"And arrogant," Anita added to what I said, grabbed my bag with my clothes, and handed it to me. "Now grab this and head to the truck. Robert arrived saying everything's ready for your arrival at the Jerez circuit. There are a lot of paparazzi there, so remember to be friendly, but don't say too much."

"Of course, the same thing we agreed on earlier."

"Exactly," she pulled me by the shoulder, making me turn around immediately. "And later, I want to know what happened last night at Navarro."

"Oh, but Juan already spilled the beans to you."

"He only mentioned the meeting between you, Dolores, and Jacob with Eve."

"There was nothing important. He just almost drove me crazy." She looked at me with concern.

"Please, what are we talking about now? Don't fall for this idiot's nonsense."

"I promise I won't, but if he provokes me on the track, it will be impossible for me to stay calm."

"Okay, we'll talk about this later," Alex interrupted. "We need to be at the circuit. The whole team is there for the first test."

After that, we left and got into the truck with Robert driving, clearly excited. The first test day is always like this—the excitement to see all our hard work on the track, live and in full throttle, is one of the best moments. When we arrived at the Jerez Circuit, he had to slow down because the entrance gate was crowded with paparazzi, fans from all over with posters with my name, other riders, and our numbers.

Robert slowly passed through the entrance while answering the quick-fire questions from journalists and curious paparazzi. I answered as Anita had instructed me, and we continued on. After a few minutes, we entered. I was moved when I saw that circuit, the first of the season. As soon as we reached our area, I saw our whole team waiting. My heart raced with emotion at that moment. It's not just my dream, it's theirs too.

I got out of the truck, receiving a warm welcome. I hugged and greeted everyone. Most of them have been working with me and Alex from the beginning, others we met after the wins in Valencia and the Isle of Man. We went into the locker room, Anita led the way, helping me get my thirteen-piece leather suit ready. This year, she made sure it was even more comfortable and protective.

All the suits are equipped with advanced full-body airbags. This airbag has two charges and remains inflated for 5 seconds after a fall. The suit carries highly advanced sensors capable of distinguishing whether the rider is on the track or not. It's the difference between a fall and a "saved" fall. Its activation is almost instantaneous, allowing it to be active even before the rider touches the asphalt. This is something we don't skimp on, as the material is also abrasion-resistant. Our team thought of everything for the world championship, and I'll give my best when I'm on the track.

I got dressed after Anita left. When she came back and helped me, I looked at myself in the mirror and felt very proud of how I looked in that suit. The colors are red, purple, and black, and my number is 93, very well represented. At first, many just called me by the number, then García. As soon as I left the locker room, the team applauded. They cheered, and Alex called me over, leading me to where the bike was being prepared by Tenner.

"Remember everything we talked about and practiced in Brazil, but here there are thirteen curves, eight to the right and five to the left. This is one of the slowest circuits in the Championship due to these very technical turns. There are several overtaking zones, but the most obvious ones are at the end of the straight, so stay alert."

"Alright, Alex, I'll pay attention to the curves, don't worry." I put on the helmet they handed me and my gloves.

"I know you'll give your best, don't forget that you can and will succeed."

"Thanks to you." Tom and Robert held the bike, already prepared and running. I mounted it and got into position, then accelerated. The roar of the engine quickened my heart as I took off for my first lap on the Jerez Circuit.

A dream that is coming true, fueled by adrenaline I had never felt before, it's even different from racing at the Isle of Man, one of the most dangerous in the world, which brings an immense thrill. That's why I love being on two wheels, no race is ever the same, even if I've already been on that circuit.

The thrill is unique in each one, the pleasure I felt from making the first of the thirteen curves of this circuit is what I would call an Epinephrine bomb, like an electric current running through my entire body. I accelerated and prepared for the next turns, at 160 km/h, shifting my body outward from the bike's axis towards the inside of the turn, creating the pendulum effect. It was clear that the bike has a perfect global evolution to be explored in the curves. I celebrated internally, feeling a unique emotion that I'm sure I would never forget.

CHAPTER NINE

Dolores

I spent the whole night thinking about that bastard. As I said before, a handsome man is a walking danger. I knew that if I laid eyes on one, he would take away all my peace, and with Guilhermo, it's been more than that. Everything I felt when we embraced, his body against mine, was new and very, very crazy and intense to ignore. But that's what had to happen; I can't be with him, especially being the brother of who he is, the flesh and blood of those Rivers Nolan.

"What are you thinking about?" my sister asked me, too curious as usual. It's obvious when my mind is boiling; I'm always talking, in fact, I'm the most restless person in the house. When I go quiet, everyone here gets suspicious and knows something is wrong, and they have no idea how big my problem is. How delicious he smells, how handsome he is, with that look..."—"Earth to Lola!" She snapped her fingers in front of me and then stared at me, smiling.

"What happened last night that made you get home so early and still be restless, walking around the house?"

"It was nothing, just anxious for today," I made up an excuse that I knew wouldn't fool Olivia; she knows me too well and knows I'm terrible at hiding things.

"What's happening today that I'm not remembering?" There was nothing, but I was stalling her, just didn't know which excuse to give to avoid talking to my sister about what happened last night.

BOUND BY FIRE AND FUEL 63

"Today we have an exclusive lunch at the restaurant, and I need to do well on the choreography tonight, so..." I rubbed my face, expressing my exhaustion. "I need to do well in both my jobs, and yes, my mind is boiling."

"I can imagine it's hard for you, but staying up all night restless, Lola?"

"Don't worry, Oli, everything will be fine." I gave her a big smile to make her less suspicious.

"You know I'm the mother of patience, and you're clearly hiding something you don't want to tell me now, but remember, I'm here and you can count on me when you're ready."

"Thanks for worrying and being here with me. Now tell me, how did she behave yesterday?" I asked about our mom, and she smiled.

"She was calm, even sat on the couch to watch TV with Luna and me, that series we love. Actually, she had fun and laughed with us."

"Oh, *Friends*, she always liked it, she used to watch it with me sometimes. I'm glad she managed to get out of that slump and sadness."

"At least a little." I finished the scrambled eggs, and we had our coffee. Luna and Mom always sleep in late. I woke up earlier because I still had a few things to sort out downtown and go to the dancer selection for the MotoGP event at the Jerez circuit. Oli and I chatted a bit more, then I sent a message to Nina, my best friend; she was coming with me to the selection. I didn't tell anyone at home about it because I didn't want them to get their hopes up. If it works out, I'll surprise them."

I finished getting ready and went straight to Nina's house after giving my mom and Luna a kiss. As soon as I arrived, she asked me to wait since she was still getting ready, but knowing my friend, she'd take a few more minutes, and that's exactly what happened when she opened the gate for me in a bathrobe. I smiled to myself; my friend is the most scatterbrained person I know. Every time we go out, she hands me a huge bag with the outfit she made for the selection.

"Sorry for the delay, I promise I'll just put on the clothes and brush my hair real quick," she shouted from her room. I opened the bag and saw that she had nailed it with the leather and colors used in the race suits from last year's riders.

"Nina, this outfit is amazing!" I complimented her, and she came into the room, zipping up her jeans and tossing her long hair back. I admire my friend; she's very beautiful and loves fashion, which really suits her personality. She's always on top of trends and likes to create pieces that reflect each person's individuality.

"I knew you'd love this outfit. Are you really going to do that choreography?"

"Yes, I'm still going to do it like I showed you, by the way, these pants are perfect for all my moves. Wow, when I tried them on, I didn't think they'd fit so well."

"If you want, try them on again. I made a few adjustments after the fitting, and I think it's perfect now." She smiled and pulled me towards her room. "Try it on quickly, Lola, we don't have much time to get to the circuit without being late." I just nodded and started changing. As soon as I put the pants on, I felt the comfort, and when I looked at myself in the mirror, I was amazed at how well they fit and looked. The material was leather, but with several cutouts of numbers and colors from the suits of some of last year's riders.

When I turned around to see how it looked from the back, I was hit hard. My friend had put the number 93 above the surname García on the back of the waistband, just above the hip. I don't know how she managed to do that, but I knew who it referred to, and I immediately felt uneasy, my whole body heating up just thinking about the possibility of running into him at the circuit and him misunderstanding.

"What was that idea on the back?"

"What? You don't like it? It's the number of the fan favorite for the podium this year, Guilhermo García. I know you guys..."

"Oh no, Nina, he might think I'm implying something, like interest, and I don't want..." I interrupted, staring at her through the mirror when I turned to face her.

"Lola, don't freak out, it's just a different design for the outfit you'll wear for the MotoGP event selection, the opening of the championship."

"Oh my God, do you see how crazy I've become? That's what that son of a bitch is making me go through!"

"Did something else happen after that incident at Navarro? Because he left right after you."

"No, I haven't seen him again, thank God!" I quickly took off the outfit, already wanting to move on from that conversation topic. "Let's change the subject, this one's getting really boring."

"Typical, Lola, you always avoid the topics we should talk about, but fine, I'm not going to argue today. It's selection day, and I'm ready, let's go?" She opened her arms, and I hugged her. She's my best friend; we've known each other since we were ten, studied together, and she was there for me through one of the hardest times in my life. She's the person I trust the most and can always count on, we're soul sisters, as she likes to say.

"Sorry, the outfit turned out amazing and unique, you always outdo yourself."

"You deserve the best, and I'm sure you're going to give an amazing dance performance and become the MotoGP event dancer."

"God, I hope so, my friend. Thanks for everything, and especially for tolerating me."

"Oh, that's nothing, it's been years putting up with your crazy mood, don't worry." She waved it off, and I looked at her in disbelief. That's my friend.

"I know, so let's hurry before I'm late." We organized everything and left. She was already used to riding on the back of my motorcycle, though she complains a little when I speed up too much, but we always have fun, enjoying the breeze of Jerez.

The ride to the circuit was smooth. We arrived too quickly, and I felt that little flutter in my stomach, the one you only feel when you're about to take the most important test of your life. The worst part was knowing I might run into the most famous rider of the moment, the one who makes my heart race and my legs weak. As soon as we arrived, we were directed to the area on the opposite side of the track where the presentation tests would take place. Nina couldn't enter, so she left me at the door of what would be the dressing room with my outfit. After I dressed, I quickly did my makeup. After so many years having to get ready alone, I knew exactly how to handle it, as I always have in my life.

I looked at my reflection in the mirror, and even though my whole body was trembling with anxiety, the courage and desire to fight for my dream were greater than anything. No one knows what it's like to carry the world on your shoulders like I do, which is why I can't afford the luxury of a relationship. I don't stop flirting with some men, I just keep my distance from guys like Guilhermo García. He's a walking danger, I have to keep my sanity, it's for the good of my family. Two encounters with him, and I've already felt the weight of the intensity in his gaze and body. We would definitely set Jerez on fire if we gave in to all that madness of attraction.

CHAPTER TEN

Guilhermo

When I left the pit and headed toward the stands, I had an unexpected encounter with Jacob River Nolan. He stared at me, his eyes sparking, the challenge crackling between us like flames, something I had never experienced before. There was competition with other riders, but always in a healthy and professional way, nothing more than that. Unfortunately, for the first time, I wanted to punch a rival rider in the face, because he's my brother, but I don't consider him as such. We didn't grow up together, we don't even know each other, to me he's just a spoiled, arrogant bad boy. He grew up under the wing of our father, and as much as I say it doesn't bother me, it does. It torments me, a lot.

I clenched my fists and held myself back, controlled my breathing, and just returned his expression, letting him know that soon, we would settle this score. We held each other's gaze, filled with fury, and after what seemed like minutes, we walked away, leaving an explicit message of confrontation hanging in the air. It's all nonsense, I know that, but I couldn't stop the rage that hits me every time I encounter him. It's funny how things work, imagine, Jacob has always been there and never affected me, but he's been away this whole time. Now, he's in my path, and on top of that, he's become my biggest adversary, not just on the track, but because of how he looks at Dolores. I know he feels an attraction to her too.

What's my problem with that?

Oh my God, I'm completely lost for this woman, a dancer who loves motorcycles. Another woman with the same taste as mine. Another thing I'm sure of, just by her gaze, you can tell she would be up for any madness with me. However, this time, I can't let anything happen to her, like it did with Mari. I couldn't stand losing anyone else. It's out of the question. *But what do I do about this overwhelming desire that takes over my body when I see her?* Every time I'm in the same space as this woman, I feel the urge to touch her, claim her, and make her mine.

I shook my head, refusing to think about her at that moment, then walked down the corridor to get back to my team. But I heard a song that intrigued me, making me wonder where it was coming from. The beat was familiar, so I approached the door to peek. Through my line of sight, I saw Dolores moving her body in front of a motorcycle, and her leather outfit caught my attention. Above her waist, on her hips, my last name and number were embroidered with sequins. Even more intrigued, I opened the door a little further, and to my surprise, I recognized the dancer's identity as soon as she finished sliding her legs open to the floor in a perfect 180-degree angle in front of the bike.

I clapped before I could even think about what I was doing, as all eyes turned to me. I was an intruder, not invited into that room, but those who understand dance were there. Still, the music and the fact that the dancer was wearing my number on her outfit intrigued me. Even more so after seeing that the one performing that perfect choreography was none other than Dolores López.

Her eyes locked with mine, her striking green eyes turned bright, almost hesitant, but still as hot as only she could be, dear God. Lola is absolute perfection! I stood there staring at her, unable to look away. It's surreal how much she affects me, totally hypnotizing. I could have slipped away quietly, but I couldn't resist, seeing from her outfit that she admires me as a rider. I smiled to myself, unable to contain it, and one of the women in front of me recognized me, grinning and calling out.

"Guilhermo García!" she called out loudly, drawing the attention of all the other women in the room. I heard my name echoed in unison. "What an honor to have you here at our auditions! Don't tell me you already know about the performances we're having before the races?"

"I didn't know about this, but I was passing by the corridor and heard the beat, I must admit I was intrigued," I said, trying to sound as normal as possible, not as if I had just been swept away by Dolores' incredible choreography. She just smiled awkwardly, and I could bet she wanted to escape that situation. I felt that she wanted to get out of there, and I understood her, because it felt like we were being exposed. I know it's just a wrong impression, but I was sure she felt the same.

"It's alright, we'd like to invite you to stay for the performances. We're choosing which dancers will be the official ones for MotoGP."

"This is the first time I've heard about performances before the competition. It's a show in itself, and the dancers are killing it. Congratulations on the innovation."

"We appreciate your compliment and support. Feel free to stay and watch the rest. Make yourself comfortable." She turned to the girls after flashing me an excited smile. "Let's keep going, girls, you're all doing great, but only three will be chosen."

With a smile and knowing I couldn't stay there, I sat in the first row to watch the next performances under Dolores' sharp gaze. I still kept my good humor. I was irritated by the unpleasant encounter with Jacob, but it all passed the moment I saw the identity of the dancer performing. This was getting more and more interesting, and I should run, as fast as I could, away from her, but instead, I only found myself moving toward her faster and faster. Crazy, right?

Dolores

I KNEW I RISKED BUMPING into Guilhermo or Jacob at the circuit, but I felt a bit relieved when I realized there was no one I recognized walking through the halls of the Jerez Circuit. However, fate, not satisfied with our other unpredictable encounters, decided to play a trick on me right in the middle, or rather, at the end of my performance, and surprise me with the presence of Guilhermo, who was the first to applaud my choreography. Of course, he must have seen his name and number embroidered on my outfit and was probably feeling like the king of the world. That's why he sat in the front row, smiling, looking in a good mood.

I felt his gaze wander over my body, and I didn't look away until he smiled slyly, as if he didn't care that he had been caught. It's truly arrogant of him. I rolled my eyes, trying to keep calm in his presence, which was very difficult, but I wouldn't let anything ruin my moment. I needed and really wanted to be one of the three dancers chosen for the opening ceremonies of the races. It's a unique and extraordinary chance to be seen by so many countries and different people. I never imagined the MotoGP would do something like this, but it looks like they want to innovate this year.

Two more performances followed until they asked me to do an improvised choreography to the song *Faster* by Within Temptation. Ecstatic and suddenly inspired, I walked toward Guilhermo and asked him a favor: to bring his motorcycle. I saw him quickly type a message on his phone, and his phone beeped.

Everyone turned to him as he apologized and got up, heading to the back of the room. I heard him mention Alex's name, arguing about something I couldn't understand, but in the end, he said to bring it. Just in time for the last performance, Guilhermo's team arrived with the motorcycle. I smiled, euphoric and emotional. My heart racing, I approached them and thanked Alex, who smiled and winked at his friend.

"What are you going to do?"

"Wait and see. I want you to feel the excitement when you're putting on the show, especially when you're on the track."

"You don't exist, Lola! But be careful, it's not like your bike, you know you have to be careful when braking." His voice was low and raspy in my ear, sending a chill down my spine. I took a deep breath, and as soon as the other dancer finished her choreography, I jumped onto Guilhermo's bike.

"Don't worry, I've been watching motorcycle races since I was a kid, so I won't do anything too risky." He nodded, his eyes shining, giving me that characteristic sideways smile. The Wacco Racing baby is truly amazing, under the pilot's fixed gaze. I started the bike and did a lap around the space. Alex cheered when he entered my field of vision, and I heard him say that I was good. After two more laps to get somewhat familiar with the bike, I did the final lap, signaling for everyone to join me on the track. To do what I had in mind, I needed the space of the track.

As soon as I heard the guitar riff from *Faster*, I brought the bike onto the track and performed stunts with it. It wasn't exactly ideal for what I had planned, but it would work to complement the performance. I managed to stand up and dance a bit, then turned off the bike and put the stand down. In front of it, I did some contemporary and striking moves that earned applause from everyone, finishing with a gesture as if the bike were the kryptonite of the entire championship, just like the instrument for a band like

Within Temptation. The song says a lot about what riders and their teams go through in the races. In their case, they race faster to reach the podium and be champions, even though the song talks about racing faster for love, and I realized that the song actually said a lot about what I felt for Guilhermo.

Everyone applauded, and I couldn't process anything because his eyes were on me in such a fiery and intense way that I longed for us to be alone in that moment. I couldn't stop myself, nor could I avoid it, I would race faster toward him, his body, and let him burn me alive. My God! What was I thinking?

"And the chosen ones are Rosie, Marta, and Dolores! Congratulations, girls, you put on a great show, especially you," the woman said, smiling and pointing at me. "We want you to perform this last choreography at the opening of the race. You'll have time to rehearse, and everything will be fine. This is the kind of emotion we want to convey with these performances, the same one we see in the races."

"Oh, thank you! I'm happy to be a part of this. It's an incredible honor and opportunity," my heart raced frantically, and my entire body shivered, but with emotion and happiness, something exploded inside me in a unique way.

"That's right! And next week, you can start rehearsing and thinking about your outfits." I thanked her again, then hugged the first person I saw. I only realized it was Guilhermo when I felt his arms and perfume. He didn't let go of me, taking me to the other side, leaving everyone behind, even his bike and team.

Unable to stop him, I screamed his name at the top of my lungs, and he only stopped when we reached an empty space. He pressed me against the first wall and kissed me wildly, igniting fire all over my body. My hands roamed over his back, trying to feel his skin. I slipped my hands inside his shirt, scratching his back, consumed by wild lust.

I jumped into his lap under his stormy gaze, filled with a desire that mirrored mine. I wouldn't let go of his lips either, so I tugged at his lower lip with my teeth, and he groaned hoarsely. My tongue explored every inch of his mouth, and it felt like we were about to swallow each other, the hunger taking us both. What I feel for Guilhermo is like fire running wild, spreading everywhere, and in his case, he feels it all over my body. I'm so screwed, God! How can I stay away from this man?

CHAPTER ELEVEN

Guilhermo

Without saying a word, she looked at me with those intense and exotic eyes, making me long to touch her. Dolores had no idea that in my crazy mind, I was already on my motorcycle, grabbing her with all the wild desire that had consumed me since the first time I saw her. Lola is a woman, hot and sweet at the same time, a bomb about to explode, just like my mind at this moment.

We were both resisting, but how much longer could we deny what our bodies longed for? My heart beat fast as she got closer, even though we were in the Circuit of Jerez, filled with people. I took her to a quiet spot. I pulled her towards me, pressing her body against mine and pressed her against the box wall where I was supposed to leave. Unable to control myself, I pressed my mouth to hers, hungry for her taste. I never imagined that our kiss would be so delicious. Her full lips and tongue tangled in circles inside my mouth, leaving me as hot as hell.

I wanted to devour her alive, take everything she could give me, so I consumed her low moans of pleasure and spread my hands over her delicious ass. I bit her lower lip, and we locked eyes, her gaze full of lust was all I needed. I undid the button of her leather pants with her help, moved her panties aside, and, keeping her gaze on mine, I caressed her wet entrance for me.

"Damn, Lola!" I cursed in a guttural voice, desperate to be inside her soon. "Are you sure you want to do it here?" The little minx smiled sideways and rolled her eyes, mocking me. I spread my hand firmly across her ass, and she moaned loudly. I placed my finger in her mouth, wanting to silence her, but Lola did something that made me even more crazy to have her, not just between her legs, but in her mouth too.

"There couldn't be a better place for this, hurry up, I want to feel the same speed you put into your beautiful bike."

"The same?" I asked, gazing at her, my expression filled with lust, feeling the weight of her question as a challenge. I massaged her clitoris and felt her body wriggle under my hand, then I slowly inserted two fingers inside her, and she threw her head back, giving me a beautiful view of her enjoying what I was doing.

It wasn't long before I heard the rain fall where we were. Despite being leaned against the box wall, the roof didn't cover part of it. I felt the cold rainwater on our hot bodies, and that didn't dampen my desire to fuck until we collapsed from pleasure. So, I began to move my fingers inside her faster and faster, capturing her mouth and kissing her savagely without holding back.

Lola didn't fall behind. She moved her hips against my fingers and moaned into my mouth. When I felt she was close to orgasm, she bit my lower lip hard, making me go wild with desire seeing her reach her peak with my fingers inside her wet, hot pussy. Thinking of that made me remember that my dick was about to explode in my shorts. I gave her a few minutes, but I couldn't control myself, I grabbed the condom from my wallet, and she looked at me. Without saying a word, I lowered my shorts and underwear, and my hard, ready cock sprang out, prepared to enter her pussy. I opened the condom wrapper and slid it all the way down my length.

"I want and need to be inside you, Lola," I said after she grabbed my cock, making me moan as I felt her hands moving along its length. She jumped into my lap and leaned against the wall, never taking her eyes off mine. I positioned the tip of my cock at her entrance, and we both moaned at the contact. I just wanted to lose myself in those eyes, her mouth, and her delicious body. My cherry, yes, this woman has the most incredible cherry flavor, the sweet, red one.

"Guilher..." she began, but I didn't let her finish. I entered her slowly, but she nodded for me to go faster. I pushed all the way in and started a delicious rhythm. I didn't know whether it was sweat or rain. Everything mixed, I captured her full lips, and we kissed while I kept thrusting into her without stopping. When I felt her body tremble and contract, I bit her lower lip and didn't stop thrusting, pushing her to the limit, just like me, as I came so hard that I couldn't control the guttural sound I let out, moaning her name. Her eyes looked at me, still full of fire, but something suddenly darkened them. Without saying a word, she pulled up her pants and buttoned them. I couldn't move; I just watched Lola run off in the rain.

I dressed quickly and let the water fall on me. I was already wet anyway, and not even that could cool me down. My body was hot and ecstatic. How could I have acted so impulsively? How stupid am I, Guilhermo! I lost track of time and only realized where I was when Alex came running.

"Guilhermo, what are you doing here in the rain?" he asked impatiently, and I couldn't respond, not after everything I had just experienced with Lola a few minutes ago. I ran my hands through my hair, nervous and confused by the way I was still feeling.

"I couldn't control myself, Alex, I couldn't help it."

"What happened? We were all looking for you."

"What happened is that I couldn't escape the desire I felt for Dolores. But I don't want to talk about it right now."

"What? You're going to tell me this story properly because I knew there was a reason you rushed off pulling the girl."

"Can we just get out of here?" I just wanted to escape. I could still hear the wild sex I had with Lola and her delicious moans in my mind.

"Right now, that's why I came after you. Also, because we wanted to train on the wet track with the other tires."

"That's perfect, I just need to put the suit on again."

"But you need to tell me this story properly afterward. I'm way too curious, and you, of all people, losing control with Dolores. Speaking of her, what a woman she is on your bike, now I get why you were so excited."

"Shut the fuck up, Alex," I snapped, and he looked at me, smiling.

"Man, I don't know what you did with a woman like that, and you're in this bad mood. I swear to God, I can't understand you," he said, and I didn't answer. When we reached the Wacco box, I went to the locker room and took a quick shower. As I was drying off, I turned to place the towel on the bench and saw that my back was scratched. Fucking wild woman. I threw my head back, trying to shake off those memories, but the only way to clear my mind was to hit the wet track again to try to forget how she had taken over me.

I put on the suit and went out to prepare. Alex came over with Tenner in tow. He looked at me and smiled.

"Is everything okay?"

"All good, I'm ready."

"Great, let's time it." I put on my helmet, and soon two guys from the team brought the bike. I got on, and with Alex's nod, I started it up and accelerated. Feeling the adrenaline pumping through my veins, I did well on the Expo 92 turn, kept the same pace, and was careful with the upcoming turns, but without losing speed. I managed to complete twelve laps at 362.4 km/h, and the team was really excited. That's why I love what I do, it feels good. After the intensity of what I lived with Lola, I needed to ride to clear my mind and realized that I shouldn't have let her go like that.

"Hey, Guilhermo, there's no way you're not the winner in this circuit, even with eighteen bikes and good riders on the grid," Alex commented.

"Ah, I just want to give my best on this track. This is my home, where I was born, and nothing could make me prouder than this."

"We're already proud of you!" he said, then left. I went over to Tenner and gave him my feedback on the bike, which was well-developed, and the tires did their job on the wet track. Although I knew it wasn't going to rain, the trend was for it to warm up and the asphalt to reach 59°C. After chatting with my team for a while, Anita arrived with some of our sponsors for official photos with the bike. This was a must after every race, and they filmed my test. They would send all the footage for us to post on our social media.

"So, are you going to tell me what happened with you and Lola?"

"Dios mio! Alex, you're like a little old lady with how much you gossip."

"Well, he is a snitch, but I'm curious too. Despite that, I promise I won't tell him anything. I know you didn't reveal anything to our troublemaker friend."

"I just want to go home. A few more days and we'll be in another place. Speaking of which, have you checked the hotel in Qatar?"

"Of course, I have. By the way, I made a list of the best hotels in the other countries we'll be visiting. But don't change the subject, tell me already." I grabbed my backpack and sunglasses and put them on my head.

"I just want to go home. I'm tired. It's been a long day, and I still need to work out a bit today."

"But are you crazy? You already worked out in the morning! Let's go home now, but tonight we're going to Navarro's. He called me and invited us to celebrate Lola's success since she stood out in the presentations."

"I think it's better to rest since tomorrow..." My friend and agent looked at me, surprised.

"No, sir, we're going together, and stop trying to avoid Lola. You can't keep acting like an idiot. Dios mio, I'm telling you!" she snapped, and when she used that louder, more authoritative tone, I knew there was no way I could deny her. After that, all I could do was go home, take a shower, and go out with Alex and my persistent, stubborn friend.

When we arrived at Juan's bar, I didn't expect to run into Jacob's girlfriend on my first trip to the bathroom. She looked at me with interest, I'd even say desire. Her gaze was anything but innocent when she stared at me and smiled, all mischievous. Bold as ever, she licked her lips like a hungry cat, and it just made me feel incredibly awkward, wanting to run as far as I could.

"Guilhermo García, no point looking at me like that, I still want you in my bed, devouring me with lust and giving us both the greatest pleasure in the world."

"I never..." She silenced me by putting a finger on my lips, leaving me stunned.

"Don't say never, darling. You don't know what tomorrow will bring, and I'm just telling you that when I want something, or someone, I simply get it, and you'll beg for it." With that, she walked off, swaying down the hall, and when I turned around, I saw Jacob at the end of the hallway, staring at me with a not-so-friendly look. That was the last thing I needed!

CHAPTER TWELVE

Dolores

After running as fast as possible from that box, soaking wet from the rain, I stopped only when I realized I was heading towards the exit. My heart was racing, just like my body, and even though I had been caught in the rain, I was still burning hot. What did I just do? I leaned against a wall, needing to process what had just happened, but my mind kept spinning. Because never, despite having had a few relationships, had I felt this way. The way Guilhermo and I kissed, the way he grabbed me. I threw my head back and hit myself.

How could you, Dolores?

I closed my eyes and tried to breathe deeply, releasing the air I was holding in, making me even more nervous. My heart rate began to normalize, and I let out another breath, relieved, but as I closed my eyes, I could only see images of me and Guilhermo kissing, tearing off our clothes, surrendering to that insane and overwhelming attraction. But I can't help but emphasize how fabulous and amazing it was to be with that reckless rider. I could feel the adrenaline coursing through my veins in a unique way. The heat that spread throughout my body and the pleasure I felt as soon as he entered me, the intense way he touched me, his rough and strong hands, just thinking about it makes me feel hot and wanting to repeat it for an indefinite amount of time.

Unable to hold back, I distracted myself with the memories, also feeling his woody scent still lingering on me, mixed with the rain and sweat. I didn't even realize when I felt a slap on my arm. I opened my eyes and found Nina staring at me with a furrowed brow, looking angry.

"Why are you walking around with that goofy smile on your face?" She yelled, catching the attention of people walking by, and then I realized I had disappeared for quite a while.

"That smile is because I'm the new dancer for the MotoGP presentations, did you forget?"

"I didn't forget, but you disappeared with that rider you said you wanted to stay away from. What happened?"

"Nina, I need to tell you I was trying to escape from him, and then it started to rain."

"That's not what happened, your lips are swollen, and you have some red marks on your neck, and your hair is a mess. Don't hide anything from me, I know you two hooked up, and it looks like it was insane." I rolled my eyes and smiled, surrendering to my friend. I couldn't hide anything from her. We've been friends since childhood and always tell each other everything.

"It was crazy, Nina, despite all that, I'm so torn. We need to talk, but not here." She pulled me and we quickly left that place. The rain had already passed by then, and we were able to get on the bike and head to Navarro's.

"We have to celebrate, Juan called me a hundred times, that crazy guy," she said exaggeratedly and smiled, removing her helmet and tossing her long hair over her shoulders.

"He was anxious and rooting for you, always wanting to know."

"You always sucking up to him, Argh!" she declared, gesturing with her hands, as she always did, something characteristic of my friend. She feels a bit jealous of my friendship with Juan, he always likes to protect me, and these two drive me crazy sometimes.

"Nina Rodriguez, you look amazing!" I turned around as soon as I heard the disgusting voice of River Nolan complimenting my friend, then staring at me, ignoring me, thinking he could hit me that way. Little does he know, it's better for him to keep his cool.

"That rider is so rude." I rolled my eyes and pulled Nina inside with me, making her forget about the rude Jacob. We saw Juan serving something to the blonde hanging around with River Nolan.

"Lola, finally! I've called you so many times, where the hell have you been? Why did you take so long?"

"Juan, my dear, don't worry, I've taken good care of our little friend here, who is the newest official dancer of the MotoGP Championship." He jumped over the bar counter, ran to hug me tightly, and tossed my hair in the air.

"Hijo de puta, you did it!" He's the best, I can't get rid of him or Nina, but they're my only friends. The ones who truly cheer for my victories and achievements, sincerely. Not everyone is lucky enough to find people like that in life, so I hugged him tightly too. "You know you deserve this, and after this, you can be sure you'll have the world at your feet."

"Thank you, my friend! Do you know how happy I am?"

"I can imagine, but this feeling is unique and yours, you need to live it and celebrate it. Today we're closing the bar to celebrate your achievement."

"You're crazy, you can't close the bar!" I yelled at him, and he smiled slyly and looked at me with a mischievous gaze.

"It will only be open for exclusive people, and nothing would make me happier than leaving the stage open for you to do whatever you want."

"Wow, that's going to be amazing!" Nina exclaimed loudly, excited for our celebration night.

"We'll do that Spanish night, but with plenty of Reggaeton."

"Done, it will be only invited people and VIPs," Juan said, then left excitedly to organize everything.

"I just need a shower to go to the restaurant, with the rehearsals, I'll have to quit that job. Also, from what I heard the girls say, they'll pay really well."

"That's perfect, and don't worry, your restaurant job was only for a short time since you really want to live off dancing."

"Definitely, my friend."

"Now, go take a shower. Do you want me to call Olivia?"

"Yes, please, but wait a bit. I want to talk to her." I left, but came back, and she was already finishing the call.

"Lola, is something wrong?" Olivia answered, speaking frantically.

"What happened is that I signed up for the dancer selection for the MotoGP presentations. I'm the newest dance sensation in the Motorcycle Racing Championship!"

"What a dream, mi hermana! You totally deserve this achievement, it's the first of many! But you didn't tell us anything at home!"

"I wanted to surprise you, I'm so happy, and we'll celebrate today. How is Mama Dulce?"

"We'll celebrate, yes, and as for Madre, she's doing really well. She started cooking, looking cheerful. You can relax."

"How wonderful, Madre is doing well, I'm even happier to know that, take care of her because I'll be getting home later today."

"That's right, hermana, we'll celebrate tomorrow because today I'm here taking care of Luna and Dona Dulce so you can enjoy yourself."

"It's a shame, but we'll be together tomorrow. I'm going to the restaurant to quit my job."

"It's fine, don't worry. I also need to study for a test, it'll be easy. Enjoy the moment and celebrate a lot, you're always working."

"Thanks, Oli, you're amazing. Love you!" We said our goodbyes and I went to the bar's dressing room to take my shower. Luckily, I always leave clothes there because I work every night presenting at Navarro. I stepped into the shower stall and let the water fall over my body, but the truth was I didn't want his scent to leave, just like the memories that had deeply rooted themselves in my mind. Just like on the tracks, Guilhermo was intense and bold, unforgettable.

The man, besides being an extraordinary rider, is handsome and seems to be a good person, at least that's the impression I had. He's a River Nolan, but he doesn't care about that last name, which moves mountains. He uses García from his mother, who raised him alongside his grandmother. That's what the newspapers, magazines, and social media say. Always discreet, and I've never seen anything more about him. I researched the women in his life and only one was ever in the spotlight with him, Mariana Salles, and she was the one who held his heart for more than three years. As far as I know, no one has been in his life since, and he always skips this part in interviews.

I dried myself, remembering his hands claiming me and wanting more. He seemed hungry, and by God, I was too. I couldn't deny it, and something about my performance on one of his bikes drove him crazy with desire. My legs turned to jelly when he started thrusting into me. I don't even know how I managed to walk after everything. All I knew was I couldn't look him in the eye. The weight of what happened quickly took over my mind. That's what happens when you give in to unrestrained and unreasonable desire.

"Lola, are you done?" Nina yelled from outside.

"I'm coming out," I answered, wrapping myself in a towel and pushing away those indecent thoughts that hit me. The truth is, I'm afraid of all the intensity of Guilhermo. He has such a past, and it doesn't fit into this moment of my life.

"You know, I thought you had drowned under the shower," Nina said impatiently.

"Wow, what's wrong with you? Are you on your period, or is something going on?"

"It's just that you've been lost in your own world, thinking too much. I don't know exactly what happened on that circuit while you were gone."

"I was with him, you must have seen that crazy guy pulling me away with no control."

"I saw that, but what happened afterward?"

"He took me completely, Nina, and I can't think straight anymore." She stared at me with her wide blue eyes.

"My God!"

"Nina, now is not the time for you to be calling out to the saints!" I shouted at her.

"Sorry, it's just that I'm shocked. You two kissed and then?"

"Then we had the most insane, wild, and unreasonable sex of my life, and I don't know what to think! I mean, I'm confused."

"Lola, I knew this was going to happen sooner or later. You two together, it's almost impossible not to feel the energy between you. I noticed it the moment he walked into that room. His gaze at you could set everything on fire."

"I know that, but I can't get carried away. I need to focus on my dance career. Look at the opportunity I'm getting."

"Lola, I get it. Today we'll celebrate, and later, when things have calmed down, we'll talk about Guilhermo and all his fire." She poked me while I got dressed, and after I finished, I went back to the bar, where Juan served me a lemonade with plenty of ice, just what I needed.

"Today was also Guilhermo's first test. Did you meet him there?" I was drinking the juice and almost spit it on Juan's face. I choked a bit, and Nina started patting my back.

"What was that, Lola?"

"It just went down wrong, and I choked," I deflected, realizing my friend was staring at me with curiosity, but I knew he wouldn't ask any more questions.

"We saw him quickly, but it was really rushed."

"I know. I already sent him a message, as well as to Anita and Alex."

"Wow, that gorgeous dark-haired guy is coming too." Nina smiled devilishly. She thinks he's handsome; he really is, although I prefer the rider.

"You're impossible!" Juan said to Nina, who glared at him angrily.

"Look who's talking, the one who's with Anita. Stop being a hypocrite, Navarro!"

"I was just teasing you, Nina, but I forget you hate that."

"Always."

"I'm going to leave you two here and go quit my job at the restaurant. Soon, it'll be your turn, Juan."

"I know. I'm sad to lose one of my best friends, but I'm so happy to see you soaring higher, and I'm sure this is just the beginning," he said, took my hand, and kissed it gently. After that, I thanked him and left the bar. I mounted my bike and headed to the other side of Jerez. I quit my job, happy to leave a position I didn't like, but one that had helped me support my family for long enough.

Later, I returned to Navarro's, and it was already dark. The street was full of cars and bikes. As I passed through the back entrance, I was met with loud music and the usual buzz of the bar, which really felt more like a nightclub. Juan expanded his father's business. He said he was going to make some changes to the bar, and when he reopened it, it was a success. Tourists love coming to experience one of the oldest bars in Jerez, serving both modern drinks and the region's famous Sherry wine.

I approached the bar and soon heard my name shouted loudly by my friend Juan.

"Today is a celebration day, so we'll close the bar at 9 PM. We're celebrating Lola, our newest official MotoGP dancer, who is innovating this year with a new performance to open the grid."

Everyone cheered my name, and I smiled and thanked them, feeling so happy for the love from my friend. "Play the music, DJ, today the stage and the track are hers, our flamenco queen."

I got on stage as soon as the opening of "Despacito" by Luis Fonsi ft. Daddy Yankee started playing, immersing me in the beat of the music. I called my fellow dancers to join me, and as soon as I spotted Nina among the crowd, she came over bringing Anita and Alex with her. I was sure Guilhermo was somewhere in that bar too. But I decided to enjoy my celebration, and I immediately started a move for everyone to follow. It was delicious to see even Juan dancing with a flair only he has.

We grooved to the sound of "Mi Gente" by J Balvin, and everyone made space for me to dance in the middle. I threw my arms in the air and shook my hips to the ground. When I came back up, my heart skipped a beat as I felt Guilhermo's body too close to mine, putting on a sensual show for everyone. I didn't care, I wanted to feel it a little and allow myself, so I turned to face him and felt his gaze burning me alive with such intensity. I swallowed hard, tried to contain myself, but that rider was just too much to absorb on a dance floor.

CHAPTER THIRTEEN

Guilhermo

I should have stayed home, as I'm about to start a world championship, and we're going to be touring across Europe. But just the thought of missing Dolores' celebration, I don't know what got into me. I got ready, and before I knew it, I was at Navarro's with Alex and Anita, who had barely arrived at the bar before she was already all over Juan. We arrived an hour later, and the doors were being closed, as planned. My eyes instinctively started searching for Dolores throughout the bar, which looked more like a nightclub.

The truth is that Juan transformed the traditional bar into a place where you find unique fun all night long. Then I heard Navarro's voice freeze everyone, honoring his friend. I tried to get closer, but I was too far from the stage, and all I could hear was everyone cheering and applauding the new dancer of the MotoGP Championship. She deserves this and much more. From what little I know, she works day and night to support her family— a hardworking and talented woman.

Not fully processing what I was doing, I started moving toward the stage, and as soon as I got closer to her, she was provocatively dancing to "Mi Gente" by J Balvin. I decided to follow her lead. When she turned to face me, I felt her eyes meet mine, her green iris filled with a fire I had seen before on the Circuit, when we lost control and gave ourselves to each other in such a wild and unique way that I can't erase from my mind.

"What do you think you're doing?" she asked, as she moved closer to my body.

"Just fighting for what I want..."

"What exactly do you want, Guilhermo? Tell me specifically." Damn! Lola didn't make it easy, staring at me like that, her dark green eyes filled with the crazy energy that flowed between us. It was almost crackling, my whole body aching to feel her delicious skin, and she seemed to enjoy leaving me like this.

"I can do better." As soon as I got close enough, I took her into my arms and did what I had been imagining since the moment I saw her on the stage of the bar. The music was still playing, and I took the first step, leaving her surprised. I knew she thought I was going to kiss her. But not yet, baby! As much as I was dying to taste her and feel her tongue in my mouth again, I needed to move my body along with hers for a few minutes and drown myself in her sweet and warm perfume.

"Loco Contigo" started to play, and it couldn't have been more perfect, because the lyrics of that song said everything I was feeling for Lola, from the moment I saw her pop the bike up on one wheel on the road, something that hypnotized me. Even without knowing her identity, she intrigued me, and when I saw her on the Navarro stage, that's when I was truly captivated. I followed her steps, and we moved our bodies in perfect synchronicity. I could only stare into her eyes. We pushed our chests forward and back, making it even more intimate, our thighs pressed together, and I sang the song to her.

Tú me tienes loco, loco contigo
Yo trato y trato, pero, baby, no te olvido
Tú me tienes loco, loco contigo (come on)
Yo trato y trato, pero, baby, aquí yo sigo (okay, okay)

When the song ended, I pulled her off the stage towards the bar. When I saw that our friends were sitting, I took her to the table. Juan asked one of his men to bring us a drink. We chose the good sherry wine, typical of the region. It's fortified and liqueur-like. It's slightly salty and dry, but I like it a lot. I don't drink wine often, but since it's a special night, I wouldn't miss toasting with my friends and Lola.

I sat next to her, and it was getting harder not to admire her carefree and easy smile. Lola's joy is contagious. Despite being tough, Lola has a unique and beautiful energy. On this particular night, she wore a red bodysuit with a generous round neckline and a pair of denim shorts that showcased her tanned, well-toned legs.

While Alex was talking some nonsense that made everyone laugh, acting on what my body desired at that moment, I ran my fingertips along her exposed thigh. Out of the corner of my eye, I saw her turn to look at me, but that didn't stop me. I turned and returned her look with a sideways smile. Her green eyes were wide from my boldness. Honestly, I was surprised at myself. Where's your control, Guilhermo? I kept talking with Anita and Navarro normally, although inside, my mind was literally on fire for this beautiful woman with green eyes.

Lola got restless and stood up, then returned to the stage, giving her show while the Reggaeton music heated up the dance floor. She danced under my gaze, which couldn't get enough of the beautiful sight of her, my eyes addicted to Dolores. How could I stay focused on racing, knowing she would be at every event, dancing like this and making everyone drool? What madness, look at what I'm thinking. She's not mine. Not yet. I shook my head, trying to clear those confusing thoughts from my mind, and didn't see Anita approach until I heard her voice too close.

"You still haven't told me what happened between you and her," she said, directing her gaze toward Dolores.

"We lost control, Anita. Actually, it was my fault."

"Why is it your fault?" she asked, but she already knew the answer. My friend is smart and knows me well.

"I shouldn't have dragged her into the mess I am, Anita. I just got out of mourning and..." She cut me off, as she always did, not having the patience to listen to me like this.

"For God's sake, Guilhermo. How long are you going to deprive yourself of living? Time is passing while you're sitting there worried about what's already gone. You loved Mariana and did everything you could, but we don't understand the purposes of fate, that's not up to us. Accept as soon as possible that you need to live and not blame yourself for desiring such an incredible woman like Dolores, or you'll lose her before you even have her for real," she said and left, leaving me immersed in thoughts. I know I'm stubborn about accepting that I deserve such a wonderful woman. Even though I was in an internal struggle, my body can't hold back when we're in the same room, or even when we're apart.

The living proof was after what happened. Even on my bike, doing twelve more laps at over 300 km/h, training to start the season, I couldn't forget the extraordinary feeling of having her body close to mine, and especially, her mouth.

After thinking a bit more and appreciating Dolores, I headed back to where she was dancing. I bumped into someone, and as soon as I turned to apologize, I found Jacob, who smiled mockingly.

"Look, the champion. Be careful where you walk, and especially who you bump into." That arrogant playboy is still cheeky.

"You know, Jacob! It's not worth wasting time arguing. It's better we meet on the track, where we'll see if you can be a champion like me," I decided to provoke him back.

"We'll see! And if you actually stay with her," he said, directing his gaze to Dolores, dancing on the stage.

"Know that we're not in a competition."

"We're not, but I feel like I'm in one with you by my side, fighting for the podium, which in this case is Dolores."

"How dare you talk about her like that?" My blood boiled at how he referred to her so disrespectfully. What a disgusting guy.

"I'll talk however I want, and I just wanted to provoke this reaction from you." I moved towards him, and he smiled sarcastically, seeing that he had gotten to me, but Juan arrived quickly and held me back.

"I've noted that she's your weak spot, but it won't lead to anything, since you're also a River Nolan, and from what I know, she doesn't like people from our bloodline."

"Don't put words in my mouth, Jacob River Nolan, and as far as I know, Guilhermo only uses the García surname." Dolores arrived, speaking with her nose in the air, staring at the disgusting bastard that is my brother.

"I don't think the fact that he's a García is what matters. That doesn't change the fact that he's also a River Nolan's son."

"We're getting into a delicate issue here, Jacob. I won't accept you talking about anything related to this. You know one part of the story, but not the whole thing, and I won't accept you talking about my mother. It's important for you to know that, no matter how much your father is mine too, it's always been my mother who raised me. That's worth more than blood." He clenched his fists, holding back, because he knew I was right, and then he kept staring as Dolores took my hand and led me toward the back of the bar.

We entered a corridor that led to a balcony just on the other side. I didn't even know all this existed. But Juan has lived here his whole life. His parents used to live in the back of the bar, on a whole plot of land. I felt the night breeze and could finally take a deep breath, feeling a little more at ease. Dolores didn't say anything; she stood there, waiting for me to have some time to clear my mind, and honestly, just her presence made me feel better.

"You've known Juan since childhood?"

"Yes, we met because my parents frequented this bar a lot, and our families were friends. Actually, we were here almost every night, but Juan helped me when he saw me almost lying on the table, half asleep."

"So that's how you became friends," I affirmed, because they are like brothers.

"Yes, he brought me to this balcony. It was a bit different back then, but I felt welcomed, and he understood my situation without me needing to say a word."

"Juan is very intuitive and a friend for all occasions. I'm happy you have him in your life. I'm sorry for what you had to hear in there. Jacob..." She came closer and silenced me by placing her hand over my mouth, never taking her eyes off mine. Just feeling her closer made my heart race, captivated by her presence and complete attention on me. I felt more and more fascinated by this fearless woman.

"Don't say anything, Guilhermo. What happened today on the Circuit hasn't left my mind, and it feels like you've imprinted yourself on every part of my body. I want to know what we're going to do about this because I'm so lost..." I didn't let her finish, because I put both my hands on her face, acting on what I was feeling in that moment, consumed by a crazy and tempestuous attraction. I pressed my mouth to hers, tasting that delicious flavor of hers, which completely unraveled my senses. I pulled her lower lip, drawing a moan from her, and then her hands tangled in my shirt, making our bodies press even closer together.

Damn! I was already hard and desperate to be inside her, to lose myself in pleasure until we couldn't take it anymore. Once again, we were lost in each other, and nothing would stop me from living this with her because it was something we couldn't control. It was irresistible.

Just like what happened on the circuit, Lola ran off and left me alone again. Baby, this is becoming a recurring thing. But, without thinking, I kissed her, unable to control myself, and that must have made her pull back, just like when I pulled her into that box.

Damn it, Guilhermo! Why are you acting like this?

CHAPTER FOURTEEN

Dolores

The days passed quickly, and I was dedicating myself to rehearsals for the first performance. I felt anxious, wondering if they would like the choreography, and on top of that, I did everything I could to avoid bumping into Guilhermo at the Circuito de Jerez. After that kiss at Navarro, we hadn't seen each other again. He left, didn't return to the dance floor, and I understood perfectly. We were losing control, and I needed to put a stop to it, so I ran away from him for the second time that day. Since then, I haven't had a single peaceful night's sleep. He takes over my dreams, and I wake up drenched in sweat. I toss and turn in bed, unable to fall back asleep, replaying that day in my mind, reliving the kiss, even feeling his hands on my body and his gaze.

Scorching.

Impetuous.

Hungry.

I felt like prey, surrounded by a cloud of lust, and incredibly, the sensation was fabulous. The power I felt in affecting that man was something unprecedented for me, Dolores López. I could even feel the fire spreading on my skin just by remembering his wild and powerful touch that drove me crazy in seconds. The adrenaline running wildly through my bloodstream like a runaway train, aimless, completely lost. That's how I'm feeling right now, confused and unsure how to act in the face of such a powerful attraction.

As if that wasn't enough, he managed to find the rehearsal location and always lurked around, watching me. I could feel his eyes burning into me, such was the intensity with which he watched me from the door. It drove me crazy. I tried to ignore it, but my Spanish blood goes against that, especially with his gaze, looking at me with desire. Everyone could be noticing his real interest, and I was afraid they would think I only got this spot because I was involved with the famous Guilhermo García.

"Did you lose something here, Mr. García?" The jerk smiled sideways, and yet his smile always reached his eyes—a charm that destroyed me.

"What's this, Lolita! I'm just enjoying watching you rehearse." He forgot that, even though he wasn't raised like a River Nolan, he had some of their genes. I rolled my eyes.

"The choreography is a surprise even for you, the famous rider, this year's star." My eyes caught his smile, stretching even more as he bit his lower lip provocatively. *Qué cabrón*!

"Don't tell me, we need to talk, and I'll wait for you at the back gate."

"What if I don't want to talk? We have nothing to say, and we can't..." He moved closer, staring into my eyes seriously, but still with all that intensity.

"It would be better if we talked. Next week, the Championship starts, and we won't have time to talk because it's going to be hectic."

"I know that, and it's better to leave it as it is. Just let me work in peace," I said, keeping my eyes on his. I'm not short, and I love the fact that I'm always at eye level with these men. I'm 1.75m of pure boldness; I could face the handsome 1.85m guy without any trouble.

"You know best, but we can't..."

"Look, Guilhermo, when the time is right, we'll talk about what's going on. But I need to focus on the rehearsal, and it's not right for you to come here just because you're a famous rider, thinking

BOUND BY FIRE AND FUEL

I'll drop everything to attend to you." He raised one eyebrow as if considering what I said, then furrowed his brow and nodded in agreement.

"You're the boss, Dolores López." He straightened up and left, leaving me behind. *Qué te jodan*! I urgently needed a glass of sherry and a spicy pasta to soothe this fire burning inside me. I didn't know if it would help, but you have to try.

I returned to the rehearsal with my colleagues, who didn't ask me anything, just stared at me, probably thinking I was crazy for sending a rider like Guilhermo away like that. But if there's one thing that drives me crazy, it's being interrupted when I'm working. Many people don't see dance as work but as fun. But for me, beyond personal satisfaction, it's my livelihood. Those who think we live off glamour are mistaken; everything is earned through determination. We must love what we do, but we also need to dedicate ourselves and not give up on our dreams.

We rehearsed the choreography for another hour because the race would be on Sunday, and I was feeling more and more nervous. We would open the Championship, and after our performance, the motorcycles would make their procession. Besides the excitement of being part of such a moment, we would have an exceptional opening, something never done before in MotoGP history. Of course, I was nervous because I was part of something so significant in the history of motorsport.

Many people love and are addicted to Formula 1, but in Spain, especially here in Jerez de La Frontera, we love motorcycle racing. That's why the expectations for the start are high. MotoGP is the premier motorcycle racing category in the world, with seventy years of history, making it one of the oldest motor sports competitions in the world. I know this information because I truly love this universe, and it's a huge pleasure, and an honor, to represent dance and Spain in every place they will go.

By the end of that night, at Navarro, I did my show and didn't spot Guilhermo anywhere in the bar. What was he doing? This is the end; I was becoming one of those possessive girls, chasing after her man. Considering he wasn't going to show up that night at Navarro since Alex and Anita were there, I went to the dance floor and let myself go. I danced until I was drenched in sweat, then went to the bathroom to splash water on my face, neck, and catch my breath. That's when I bumped into Jacob at the door. It could only be a joke. I bet Eve was inside. I turned around, passed by Jacob, and tried to ignore him, but the guy was so arrogant and annoying. He never misses an opportunity.

"Did you give up, darling?" he asked mockingly, something typical of him.

"Is that any of your business? Mind your own, River Nolan," I said, glaring at him in anger. I can never have peace with this family.

"Are you mad? Is it because your rider didn't show up today? He's probably avoiding you."

"What do you know about him, Jacob?"

"I know more than you think, after all, he's my brother." I let out a mocking laugh.

"I won't waste my precious time arguing with someone as smug as you."

"You know, it's probably for the best. You can use that sassy mouth of yours another way, a much more enjoyable way," he said, moving closer and looking at me with a desire that disgusted me. Jacob isn't someone to throw away, but his arrogant and untamed attitude makes me sick.

"Stay away from her." I heard Guilhermo's guttural voice behind me, and my skin tingled. Just hearing that annoying tone, I knew things could get messy.

"I can handle myself, Guilhermo." I turned around and stared into his eyes, which now looked like a stormy sea, but this time it wasn't desire—it was fury. Jacob cleared his throat, and when I looked back at him, Eve was already glued to him with those blue eyes full of arrogance and snobbishness.

"Look who finally showed up." River Nolan can't control himself, which annoyed Guilhermo. He clenched his fists tightly, and I looked at him, worried about how this would end. I ran my hands over his and he turned to look at me, his eyes sparking. No words were needed; the silence between us was so significant and strong. He pulled me and we left in silence. With each step, my heart beat faster, and my body entered into a wild, unstoppable frenzy. We passed through the crowd until we reached the hallway leading to the back. We arrived at the parking lot on the other side. He leaned me against his motorcycle and trapped me there with his strong arms. My eyes caught his tight t-shirt, his well-defined biceps showing part of his tattoos. *De puta madre*[3]*!*

I'm really *fucked* with this man. His woody scent hit me hard, and he followed my gaze, smiling arrogantly.

"Don't do this, Lola!" he said, his voice low, rough, and deep, which affected and ignited my body.

"It's impossible not to," I whispered, not breaking eye contact, full of meaning.

"Fuck it, who cares!" He looked at my lips intensely, took my body as his, throwing my self-control out the window. I grabbed his hard biceps tightly and clung to him even more, kissing his mouth in a rush to feel his taste and have more of him. Our tongues danced in circles inside each other's mouths. I jumped into his lap, and he palmed my ass hard, pulling a moan out of me without control.

"I need you more than I want," I said when he pulled away, staring at me, wanting my consent to continue the mess we become when we surrender like this. "Don't say anything, please, I just need you," I continued, and he silenced me with a devastating kiss that said everything about our lack of control for each other. I didn't want to understand why I felt so out of control, going against what I feared most. Men are dangerous, and here I am, involved with one who is pure nitroglycerin.

"Stop thinking so much, Lola," Guilhermo mumbled when he pulled his mouth away, his eyes full of wild desire.

"I can't, but all I know is that I can't understand why I want you so much."

"Damn, even this!" He smiled, and I ran my fingers through his hair, which was trimmed on the sides and full in the middle, that charming pompadour now messy because of me. I smiled even more, so satisfied to have him like this at my mercy.

"What are we going to do about it?"

"Nothing, let it happen," he said, suddenly looking tired.

"What happened, Guilhermo?"

"That's why I wanted to talk to you earlier."

"I know, but I was trying to avoid it messing with my new job, the one I worked hard to get."

"Sorry, for today. I was too arrogant, only thinking of myself. But the truth is, you drive me like this."

"So it's my fault, then?" I asked, confused.

"Partly, but you drive me crazy, Lola! All I know is that I want you, and I don't know what to do with the intensity that takes over me every time I see you. I can't even sleep, and when I do, you're in my dreams, all over the damn place. I get to the Circuit and remember you're around. Even when I'm on the track, racing fast, I can't forget you."

"*De puta madre*, Guilhermo!" I let it slip and laughed loudly because that's exactly how I feel about him.

"I'm serious, Lola," he said with a puppy-dog face.

"I know you are, but you just described everything I've been feeling, but added to a huge fear of getting hurt in this madness we are. Because I feel like, just as this wild desire hit me, I feel the danger lurking, and I'm scared for my heart. I don't want to end up in the last curve of this crazy race that is our attraction, shattered, Guilhermo. I can't let myself fall; I have a family that expects me to be strong and be there for them," I revealed everything I felt, unable to hold it in any longer.

"I understand, I feel that fear too. I've been in the shit for months, this last year wasn't easy, and I can't even clearly say what I feel about it."

"You don't have to speak, only when you feel ready, but then what are we going to do?" I ran my fingertips across his face, admiring every feature, memorizing each one. I didn't know what would become of us, we were confused, and we were living our professional dream. Taking that into account, what would happen after it ended?

"I know what you're thinking right now, and I can't deny it, I've thought the same."

"What's happening with us? You know exactly what I'm thinking, this is a serious problem," I said with a smile, and saw him smile back with that confident grin.

"I don't know, but I can hear your mind exploding with thoughts and by your gaze, Lola!"

"So, can we rewind the tape? Back to that moment when your hands were gripping me and your mouth was taking mine deliciously?"

"Fuck, you're something else!" With that, he grabbed me again, and we kissed without being able to control what we felt for each other, and I accepted that there was no turning back. We're stubborn, but we can't deny the attraction we feel for each other, and I wanted to feel the danger burn us alive. As Nina would say, let it burn.

CHAPTER FIFTEEN

Guilhermo

I didn't understand what I was feeling for Lola, because the lack of control blinded me—this feeling of possession and hunger. Yes, it's horrible to say this, but it's purely and simply what I feel for her. I want her to be mine, and if I could, I'd take her lips and body every day. It's something that doesn't go away. It just burns like embers, and I can't control myself in front of such a burning desire.

Overwhelming.
Uncontrollable.
Lustful.

Right after we kissed that night, again at Navarro, she left me with my body on fire. That's why I dedicated myself to training over the last two weeks. The big moment arrived, and I couldn't see Dolores these days, which was probably for the best. The rush leading up to the first race day is always total madness. We made the final adjustments to the bike and tested it with different types of tires.

Alex and Tenner led the teams because in these last few days we made several revisions, even though this is done as soon as the bikes arrive completely disassembled. Nothing comes ready, and that's how the revision stays thorough. No fluid is reused, the radiator is completely dry, and every part of the bike is meticulously cared for. Despite the short time, I managed to follow this process a bit and stay on top of everything regarding the bike I'm going to ride.

I abandoned the gym. Alex managed to organize everything so I could use the track itself to exercise. With all the cycling equipment, I did some laps on the bike at a strong pace. I also did running drills on the track, as this physical preparation is essential for us, besides helping a lot with getting used to the track and memorizing it better.

The frantic pace of riding requires a lot of strength and endurance, which is why we maintain a strict weight control. I'm lucky not to have a smaller frame, because the bikes are heavy, and with the rider, this can mean less aerodynamic drag, but also less physical strength.

Danger is always present, so training well and knowing the curves of the track is necessary. I've been to this Jerez circuit before, but on a Moto2 bike, with the 250cc engine. Now, with a 1000cc bike, the difference is huge. That's why I didn't meet up with Jacob earlier. I knew he was racing in some competitions to get to MotoGP, like MotoE, the electric bike category, and that's where he made a name for himself.

Without further ado, I managed to get dressed with Anita's help, because those racing suits have all the possible protections, and even so, we still take risks. But everything is done very carefully to prevent anything worse in case of a fall. I put on the cap and headed to the studio. Besides riding well and qualifying in a race, there were all the behind-the-scenes work. Contracts with sponsors involve many photos to keep marketing at its peak, and it's nine months of craziness like that. We MotoGP riders have three months of vacation, a little rest, and the rest is all dedicated to traveling.

When I got to the photo booth, I greeted the other rider who would be with me. We're a duo that worked well in Moto2 before, and now we're back together as the Wacco Factory requested, along with the whole team. After I finished the photo session, I finally headed to the track.

"Are you ready for another test?" Alex asked me while Anita looked at me with gleaming eyes. Yes, she stayed with the team, a large group of men, and they all were terrified of her, actually out of pure and simple respect that she earned. She cheered for every turn and went wild with the guys.

"Yes, you know I was born ready," I replied with a smile. I was feeling very emotional about finally being able to step onto that track and give myself fully to it. Racing is much more than competing for me; it's how I feed my soul that craves adrenaline and intense emotions.

I got on the bike after putting on the helmet and handing the cap to Anita. I revved the engine loud and headed out for twelve laps to finish. The excitement at the starting grid was even higher. But no matter how it goes, it will always be an indescribable feeling to ride a track like Jerez.

In an instant, I hit maximum speed, but slowed down a bit when entering the curves, using my knee to touch the ground, which always helped to lean the bike. Consequently, I use my elbow lower, coming off the bike in the turns, allowing not just my knees but also my elbow to stay in full contact with the asphalt. This is thanks to the evolution of the chassis, suspension, and tires trio.

After completing twelve timed laps on the track, I stopped in the Wacco pit and saw them celebrating the great time I posted during the test. I know that in the free practice sessions, I'll stand out on the pole position, setting a good time. When we left the circuit and headed home, all I could think about was Lola. When I closed my eyes, I remembered her green eyes staring at me intensely, as well as her lips.

Fuck!

All I could do was think about and remember her. These days I tried not to meet her because I knew it would mess things up for both of us. Then, we would be caught up in the rush that MotoGP demands. We're going to several places; the second circuit is the Qatar GP at Losail International. We'll run into each other again, and if that happens, I'll let her decide what will happen between us. Whether we'll live an adventure full of adrenaline and pleasure or leave this attraction behind. There's no middle ground; we have to decide, and just like me, Lola seems to be a woman who goes after what she wants and doesn't give up on the best, and that's exactly what we'll do.

"You know I have her number, if you want to send a message, I can give it to you on WhatsApp," Anita said to me while drinking her beer and looking at me mockingly.

"You're mocking my situation, and you don't know anything."

"I know Lola disappeared that night at the bar, and when I got here, you weren't around, and nothing convinces me more than the fact that you went to Navarro that day. Don't fool me anymore, Guilhermo," she said. I frowned and pretended a little, and she let out a loud laugh that reverberated through the whole room, making Alex come back from the kitchen quickly and lie down on the other sofa.

"What's the joke, Anita?"

"She's messing with me here, thinking I went to Navarro that night when I just went out for a walk to clear my mind."

"*Fuck*, Guilhermo! Tell me another one." He turned up the music, which started playing Charlie Brown Jr., a Brazilian rock singer I fell in love with the first time I heard him. When I lived in Brazil, I discovered a huge variety of music with different rhythms from every region.

I first heard the song "Pontes Indestrutíveis" and started listening to all of Charlie Brown's other songs, which became my favorites. And listening to those songs always brings back memories of Mariana. She introduced me to her country in a unique way. She was completely in love with her country and had an enormous pride in being Brazilian. *Meu Novo Mundo* started, and I couldn't help but sing along, nodding my head to the beat, which got Anita and Alex singing along with me.

As if silence said it all
A good feeling that takes me to another world
The desire to see you is now greater than anything
There are no distances in my new world

Despite everything that song made me feel, I thought of Lola, and that gave me the certainty that, for the first time, I'm moving forward. And even though I still feel the pain of the loss I suffered, it's different now. Only the longing and the memories of unforgettable moments I lived with Mari remain. She followed me through all the races, traveled the world with me, and I know she wouldn't want to see me like this, stuck in the past.

"You know, I'm going to tell you what's going on with Lola."

"Finally." Alex lowered the volume of the music, and I saw Anita watching me with total attention.

"We have this crazy, uncontrollable attraction, and I avoided Lola these past few days because I needed to focus."

"She's a real woman, my friend." I shot Alex a deadly look, and he swallowed hard and stared back at me. "Sorry, that was out of line. But she really is beautiful, and that determination of hers makes her even more stunning."

"Yeah, I can't fight something I can't control. I'm just afraid of what will happen to us in the future. Our careers don't allow us to stay in one place, and you guys know I can't stand losing another person."

"My God, Guilhermo. Just focus on the now, live in the present, and forget about the future, that's not under your control. I'll send you her number, and please, send her a message."

"But what should I send?" I asked my friend. She smiled, as she always did when she saw me so lost.

"I don't know, Guilhermo. I've done my part. Take your phone and save the number of the fiery Spanish woman who dances like a goddess and don't let her slip away."

"Wow, Anita, that's some way of talking about her!"

"*Fuck*! Stop it, you know I just mean you shouldn't mess this up and let the opportunity slip away to be with a woman as amazing as her. And I know Lola is much more than that."

"Has Juan talked to you about her?"

"Yes, she's like a sister to him. The guy's already worried about what will happen when Jacob finds out you two are really together."

"What?" My blood boiled with anger just hearing that name, and worse, knowing that he could affect us somehow.

"You know, Juan told me Jacob has always had an interest in Lola, and she's never given him any hope, but with you, it's different."

"But doesn't he date that slutty blonde?" I asked, feeling deeply uncomfortable knowing this fact.

"They have an open relationship, and from what it seems, they live that relationship in a completely wrong way. If it were me, I wouldn't accept what he does with her, but it's never going to happen."

"Be careful with that word, never say never." Alex interjected, making Anita roll her eyes in disbelief.

"My God, Alex, I know that, but it was just a way of saying it," she replied, waving her hand and then tossing a cushion at him.

"The point is, Jacob won't stop me from being with Lola, who does he think he is?" I was pissed off just thinking that Jacob could cause trouble with me and Lola, as if he were her boyfriend.

"Your brother is a cocky and arrogant River Nolan," Anita already knew his reputation behind the scenes. "By the way, did you hear what they said about him being too forced with his charm? Jacob tries to be charismatic, but he doesn't convince anyone."

"I've heard he's a worthy opponent, daring and fast."

"Okay, okay, not more than you, because you have the best team any motorcycle racer could dream of."

"That's true. Now I'm going to try to get some rest. Good night, you two!"

"Yeah, go send her a message, we know." I left through the corridor, smiling at them. Despite everything, we're family. They know me and understand how stubborn I am, but when I want something, nobody can change my mind. I grabbed my phone and saw a missed call from my mom. Since I didn't answer, she left me a voice message on WhatsApp, which made me smile as soon as I heard her voice.

"I miss you, *mi madre*," I said aloud, alone in my room, my heart racing, bursting with longing. She said she would surprise me in a few days, and I was curious. For sure, Anita knew something, I couldn't forget to pressure her to tell me.

After listening to the message and becoming curious about what my mom was planning, I scrolled through the chats and went straight to Anita's. When I saw the photo of Lola and her number, my heart leaped at a crazy speed. That woman, even from a distance, had a power over my body. The energy flowed, and I felt like I could stay up all night. I opened the chat and saved her number under her nickname, which I particularly loved. I started typing and deleting several times, not knowing what to send. So, I decided to send what I was truly feeling.

Lola, I can't stop thinking about you

CHAPTER SIXTEEN

Dolores

Unknown number: Lola, I can't stop thinking about you.

Since my phone buzzed with a new message and I unlocked it to read, my heart raced. I almost fell off the couch; I was watching a movie to help me fall asleep, and when I checked the message from the new number, I was shocked. I could barely contain the electric current that ran through my whole body. I fanned myself and admired the image of that man.

"Qué cabrón!" I exclaimed, then quickly covered my mouth, hoping not to wake anyone, as I didn't feel like explaining the reason for my excitement. I zoomed in on the photo, like everyone does to see better, in this case, the tattoos on Guilhermo García's chest and arms. I counted the abs on his toned and tanned stomach, which made my mouth water. He looked sculpted, so perfect, dressed only in worn black jeans hanging to the side, revealing his white Calvin Klein underwear.

Blessed temptation of a man. I couldn't help but notice the veins popping on his perfect biceps, nor the most indecent details, on his stomach near the underwear showing. I salivated, wishing I could run my mouth and tongue across his stomach and keep going faster towards the dangerous and delicious zone. A danger and a walking temptation. I exited the photo, went back to the message, and those words seemed to leap off the screen of my phone, just like my heartbeat. I started wondering how to respond to that message; he's thinking about me, my God.

"Esto es la hostia!" I said aloud to myself again, staring at the TV as if it would solve my problem. It was late at night; what could he be thinking?

We hadn't seen each other these past few days, and despite the absence, I had been thinking about him all this time. Now he sent me this message, which made me wonder how he got my number. It must have been Juan or Anita, more likely it was his press agent and friend. Navarro wouldn't give my number to Guilhermo, at least I don't think my friend would do that. I saved his number, read the message again, and my fingers came to life as I replied.

Dolores: Do you want the truth?
Guilhermo: Always.
Dolores: I'm lost, Guilhermo.
Guilhermo: Am I the reason you feel lost? If so, just tell me if it's good.
Dolores: I don't know what to do with what I feel for you, and I've been thinking about you too.
Guilhermo: Fuck, Lola! You're making me even crazier, if that's possible.
Dolores: Anything is possible when we feel this way.
Guilhermo: Is that so? If I wanted to show up at your house right now to see you, would it be possible?
Dolores: I don't think you'd go that far, you don't even know where I live.
Guilhermo: Don't challenge me, Lola.
Dolores: I love challenges with you.
Guilhermo: Of course, I'll let you win.
Dolores: Your arrogance is what kills me.
Guilhermo: If it's from passion, my love, I'm done for, all I want is you.
Dolores: I need to sleep, tomorrow

>   I have a full day.

Guilhermo: I know that, but know that you
will be in my dreams, and who knows, maybe tomorrow
we'll see each other and I'll take you by surprise. I hope that
I'm in your beautiful and hot dreams, Lola.
Save my number, we'll talk a lot here.
A long kiss on those beautiful lips.

I couldn't respond because I turned off the TV and went to bed, my body on fire. While we were texting, I kept imagining his expressions and that cheeky smile of his. What's going on, Lola! Who are you trying to fool? You already like that walking danger, or rather, danger on two wheels. I lay on the bed, tossing and turning, unable to stop thinking about him. Guilhermo is going to be my end, oh my God! What a mess I got myself into, getting involved with that famous rider and another River Nolan.

I thought about it so much that sleep finally took me, and I dreamed about him, it couldn't have been different. In fact, I don't even know what we have; it's so confusing trying to understand where this is going, and now these messages. He avoided me for days, and now he says he's thinking about me. I jumped out of bed when my alarm went off, I got up and went to take a shower to cool my head. But nothing seemed to help with what I was feeling, it was burning inside me like a wild fire. Faster and faster, spreading warmth throughout my body, and I ended up closing my eyes and touching myself, imagining his strong hands caressing me to the point of ecstasy. Fuck, Lola! Where's your control?

"Are you going to take long in there?" I heard Olívia shout from outside in the hallway, and then I jumped out from under the shower, realizing I had let myself get carried away by the lust I was feeling for Guilhermo.

"I'm coming out, just give me five more minutes." I finished my shower, washed my hands, and finally my face. I applied my moisturizing oil and rinsed off, quickly drying myself. That was the last thing I needed. I rolled my eyes, put on my bathrobe, and wrapped my hair in a towel as I always did. I opened the door and found Oli with a stern look on her face.

"Wow, I thought I'd have to break the door down, it took forever!"

"Sorry, the water was so nice, I decided to relax a bit."

"That's good, but I have class and still need to drop Luna off at school."

"Got it, I'll brush her hair and get her ready."

"Great, that helps. *Madre* hasn't gotten up yet."

"Do you think she's okay? I'll check her room." I went down the hallway to my mom's room and gently turned the doorknob so as not to wake her if she was still asleep. But as soon as I opened the door wider, I didn't see her in the bed, and I was startled. Immediately, I forgot about everything and became worried.

My mom hadn't had a relapse in the last year, and only God knows how hard it was to help her recover. Life is not always a bed of roses, there are so many thorns that are too hard to overcome. *Mi madre* began having problems with alcohol after my father passed away. She couldn't accept his death, and for years we've been fighting this battle together.

She's been having tough days, especially since they would have celebrated their wedding anniversary recently. They were deeply in love and couldn't imagine life without each other. But *mi madre* couldn't move on, didn't handle the struggle well, and gave in to alcohol. Since then, I've had to support her, looking for help groups like Alcoholics Anonymous. She resisted a lot at first, and it was painful until she accepted that she needed help to regain control, and we found a psychologist for her. That's when we discovered the extent of the fear *mi madre* has of being alone, abandoned like our grandmother was when she lost my grandfather.

"She left? She's not in her room?" I started searching the house until I found her in the kitchen, quietly making eggs in the frying pan and staring out the window.

"Madre!" I said too loudly, but relieved to see she was home.

"What's wrong, Lola? You look as pale as a sheet!" She looked at me, concerned and curious.

"I couldn't find you in your room, and I was afraid that..." She rolled her green eyes and interrupted me.

"That I was in a bar, and it was just another relapse, right, sweetheart?" She said angrily. She didn't like us doubting her, but it's more than that—it's concern.

"Yes, we get worried about that, unfortunately, but because we care about you and don't want anything bad to happen. There's no point in getting angry, it's normal, after everything we've been through to get here." She came closer and hugged me.

"Sorry, Lola. I know I worry you guys, and I swear I'm trying to get better so I can take care of my daughters the way they deserve."

"You're doing great already. I know sometimes we overdo it with the worrying."

"You are the most wonderful daughters a mother could have, and I'm so proud of how far you've come."

"Thank you, *mi madre*!" Oli entered the kitchen, and we finished setting the table for breakfast together. It felt good to be with the women in my life on a morning like this. It was the day to start the MotoGP free practice sessions, including Moto2, Moto3, and MotoE. Now, the real excitement and rush at the Circuito de Jerez would begin. The official race starts on Sunday, and the free practice sessions are for qualifying for the starting grid. Those with the best times will be in the front positions for the race. When I remembered that, my heart started beating fast, and I felt anxious, a good little flutter in my stomach, as there were only two days left until the most anticipated and electrifying journey of my dance career would begin.

At the front gate of the house, *mi madre* blessed me and told me to go to work without worrying, that she would be fine. In her eyes, I could see hope; she wants to be well, and that's already a huge relief. I smiled and kissed her cheek, telling her I loved her more than anything, and went to work.

The day would be long, as I needed to rehearse two choreographies and be present for Moto3 practice, as we would open the starting grid, and just thinking about it already got me excited.

I didn't check my phone while at home. If he had sent me a message, I would check it later. Despite everything, my mind wandered to the memories of his kiss, his touch—it wouldn't leave my crazy mind. This is all so recent for me, I never imagined I would give in to this man like this.

When I arrived at Navarro, since it was still early, I was able to rehearse the choreography calmly. The girls picked up the steps quickly, and we finished the night's rehearsal. I had lunch with Juan, who started bombarding me with questions. Soon, Nina arrived, and she was no different from my friend. They were both dying to know everything I was feeling about my first performance at the Circuit and about Guilhermo.

I managed to divert the conversation, and we started talking about the choreography I created with the other dancers. We were excited to reveal to everyone how full of emotion and adrenaline it is, just like how the riders make us feel in the stands. As soon as I saw the costume fitting that Nina was preparing for the first dance, I screamed with happiness.

"What perfection!" I said excited and euphoric with all that leather fabric.

"All the costumes will be leather, but each one personalized for your choreography and the highlight bike."

"The sponsors are going to love you, you're a fashion genius, Nina!" I felt so proud of my friend, she has an extraordinary talent for fashion. She is studying to go further because nowadays, nothing works without education. Just like her, I studied dance at one of the best dance schools in Barcelona, and it was the best time of my life, because that's when I truly found myself and realized that I was born to dance. I had many doubts if this was the right path for me, and I discovered that all we need to do is love what we do, stay focused, and be determined to go further and further.

"They already love it, because I asked for permission to use the logos, you know how complicated that can be, and when I talked to Anita, she warned me about this detail."

"Ah, Anita is truly amazing. But you, my friend, are more."

"And Guilhermo, don't you have anything to tell me about him?"

"We haven't seen each other since that night at Navarro that I told you about." I tried to sound casual, but she knew me too well.

"You're not fooling me, Dolores! Start talking."

"I can't hide anything from you, can I Nina?"

"I'm your best friend, and it's impossible to hide anything from me."

"Hostia Puta!" I said angrily, frustrated for not being able to hide it from her. "Okay, he sent me a message, and after almost falling off the couch when I saw his photo and tried to process what he said, I'm doing fine. But no, I'm in knots just thinking about everything we talked about yesterday, and I don't know how it will be when I see him again."

"What the fuck, Lola! You guys are really on fire, and you can see it from miles away. Please, don't avoid this desire."

"But how can I not, Nina! You know I could be swallowed up by the craziness of the River Nolan family."

"Guilhermo is a García, Lola, not a River Nolan. He might have the same blood, but he was raised by his mother and grandmother. It's impossible not to see the difference between the two. Jacob is arrogant and pretentious, thinks he's the best, and doesn't hesitate to attack others. While Guilhermo is completely the opposite, from what little I've seen."

"I know that, but in the end, I'm scared of everything that involves those two, and I'm really worried about my heart. That's why I should stay away from him and avoid hooking up with Guilhermo."

"You're the one who decides, but I've been your friend for as long as I can remember, and I've never seen you like this for any man. It's clear, the rider is driving you crazy, Lola. Don't miss the opportunity to live something unique with him. Don't forget, we only live once, and you might not get the chance to enjoy such a powerful feeling again."

"Nina, you're impossible. I know, but..."

"Don't finish that thought, Lola. Enjoy it, and let Guilhermo and Jacob sort out their differences. That's not your problem."

"I hope so, I can't even promise myself that I'll stay away from him," I ended up confessing to her what my heart was telling me.

"So, what are you waiting for?"

"I'm not going to look for him, but I feel like today we're going to run into each other. It will be impossible not to bump into him at that Circuit."

"That's my girl, enjoy it and live it. There's nothing better in life than finding that intense feeling, and I'll be here for anything you need."

"Thanks, Nina. I'm here for you too, always. Now, let me get ready and hurry up so we can get to the Circuit. I have an appointment." She agreed, and after a few adjustments, we organized everything and headed out for the most exciting afternoon of our lives. As soon as I arrived at the Circuit, after passing through the pits, I bumped into Guilhermo. His gaze burned me alive when he checked out my body in that tight leather outfit with his number and last name printed on it. I felt my phone vibrate in my hand.

When I unlocked it and saw his message, I smiled and felt even more powerful.

> **Guilhermo:** This look of yours, when it meets mine, needs no words, Lola. You know what I'm thinking, don't you? You look stunning.

CHAPTER SEVENTEEN

Guilhermo

The big day has arrived, the one where everything will really begin, and my heart is already beating like crazy with so much anxiety and anticipation for today's free practice. The free practices are qualifiers for the starting grid, meaning the position where the riders will be before the race starts. It's like in motorsports, the starting positions are determined by the fastest laps in the qualifying practice. I really want to do well so I can be in a good starting position, which is crucial for any rider.

The days flew by, we made improvements to my bike, some adjustments that were necessary after the tests, and I'm very confident I can stand out. My big dream is to reach the podium in the last race of the season, it's a lot of adrenaline, and my heart is more than ready to live this moment.

I arrived at the circuit earlier, with Alex and Anita, and we met Tenner, who looked at me with a smile full of expectations. I saw some dancers approaching, and then my eyes caught Dolores'.

Holy shit!

Just that glance between us made my heart race and my body ignite with the desire to touch her right there, not caring about the chaos around us. But I just stared at her intensely and didn't need anything more. I sent her a message on WhatsApp to let her know what I had thought when I saw her wearing that tight leather outfit, outlining her delicious curves with my number and surname embroidered. And once again, it got me excited, making me feel like that day I saw her dancing in one of the boxes' rooms.

We exchanged messages that night, and I found myself smiling at my phone, something rare for me. I'm not really a virtual guy. I like physical contact, seeing expressions, and feeling the energy that comes from each person, which the phone takes away. But it was fun and very interesting to talk to Lola, it's incredible how everything becomes so intriguing with her, it's not the same with others.

I'm no saint, and even though I loved Mariana and enjoyed life before her, what I'm feeling for Dolores is completely unique, and it's been extraordinary. More than I expected and thought it would be, because I even thought it would be a passing thing. But after that day we hooked up in the empty box, I can't get her out of my mind, and I can't calm my heart. My body longs for hers like someone with an insane and uncontrollable thirst. That's why I sent her that message, and shortly after, I wished her good luck, even though I knew she was going to drive everyone wild in the stands. Practice day always has fewer people watching, everyone saves it for the official race day.

After I passed her and went on my way, I went to get ready for the starting grid, my heart racing and filled with anxiety. I put on my helmet and took a few photos before mounting the bike. The bike was already on, while Alex held it, and with the headphones, he gave me a nod to get on. I heard the engine roar, which made my heart vibrate, just like my body. I love living for this, and there's nothing that brings me more pleasure in life.

I left the pit toward the starting grid, feeling my whole body shiver and the adrenaline rush through my veins as I arrived. The stands were pretty full, much more than when I arrived earlier. I saw many people with flags bearing my number in red and purple, which made me so excited and emotional. Having the support of people I don't even know but who passionately cheer for me is something I can't express.

I positioned myself in the second column of the grid as planned and waited for the flag signal, but it only went up after the dancers performed. The beat of *Faded*, Alan Walker, filled the circuit, two of the girls started dancing, and when the chorus came, one of my bikes passed by me with Dolores standing on it, and the crowd in the stands went wild. She performed a move on the bike, making everyone go crazy with the boldness of the choreography.

Then she got off and moved her body flawlessly over the bike, and one of the other girls handed her the black and white flag for her to wave. As she glided with mastery across the track, dancing with her arms, she demonstrated how it feels when we're on the track, and the crowd can feel a bit of that too. I felt emotional and inspired to give even more of myself at the Circuit de Jerez. She ended with the other dancers, waving the flags, then mounted her bike and left, leaving the crowd in madness with applause and cheers for such a well-represented and meaningful performance for those who love motorcycle racing.

After that, I closed the visor of my helmet, wished Jacob good luck, who was positioned beside me, and he ignored me. I focused on the flag and the signal that remained on the grid, indicating the start of the race. As soon as the green flag went down, I gave it my all because I wanted to set the best time. I focused and shifted my body out of the bike's axis toward the inside of the curve, bringing my body as close as possible to the ground. With my heart racing and filled with the energy that always fills me when I ride, I felt the danger.

I brought my right leg forward during the braking and squeezed the front brake with force, transferring the weight to the front of the bike, which made the rear wheel almost lose contact with the ground. In that moment, I took my foot off the inside peg of the curve and moved it forward, lowering my center of gravity, improving stability, and increasing the aerodynamic drag, which helped me reduce the braking distance and steered the bike into the curve, doing a *leg dangle*, a reference from our great Valentino Rossi.

After that, Jacob bumped into my bike, near the end of the 5th lap, but I managed to keep going, passing other riders, as I had already found my rhythm, feeling the bike lighter, at full speed, and gaining second place. The feeling is completely indescribable, adrenaline and danger, an insane combination that makes our blood boil.

I wanted to risk it for first place, and as I crossed the finish line, I felt the emotion take over my chest, burning like embers, but with happiness for setting a good time in the first practice.

I celebrated as soon as I saw the flag rise and passed over 200 km/h on the final straight, standing on the bike and throwing my arms up, celebrating with my team in the paddock and everyone in the stands. The race's backstage is always a madhouse; those who watch on TV have no idea what goes on behind the scenes. Amidst the celebration chaos, I was pulled as soon as I reached the *Wacco* box, the whole team in a frenzy. Alex screamed like crazy, hugging me tight.

"Damn it, Guilhermo! 1min39s044 on the best of twelve laps in the first practice! You're pure speed, my rider!" I felt even more emotional; it was better than I expected. I was still numb from the adrenaline and from setting such a great time right in the first practice. We still had two more free practices for qualification, but this first one already counted a lot, although everything could still change.

"It's just the first, Alex, we still have more!" I took off my helmet, and even though I was surrounded by important people from my team, I missed my mom. I couldn't get in touch with her, I called over ten times, but the calls just went straight to voicemail. So, when I turned around and went down, I heard her voice.

"Guilhermo, my champion!" My whole body shivered, and I couldn't hold back the tears that fell, overwhelmed with an even greater emotion. She threw her arms around me, and we hugged tightly. When I smelled her perfume, it felt like I had arrived home, *mi madre* is my home. Still with my eyes closed and crying from happiness, I heard her say how proud she was of my achievement. I love the support she gives me and how she always likes to surprise me like this when I'm at the races.

When I opened my eyes, I saw my grandmother, and I thought I was seeing a mirage. But it was really her. They wanted to give me a heart attack. I couldn't contain myself and went to hug her too, the women who raised me, who made me the man I am today, grateful for the upbringing and values they gave me. I wouldn't be anything without these two amazing women.

"Mrs. Inês, you're going to kill your grandson like this," I commented after hugging her and kissing her hands. My grandmother smiled beautifully. Her hair was whiter and shorter, yet still graceful, as my mom used to say, her soul has always been young.

"*Olé, Olé, qué grandes eres*! My dear, I'm not killing anything, you know where you were is more dangerous, but if this is what you love to do, we're here to support you. We couldn't miss this unique moment." First, she congratulated me and celebrated, then repeated what she always told me about my choice to be a motorcycle rider. She went crazy when I first mentioned it, very worried about my life being at risk.

"Oh, Grandma, thank you, having you both here with me at these moments really warms my heart. You don't know how happy I am to see you here." I turned to *mi madre* and we hugged. "I love you both!"

After that, I looked at Anita, who had tears in her eyes. I knew she had a hand in this surprise.

"You!" I pointed at her, and she came to hug me.

"I knew you'd love it, especially after doing so well in the first practice. You're the highlight, big Guilhermo García! Congratulations!"

"*Mola!* But you never miss a thing, always up to something. This time, though, you got it right."

"When do I ever do something wrong?" she asked, anxious for an answer she wouldn't get, because I could only smile and agree with her. After so many emotions, I went through several crowds when I left the pit. There were many people waiting to take photos and the media, some wanted interviews. I managed to give attention to a few people, but it was way too crowded. Anita and the security team managed to take me to the press conference room for the press conference.

I didn't see Dolores anymore. I gave a quick interview, and after a long time, we managed to get some peace to have lunch. Anita had prepared everything because we still had the second practice in the afternoon. We didn't leave the Circuit that day, and I was able to spend some time with my mom and grandmother.

In the afternoon practice, with my heart pounding, I started in first place. Even facing some difficulties during the twelve laps, I managed to set a good time again, did well, and secured one of the best positions on the Starting Grid for Sunday. I ignored Jacob's provocations on the track and kept my control. It was tough, but not impossible.

Even though we were tired, we all went out for dinner that night at a restaurant in the center of Jerez. My mom was happy to be in her country, or as we say in Brazil, her homeland. She said Jerez has a vast array of architectural styles, a unique characteristic of the place. Over the years, it has accumulated and blended designs and typical features of Gothic, Baroque, and Neoclassical styles. *Mi madre* loves to talk about the culture and historical richness of places, because she's traveled the world and always appreciated everything.

When we got to the restaurant, we ordered the traditional sherry wine of international renown, made right in Jerez, at the famous bodegas. While we were waiting, my phone buzzed in my pocket. I grabbed it quickly, eager to see a message from Dolores. I felt euphoric when I saw it was her response to the message I had sent earlier, and she probably hadn't had the time to reply.

> **Dolores:** You have no idea what I can read in your eyes, or better yet, you do. We just needed to do what we both wanted in that moment.

Damn, Lola!

She knows how to drive me crazy with every message we exchange, and it just makes me more eager to see her.

> **Guilhermo:** I can imagine everything, you just don't know what I'm capable of. Wait for me at the Navarro door, I'll pick you up as soon as I put my girls to bed.

Yeah, I'm definitely completely out of control now, but there's no more fear. I can't hide from the feeling that takes over me just thinking about Dolores. She's already hypnotized me, and I feel like I'm starting over. This is good, isn't it?

CHAPTER EIGHTEEN

Dolores

I hadn't felt like this in a long time, in fact, it was when I auditioned to get into the dance academy in Barcelona. That nervousness, the anxiety to see if you can achieve something, that feeling of cold in your stomach, more like having a thousand butterflies flying in it. That's exactly what I felt when I got on the *Wacco* bike, dressed in the outfit embroidered with his name. My heart was beating frenetically, and my body underneath that leather, shivering. A boundless emotion that burned everything around me. Courage flowing through my bloodstream, with the potent adrenaline pulsating.

I had never experienced such a feeling before performing. Every performance was different, which makes this profession perfect. I love this mix of sensations and the way dance expresses feelings and energy. With every step, we want to say something, many would say there's none of that, but there really is, it's very meaningful.

That's why, when I entered that circuit, nothing could have prepared me for what I would feel as soon as I heard the chosen music's beat. *Faded* by Alan Walker filled the stands, and all the spectators of that speed show cheered, making me shiver even more. It was a unique emotion, being seen and admired by that crowd. The same one that came to watch the great riders. How honored and thrilled I felt down to the pores of my skin. Most of them were holding flags with Guilhermo's team colors, his number on them, just like on my outfit. I could feel his gaze burning into me while I moved, following the choreography. Even though all of that made me feel powerful, I couldn't deny that affecting him also gave me even more pleasure dancing with his bike, wearing his number embroidered on my clothes.

In fact, everything I experienced there was so unique that there were no words to express all the raw emotions I felt. The feeling of power, being there for the first time, debuting a dance performance and being the highlight at the opening of the world championship for motorcycle racing. And all of it, through my merit and hard work. I had never felt so accomplished in my life.

The two dancers began performing in front of the Grid, and when the chorus came, I passed the riders standing on the bike, moving, driving everyone wild. I did the maneuver, and shortly after, I lifted the bike on one wheel, leaving the audience euphoric. After a few seconds, I lowered it and leaned on the bike, moving my body across it while my colleagues handed me the black-and-white checkered flag, which I waved, making everyone go crazy.

I slid across the track with synchronized steps, following the other two, dancing with my arms, showing what it must feel like when a person is hooked up to an electric current. How I think the riders feel when they're on the track and how the audience feels a bit of that with them. Afterward, I finished with the other dancers and the flags, mounted the bike again, and rode off, leaving the audience euphoric with applause and cheers for the performance, which was the realization of a great dream.

As I left with the bike, I noticed the disdainful and envious look of Jacob River Nolan. He couldn't contain his indignation after my performance. Shortly after, they closed their helmet visors, and I noticed that Guilhermo signaled Jacob, who didn't even acknowledge him, ignoring his brother. I went to the place where they had directed us to watch the free practice, feeling even more emotional when I saw the flag go up, and that line of bikes passing at high speed. My eyes locked on the rider with number 93, the surname below the name, García. My heart raced as he took the curves, standing out and giving a real speed show.

The danger they were running there was no joke. My hands started sweating, my heart was pounding frenetically, and I was shivering all over, overcome by a wild anxiety as I watched him complete the laps and secure a good spot on the official race's starting grid, where everything really begins. When he passed the Ducados Curve, the last one on that circuit, my heart skipped a beat, and I cheered along with everyone. Guilhermo got the best time out of all of them, and no matter how much Jacob tried to take him down, he was no match for the new standout of motorcycle racing. I screamed like a crazy person, or better yet, like the good Spaniard I am.

"*Olé, olé, qué grande eres, García!*" *I joined in with everyone, cheering and even feeling tears streaming down my face, overwhelmed with emotion to be there, witnessing such a speed show. I hugged Nina, who came over smiling and celebrating with me.*

"It took me forever to find you, girl, this place is crazy, there are so many people," she said, looking at me, seeming happy to see me in my costume.

"It's packed! Did you see how many Wacco flags there are?"

"Wow, tons! But I also saw green and blue ones from River Nolan."

"True, there are, but most are cheering for Guilhermo. Now, look at this, it was a success! Did you manage to watch it?"

"*Esto es la hostia*! You absolutely nailed it, I was shivering and even cried, my friend, I loved seeing you there, giving a show of what the riders live on the track. Congratulations, you shone, and you deserve everything you're achieving and experiencing. Finally."

"Thank you so much, my favorite stylist! I killed it with this outfit you made, part of my success is thanks to your talent, and I'm so grateful for everything you do for me."

"I'll always be here for you. Now, tell me, did he send you another message?"

"Yes, he did, one after we bumped into each other in the hallway and just stared at each other."

"*De puta madre*! You two are on fire, and he likes you. It's obvious when you're together."

"What do you mean, he likes me?"

"He looks at you with shining eyes and stays glued to you when you dance."

"Ah, that's just typical of a bad boy, Nina!"

"Maybe, but he has a different spark every time he sees you. We can tell, my dear. And by the way, I'm not the only one who sees this. Juan mentioned something to me about you two."

"Of course Navarro had to notice something too." She fell silent, furrowing her brow. I smiled sideways, and we both watched Guilhermo celebrating on top of his bike, waving his arms toward his big fan base in the stands. It was beautiful and emotional to see him celebrating. Then, he was greeted by his team, which had been cheering since he completed the final lap. Everyone was happy because he had done well. It was just a practice, but it would determine the starting grid for the race, where the real action begins. And García secured the best position, which would count a lot on Sunday.

After that, Nina and I left. I went to a photoshoot where we posed with the bike and the other people responsible for organizing the MotoGP event in Jerez. I felt nervous but honored to be living such an important moment in my dance career. Many people think dancing is just a hobby, but for me, it's never been just that. I've known since I was young that I had the gift of dance, and even though I doubted it at times, I kept going.

In my family, not everyone believed I could make a living from it, but look, I've achieved so much with dance, even managing to support my household on my own. It's funny how no one ever came to offer help or even emotional support to my family, who I now consider just my mom, my sisters, and Nina. It's amazing how things work out—there are those who share the same blood, the same genes, but that's all. Then there are people who are just your friends, who support you more, offer a hand during the toughest moments of your life. Nothing compares to that. There's no price for true friendships.

After taking a bunch of photos, I left the Circuit, but I couldn't find Guilhermo anymore. He was still going to the press room for a conference. Since I had already done what they asked, I went to Navarro because I still needed to change my clothes and makeup for my performance that night. I ran through the choreography with the girls. Juan was happy for Guilhermo and said he wanted to congratulate him, and he kept asking if I knew anything about him. Then I remembered the message I received earlier and replied, just before stepping on stage.

> **Dolores:** You have no idea what I can read in your eyes, or better yet, you do. We just missed doing what we both desired at that moment.

It only took five minutes for him to reply, I smiled like a fool and rolled my eyes, grabbing my phone to read his message.

> **Guilhermo:** I can imagine everything, you just don't know what I'm capable of. Wait for me at the Navarro door,
> I'll pick you up as soon as I put my
> girls to sleep.

But who were "his girls"? I didn't understand, but I just said okay, since there was no turning back from what we were starting, even though I knew how it would end. I needed to try and see where it would lead, I couldn't deny what I felt for Guilhermo García.

I arrived at Navarro excited and happy for starting a new chapter in my life. From the stage, I saw Nina talking to Jacob, but she didn't seem happy. As soon as I finished, I changed once more that day, not taking off my makeup because it would take too long, and I ran over to where I saw my friend with that jerk. When I arrived, they were arguing, and of course, I was defending myself from one of River Nolan's attacks.

"What do you think you're doing, Jacob?"

"Your friend didn't like my comment about you and that so-called brother of mine."

"You know I can't stand you, right? Just because he came out on top today, and will always be, you start treating people badly, even those who have nothing to do with it."

"As far as I know, your little blonde friend here has everything to do with it. She embroidered that number and surname on your outfit, that black leather with red and purple."

"*Qué te jodan*! Get out of here, nobody owes you an explanation, and if you're upset about the practice results today, remember, you'll need to work a lot harder to catch up to him. Now, don't come mocking my friend or my performance, which, by the way, was a request from the organizers to highlight your brother." I was getting more and more angry with that kid, and he laughed in my face with mockery and disdain.

"Who do you think you are, huh, Dolores?"

"Now I'm Dolores!"

"Yeah, you always were, and I don't know why I wasted my time with a little woman like you," he crossed the line, spitting those words with contempt.

"Your ego is hurt, oh poor Jacob River Nolan, daddy's little boy," I lunged at him, still furious, because I wouldn't stay quiet in the face of his ridiculous and unfounded insults. I felt hands pulling me away from him, I knew Juan would step in. He turned to me, and in his pretentious eyes, I saw that this wouldn't lead to anything.

"Get out of my bar now, Jacob. Go cool off." My friend turned to him, and by the tone of his voice, he was angry, and rightly so. That River Nolan could drive anyone crazy. He hugged me and then pulled me and Nina through the crowd that had already parted to watch the commotion.

As soon as we reached the counter, my eyes locked with Guilhermo's. He was serious, his fists clenched. Juan must have told him not to interfere, as it could've been worse. As soon as I got close to him, he pulled me into his arms, smelled my hair, and kissed my neck like a boyfriend would, and that startled me. But what scared me the most was that it was exactly what I wanted at that moment: to see him and feel his skin, his mouth, and his hands all over my body.

CHAPTER NINETEEN

Guilhermo

After the intense emotions I experienced today, later that night, after dropping my mom and grandmother off at home, I headed to Navarro. I couldn't control the urge to see Dolores.

When I arrived, she wasn't at the door as we had agreed in the message. I became suspicious and decided to go into the bar, which was packed. Then I saw her with the blonde friend behind her, arguing with Jacob, and my blood boiled with rage. Filled with fury and unable to think, I was about to go after River Nolan when Juan grabbed me tightly, stopping me.

"What do you think you're doing?" I asked him, my eyes clouded with anger at hitting that arrogant bastard they call my brother.

"You stay here. You can't get into a fight, especially now that the championship is starting. Think about it. Let me go over there and pull her out of that argument that bastard is causing," he said through clenched teeth. He was angry too, with the mess that the spoiled kid with his bruised ego had caused.

Juan left, and I kept watching everything from the bar, trying to control my impulses. Walking back and forth, too restless. I would need a strong drink to calm this anger, but I remembered we were in the middle of the racing season, and I couldn't do that. I closed my eyes and shook my head, feeling frustrated.

Who does Jacob think he is?

I thought out loud, and a guy beside me looked at me like I was crazy. I just moved away, not wanting to explain myself to a stranger. I went back to watching, seeing Juan talking to Jacob, telling him to cool down and leave the bar. He turned and left, the blonde following him. I saw Navarro hugging her friends, and relief took over me, but I would only feel peace when Dolores was in my arms.

So, without being able to control myself, I stared at her with my fists clenched. Still, filled with the energy that surrounds us, my heart leaped in my chest. She barely approached, and I took her into my arms, inhaling the delicious scent of her brown, wavy, thick hair. My mouth came to life, and I planted kisses along her neck and face, then pressed my nose against hers and closed my eyes, soothing the overwhelming anxiety inside my chest.

"Guilher..." I silenced her by placing my finger over her lips and led her away after thanking Juan. He nodded in agreement, and she could only wave goodbye to her friend Nina. I was selfish and didn't want to share her with anyone at that moment, actually, not anymore. This frightened me more than anything.

Damn, where is my control?

When we reached my bike, I sat her on it and held her body tightly, wanting to feel her more than anything.

"I know I didn't let you say anything, but this is freaking me out, and I can't even understand what's happening."

"I feel the same way." Her exotic green eyes locked onto mine, exposing all my desires and longings. She has that power over me.

"Don't look at me like that, Lola. I hate thinking about the horrible things that idiot must have said. More than that, I'm burning for you right now, babe."

"Forget about that bastard. Want to burn together?" Her eyes were filled with fire and intensity, the desire crackling between us. Her tongue passed over her lower lip, and I took it, trapping it between my teeth, pulling a delicious moan from Lola. This woman drove me crazy.

"Only if it's in my bed," she stared at me, then turned to the side. I had to convince her that I wanted her the right way. "We're both crazy, we did it that way at the Circuit, but I want you completely, in a bed, where we can do everything I have in mind comfortably. Are you willing to live that with me?"

"This thing we have is confusing, and yet it feels so right, so good, and irresistible." Dolores is above all very sincere, honest with her feelings, and unafraid to reveal everything to me.

"I know, babe. But I can't avoid it, can't resist what I feel for you. Let's just live it and think later about the more complicated stuff?"

"That sounds more difficult to me. We're just postponing something that's going to hit us like a bomb one way or another."

"I don't care, all I can think about now is having you in my bed, not just tonight, but every night."

"We'll sort it out later, Guilhermo. Just take me to your bed already."

"Are you sure you want this, Lola?" She smiled and took my mouth with hers, and I surrendered, kissing her with lust. My hands brought her even closer, and I immediately felt hard, the insane desire taking over my entire body. Like a fire spreading, fast and powerful, as hot as hell. My emotions, when I'm with her, become raw, and they drive me crazy. That tension between us is too high to be ignored. I bit her lower lip again and sealed our passionate kiss.

Without saying a word, she pulled her phone out of her pants pocket and called her friend to let her know. I heard her talking about her sisters, and after making sure Nina would sleep at her house, she ended the call. She got off the bike, and as I turned it off, I handed her the jacket I had brought for her. She then mounted the bike behind me, put on the helmet I handed her, and pressed her body against mine. I maneuvered and started speeding through the small streets of Jerez, the engine roaring.

The emotion was so overwhelming that I felt complete with her on my back. It was completely different from anything I had ever experienced. Not even when I'm on the track, at full speed, do I feel like this. My heart raced with Dolores pressed against me, feeling the cool Spanish night breeze.

When we got to the house, she looked at me with shy eyes, thinking I would take her to a hotel. I smiled sideways and offered my hand to her as I got off the bike and put my feet on the ground.

"I didn't know you lived in a house, is it yours?" she asked, looking around.

"Well, I don't like hotels. They're too impersonal. Although, when the championship really starts, it's going to be crazy, and there won't be time to find places to rent, since it's a quick stop at each place."

"So why did you rent this one?"

"I got here long before the championship started, and since I already know the city, I plan to buy it soon. My mom is from Jerez, and I feel that at some point, she's going to want to settle here. Now, come on, let's go inside." She smiled beautifully, making me remember that we don't know so much about each other, and I wanted to know more about her and her family. But then again, this might be too much. What am I thinking?

"What's on your mind?" I didn't answer that question. The woman seems to read my mind. Just what I needed. I pulled her in, and we entered the house quietly, but when we reached the hallway, I couldn't resist. I pressed her body against mine. "Guilhermo!" The house was dark, except for the lights. As soon as we reached the door of my room, I couldn't hold myself anymore. I opened it quickly and we entered, then I closed it with my foot.

My room was the last one in the hallway, so I wasn't worried about the noise we'd make. I could only think about Dolores on my bed; she lay down on the white comforter, her wavy hair spread across it. But what fascinated me the most were her green eyes staring at me, like two flames, capable of burning everything around us.

Overwhelmed by the insane desire that burned inside me, pushing my control away, I moved closer to her, and without breaking her gaze, I began removing her clothes. But Lola pushed me away and undressed herself, looking at me with boldness—she liked to take charge too, and that only turned me on more.

I went crazy seeing her naked on my bed, and like a great temptress, she started running her hands over her body, caressing herself under my gaze.

"Fuck, Lola," I muttered, unable to hold back, my voice hoarse, overtaken by the lust that Dolores stirred in me, making me completely lose my mind. I felt my cock hard as a rock inside my pants. Acting on instinct, I let my hands roam above her, brushing against myself for a moment, but then I saw Lola beckon me with her finger.

As I leaned over her, the minx ripped off my shirt and ran her fingers over my abdomen, admiring. Having her hands on my skin only intensified the urge to fuck her hard.

Without saying a word, I helped her remove my pants, and as soon as I was left only in my underwear, she stood up, her eyes running over my nearly naked body with an intense gleam. Then she rose and made me sit on the edge of the bed.

"Our pleasure-filled journey, laced with adrenaline, is just beginning, Guilhermo," she said in a seductive tone, starting to kiss every part of my abdomen until she reached the waistband of my boxer briefs. There, she teased a bit, smiling like a devil, and pulled them down, revealing my hard, erect cock, desperate for her wet, warm pussy. She ran her tongue over her lips as if she were starving and then gripped its base, kneeling in front of me between my legs, giving me a perfect view of her full breasts. First, she placed it between them, giving me a titfuck that had me on the edge the moment I felt her soft skin on my cock.

"Damn, babe!" I groaned with a guttural voice, barely able to contain myself. She smiled, and without breaking eye contact, her mouth took me in. This had to be one of my wild dreams, the kind I'd been having about her lately. Ever since we fucked like rabbits on the circuit, despite the crowd, I hadn't stopped thinking about her.

When she took me deeper into her mouth and sucked, moving back and forth with such hunger, I couldn't hold back and thrust into her warm mouth. Her eyes started to tear from the intensity, yet even as I warned her, she continued, determined to take me to heaven with just her mouth.

"I'm going to come, Lola," I warned, and she didn't stop, continuing until it made me come faster, filling her mouth with my cum, making my whole body tremble. As I watched her clean her lips with her tongue and fingers, looking up at me like a provocative devil, I seized the moment, flipped our positions, and kissed her, tasting myself on her lips.

Fuck, what a delicious woman.

My mouth came alive on her body, kissing and nibbling lightly, setting us on fire, making her moan. She took me to another world, there was no denying it.

Savoring her taste and soft skin, I reached her pussy, which I first wanted to feel with my hand. I caressed her entrance, feeling how wet she was from the blowjob she had given me. Without hesitation, I started rubbing her swollen clit, and she writhed and began moaning loudly. With my other hand, I placed a finger in her mouth, silencing her. She gripped the comforter as I intensified my touches, feeling her even more swollen. I slid in two fingers and thrust, never breaking eye contact as her green eyes darkened more and more.

"Ah, Guilhermo!" she moaned my name, leaving me captivated by hearing that. It was paradise to hear her husky voice, filled with lust, moaning my name. Then I moved my hand from her mouth to her breasts, caressing the left one, and she writhed; with that, I added another finger and thrust quickly until I felt her body convulse and tremble in a powerful orgasm.

Without giving her time to recover, I turned to the bedside table, grabbed a condom, tore it open quickly, and she watched me with shining eyes as I put it on.

"Ah, Dolores, you're mine now, the way you truly deserve, here in my bed," I took her with kisses, pressing our bodies together on the bed. I wanted to see her eyes when I slid my cock into her warm, soft, and welcoming pussy. The moment I did, I felt like the luckiest man in the world. Her warm, soft skin against mine—there's nothing that compares to feeling her body against mine that way.

I didn't think it was possible to feel something like that. Because I felt like I had found my place, my home. A new world began when I saw everything I felt reflected in her gaze, staring back at me on that bed. We moaned as I began going deeper inside her, unable to resist kissing her lips and sucking on her breasts while I thrust, feeling how tight Lola was. Damn, she was incredible. In a silent plea full of meaning, our eyes said everything we felt.

"Guilhermo," she moaned as her nails scratched me, driving me even crazier. I intensified my thrusts inside her, feeling her body tremble again.

"Lola!" I groaned, hoarse and utterly affected by the orgasm that hit us both simultaneously, making us climax together. I saw in her gaze that she was as lost as I was, completely undone by this hot, incredible woman.

AFTER A FEW HOURS OF delighting in Lola's body and her in mine, we lay together. I remembered that soon we would be in different places, without any rest, but I didn't want to be away from her, even though our busy routine was bordering on madness. So, I started thinking about how to make sure we wouldn't lose a single second of free time we had.

"You'll be with me in Doha, in Qatar, staying at the same hotel. Anita will take care of everything, so all your nights will be mine, Dolores López," I said, not breaking eye contact, and I saw the exact moment her green eyes widened in an expressive, shocked look.

"¡Qué te den! What do you think? No one tells me what I'm going to do, where I'm going to stay, I hate being given rules," she spat the words out with a challenge clearly marked on her face and voice. Lola didn't deny her Spanish blood.

"I know, but I saw how your eyes lit up with expectation when I said you'd be with me, every moment of free time you have. You know it's rare, so this is a rarity—Guilhermo García giving up his time to be with you." She huffed, rolled her eyes, then tilted her head and looked at me with a mocking smile.

"I knew you were a full-fledged pompous ass."

"It's my charm," I replied with a smile and felt her slap my arm. I took the opportunity to pull her closer, showering her with kisses, feeling her warm body, captivated by her luscious lips that drove me crazy.

"What will become of us when all of this is over?" she asked, her voice trembling slightly, filled with some fear, just as I felt.

"We'll live in the present, and later we'll worry about it," I said, moving closer to her face, getting very close to her hypnotizing green eyes, which made me lose all control. "There's nothing that will get in the way of what we have," I explained to her. Despite my own fears, everything we've lived has been so uncertain, even though it's something irresistible. We don't know what will happen after this journey ends. But I can only promise her that I'll never let anyone come between us during this time.

CHAPTER TWENTY

Dolores

Guilhermo said he wants to live without thinking about what comes next, and although I want that too, I'm afraid of where it could lead us. That's why, after that night at his house, I haven't stopped thinking about everything that surrounds us. We can't ignore the fact that he travels constantly and has a crazy schedule with the *Wacco* team. All the responsibilities that come with being a motorcycle racer, especially at his level, are huge, and I have to think about where I'll fit into all of this in the end. It's complicated, and I hate it with all my strength because I'm already involved with him. I don't know what to do.

"Lola, are you really distracted today?"

"I know I am, Nina. But what can I do?"

"Stop tormenting yourself. You're achieving everything you wanted, it's just beginning, but isn't that a good thing?"

"It's not about that. I'm really grateful for everything that's happening, but I got involved with him. Why did I do that, Nina?" I asked her, my voice breaking because I knew I'd end up heartbroken in the end.

"My friend, you know I understand why you're worried, but have you thought about the possibility of not living everything you're experiencing with Guilhermo?"

"I know, but I'm thinking about how I'll feel once this championship ends. He said he wants me with him every night and that he'll make arrangements with Anita to stay with them."

"Then, here's what you should do." She leaned in, cupping my face with both hands, making me look at her. "Live every night like it's the last, and as for the future," she tilted her head as if considering her words, "leave it to destiny. It will show you both what to do."

"Oh my God, you're on his side. You sound just like Guilhermo." She smiled and let go of me, raising her arms.

"*Guay*! We're in sync. But listen, I've never seen you like this because of a guy. I know you might suffer, but life is like that—full of risks. We can't always avoid the sad endings. But hey, you might end up surprised in the end." She said this and grabbed her coffee cup, taking a sip of the dark liquid and moaning in delight. She loves my coffee. "*Aff*, it's delicious! How I love this black drink."

"You're unbelievable, Nina."

"I absolutely love your coffee. You always make it just right. Now go change your clothes, or we'll be late for your performance, and that would not look good for the most famous dancer in Spain," she said, dancing as she spoke. I left, smiling as I walked down the simple hallway of my house, thinking I'd be gone for nine months. Juan and Nina would take care of my mom and sisters. It broke my heart to leave them here, but the only other time I'd been away for so long was when I went to Barcelona to study at one of the top dance academies there. It was hard, but I managed to visit them on weekends when I wasn't broke. Sometimes Juan would pick me up when he had time off from the Navarro bar, which was rare, but he helped me a lot.

Navarro told me not to worry and to go ahead, because this is a once-in-a-lifetime opportunity to be seen in my field. My phone buzzed just as I finished putting on my blouse and grabbed the jacket he left with me. He told me to always wear it. The damn thing was soaked with his woody scent, mixed with those citrus notes that, when combined with his skin, are pure temptation. I picked up my phone and saw the notification from Guilhermo. That man seems to know exactly when I'm thinking about him.

> **Guilhermo:** Good morning, love. I can't wait to see you, but even more to feel your skin and kiss that delicious mouth of yours.

What should I do with this man?

"¡*Dios Mío*!" I said to myself, overwhelmed by knowing how much he wants me. I can't deny that I desire him just as much. I quickly typed a reply to his message.

> **Dolores:** I hope you have a wonderful day and that you make it to the podium. You know that for me, you're already the champion. I don't even need to say that I'm eager to feel your lips on mine, right?
> Good luck, and a big kiss.

Oh my God, I feel like one of those teenagers whose hormones are in overdrive and can't control themselves around their crushes. I smiled and grabbed my bag. The Sunday was just beginning, the day of the first official race that would qualify the riders for the Qatar GP. I walked past Nina, who was already ready. We left and went straight to the Jerez Circuit, where the gates were packed. We struggled to get in, even with the special entrance. We saw many people wearing red and purple shirts with the number 93 embroidered on the back. I felt proud of Guilhermo. He deserves everything he's experiencing. He's so focused and determined.

I headed straight for the pit. There are so many that sometimes I still get lost. There are forty-three, and they house the event teams and racing teams. The buzz of today doesn't compare to last Friday, which was just free practice. The place was filled with people running back and forth. I could bet that the *Wacco* pit was packed. People have free access to the riders, though they're surrounded by security.

Many fans manage to get the long-awaited photo with the rider they're rooting for. It's so exciting to experience this.

My heart jumped in my chest as I prepared for the first official performance. The choreography would be the same one I did for the selection, with the song *Faster* by Within Temptation, which is perfect for such a big event. I took the girls' hands, and we were all sweating, our bodies electric with anxiety. What an emotional moment it was when we passed by the motorcycles lined up on the Grid, dancing and representing each one. Each bike belonged to a different team, all competing in this championship. It was such an honor for me, I could barely contain myself when I felt the energy of the crowd in the stands rise and shout the chorus of the song at the top of their lungs.

I go faster and faster and faster
And faster and faster and faster and faster.
I can't live in a fairytale of lies.
And I can't hide from the feeling cause it's right.
And I go faster and faster and faster and faster for love.

With my heart exploding in my chest, I watched Guilhermo head toward his bike, never breaking his gaze from me. His intense look was everything that song embodied. A whirlwind inside my body, and we finished by raising the flag. The stands erupted in applause as the riders entered, and we heard the motorcycles start, the roar of the engines, and all the energy crackling with intensity. They lowered their visors, and everything began. I felt even more anxious as I saw him start the laps with tremendous skill.

Guilhermo took control of the track in a matter of seconds, leaving everyone in awe. I screamed along when I saw him pass his brother Jacob. At every curve, my heart leapt seeing him so close to the ground. It's incredible how he throws his body into the turns without touching the asphalt. It seems so natural to him—his job as a rider, just like all the others on the track.

But I don't know—watching Guilhermo race is exhilarating. His performance shows how much he loves being on the track at high speed. The adrenaline is overwhelming. Watching from a distance, you feel everything—a mix of anxiety and fear because danger is lurking, waiting for any mistake in their focus. It's crazy. Only those who live through it know how electrifying it is. Nina and I cheered as we saw that Guilhermo took the lead. Right behind him, Jacob caused some chaos, but his brother swerved and accelerated, staying in first place.

On the penultimate curve of the circuit, the tenth lap, Guilhermo slid across the track, falling off his bike, causing my heart to race. But he got up and ran to grab the bike. His team rushed to his aid and helped him, making some adjustments to the bike before he shot out of the pit even faster. The daring guy came back with even more speed, catching up to the other riders, overtaking them until he reached 5th place. That was a great achievement, but I knew he wanted more. Showing this with impressive determination, he reached 2nd place and stuck to Jacob, trying not to bump into him. Then he managed to pass him and finish in first, sending the crowd into a frenzy. The cheers in the stands and the celebration were incredible.

I didn't know if I had the heart to keep watching—it was just too much to absorb. At the same time, it's amazing to watch the bikes race by at high speed, making perfect turns, except for the moments when they fall and slide along the side of the track, like what happened with Guilhermo. Despite that, he finished the final lap in first place, at such a high speed that I could feel the adrenaline and danger from afar. As soon as he passed the Grid, I jumped like a crazy person. What an incredible feeling of victory.

We saw him riding standing on his bike, dancing, and pointing his finger at his team, throwing punches in the air, celebrating his victory in Jerez. I rushed to his pit, and as soon as he arrived, it was a huge celebration. Everyone was smiling and congratulating him. It was clear how happy he was to have recovered so quickly and managed to win in the final laps. This was actually something that few riders manage to do, showing just how bold the Spaniard is.

As soon as he saw me, his eyes froze, the evident sparkle, and everything around me stopped. He ran to me, and I jumped into his arms without fear. I didn't care how many people were watching. First, I felt his nose in my neck and hair, then, when we looked at each other, he sucked on my lower lip and pulled it, before claiming my mouth hungrily in a hot, devastating kiss. He pulled my hair, pulling me closer, and after an unknown amount of time, he gently lowered me and sealed our lips with a smile before wrapping me in his arms.

That's when I saw the two women, as he had mentioned in his message that night and later explained were his mother and grandmother, who raised him. As soon as I saw the woman with light brown eyes and black hair approaching, I knew she was his mother, alongside the older lady with short, white hair. Their smiles clearly showed how proud they were of him.

"¡*Dios mío*! You nearly gave me a heart attack. You know I have a heart condition, my love. When you fell and went sliding around the track like a madman, I had to hold myself back from rushing out there to get you," the older woman said, then turned to me, still smiling. "And who is this beautiful young lady?" She looked at me with curiosity, making my stomach churn with nerves. That day, I managed to leave his house before they woke up. I told him it wasn't the right time, but now, it seemed there was no escape. I smiled back, though I was nervous as hell, feeling a tight knot in my stomach.

"Grandma, I knew you'd go crazy watching, but I had to keep going," he agreed with her with a nod of his head before turning to me, the smile reaching his eyes with that charming way of his. "This beautiful lady here is Dolores López, and she's with me, Grandma and Mom." He didn't label anything, and I wasn't sure whether that was good or bad. He didn't seem to know what it meant for his grandmother. I only hoped they wouldn't see me in a bad light.

"Very beautiful, don't you think, Isabel?" He turned to his daughter, who was looking at me with a serious expression, making me fear her reaction.

"I have to agree, it's a pleasure to meet what I'd say is the reason for my son's smiles," she finally smiled at me, making me exhale in relief. I was really nervous with the way she had been staring at me.

"The pleasure is all mine, Miss García," I said, shaking her hand, and the grandmother then pulled me into an embrace, taking me out of Guilhermo's arms, making him laugh. Before I could even realize it, someone shouted for him, and he asked for permission to leave, going to follow Alex, Tenner, and Anita with their security team. He was needed and had to leave me alone with his mother and grandmother. Though they had looked at me seriously, we soon moved to the other side of the pit and began talking, getting to know each other. Within minutes, I felt a little more at ease in their presence.

Guilhermo's mother is tall, elegant, and although she initially startled me, she seemed incredible. They complimented me when they realized I had performed before the race, which flattered me. Miss Isabel said that we should never give up on pursuing our dreams, which made me feel even more connected to her. I knew she traveled a lot around the world as a doctor with Doctors Without Borders. She became a well-known figure, highly sought after by hospitals, and made her name with honesty and hard work. She told me how worried she is about her son working as a motorcycle racer, but she couldn't force him to do anything else because Guilhermo loves what he does. When we love our work, nothing beats the joy of doing it to the best of our ability.

Isabel is so warm, and Mrs. Inês is a charm, the type of woman who can be tough when needed, but sweet in other moments. I was enchanted by both of them. They invited me to lunch with them, and I couldn't refuse. I looked around for Nina and then she came over, and I introduced her to both of them, who liked her right away.

After a long wait, Guilhermo climbed to the podium at the Jerez Circuit with a huge bottle of champagne in hand and popped it, making everyone scream in celebration of his victory. Jacob's scowl was so intense that he didn't even try to hide the envy he felt toward his brother. They got soaked with champagne and received their trophies. 3rd place went to an Italian, 2nd place to Jacob, and 1st place to Guilhermo, who smiled as he held it up, showing it to everyone. Guilhermo's mother and grandmother cheered with me, Nina, Alex, and Anita. The whole group was happy for the 93's first victory in MotoGP.

CHAPTER TWENTY-ONE

Guilhermo

I couldn't avoid the overwhelming emotion and adrenaline that rushed through my veins at the Jerez Circuit. On top of that, seeing Dolores waiting for me, with my mother and grandmother—it was too much. I felt like the happiest man in the world, and at one point, in the middle of that victory, I lifted my eyes to the sky and thanked God and Mari. I knew she was watching, wherever she was, cheering for me. If she were still alive, she would have celebrated my first great victory in MotoGP with me.

I pushed those thoughts out of my mind, and we went to lunch together at a restaurant in the center of Jerez. Anita was already on the phone, trying to book everything in Doha, our next destination. I asked her for a master suite, complete with a *jacuzzi*, so I could enjoy a few days with Dolores, the woman who has been occupying my mind and warming my body and heart more and more.

I introduced her to my mother and grandmother as the girl who's with me, without labeling what we have, since we hadn't talked about it. The truth is, we just spoke about enjoying our moments and the opportunity to be together in this great MotoGP journey.

Damn it, it was the Spanish GP! I thought again about the victory, trying not to lose my mind from happiness. We're just getting started, but for a rider like me, these victories are crucial.

I felt proud of my achievement, but I was already looking forward to the intense emotions at the Qatar GP.

After spending a few more days with my mother, we followed the schedule. In about five days, we'd be flying out. The rush was so much that I didn't get to see Dolores. She focused on wrapping up her performances at Navarro. I had to scramble to watch her last choreography at the bar before we left. She thanked her friend Juan in a speech that brought tears to everyone's eyes. I admire their friendship, and I don't feel jealous of him with her because they're like siblings. Now, when Jacob gets too close to Lola, I feel my blood boil with the urge to punch him until he understands that I don't want him anywhere near my woman.

Am I crazy? We're not even a couple. We're living an adventure amid a lot of adrenaline. But the feelings that have taken over us are growing faster, and the uncertainty of where all this will lead leaves me worried about what will happen at the end of MotoGP. However, I can't pull away from her. I've realized that my control vanishes when it comes to this fiery Spanish woman who fought with me at the airport as soon as we arrived.

The trip was long. We went to Barcelona, where we caught the flight to Doha, the capital of Qatar. We'd have a good amount of time on the plane, precisely six hours and twenty minutes on a direct flight. It was tough and exhausting. Anita managed to charter two planes since we had our team and the motorcycles to transport as well.

When we boarded the plane, Lola was still angry with me over our argument. I couldn't accept the idea of her staying away from me during the little time we'd have in Doha. I want to enjoy every moment with her, plain and simple. I know it's selfish on my part, but what can I do when every moment off the track, where I'm not thinking about winning and everything that comes with this world, is about her?

"Are you still mad?" I asked softly, but she kept staring out the small airplane window, pretending not to hear me. Dolores likes to

BOUND BY FIRE AND FUEL   151

act tough, so I waited for her to respond, but she didn't even turn to me.

"Damn, what did I do?" I grunted, angry at myself for being an idiot.

"You're such an authoritarian, Guilhermo García. Don't think that just because you win races, you'll win with me too."

"I know that, Lola," I said, lowering my head, but wanting her to turn to me so I could see her exotic green eyes. "I'm sorry, I won't take up all your time. Besides, we might not even get to enjoy the places we're going to." She turned to me, her eyes full of anger. She wouldn't back down so easily.

"You can't think you own me. No one dictates the rules of my life. It's never been like that. Actually, the only person I owe my respect to is my mother, despite everything we've been through." I was curious about what she said. There's something about her family she hasn't told me, and I'm walking on eggshells, not knowing how to ask without being too invasive.

"I understand, I'm really sorry. You can do whatever you want on these trips. I won't dictate anything. But if you want to be with me, I'll be there, alone in hotel rooms all over the world."

"You're so dramatic, Guilhermo. Who sees you all tough on the track would never guess how needy you are."

"I'm not needy, Lola! You're exaggerating," I said, furrowing my brow and squinting, making her laugh loudly. I covered her mouth with my hand because our friends were sleeping. She looked at me with that fiery gaze, and I had no choice but to kiss her lips.

Damn, what a sexy woman! Her full lips are my undoing, and when she looked at me like that, I lost all sense. Her kiss is sweet and hot at the same time, just like the scent of her soft skin. A true temptation. We tried to be discreet, but it was in vain since everyone was asleep, exhausted from the intense work to store everything. Dolores and I went to a small room in that plane Anita managed to charter. She'd arranged a contract with *Wacco Racing* for all the championship trips.

When we entered the small luxurious room, we threw our clothes to the floor. I grabbed a condom and put it on quickly. In just a few minutes, she was naked beneath me, moaning my name. I kissed her mouth while thrusting into her. I didn't want anyone to hear us, but what could I do? There's no control when we start making love. It's something beyond our control. We're swept away by a fog of lust that consumes our skin like fire spreading across a vast forest. The feeling of being inside her is indescribable, and it always leaves me dizzy, consumed by the pleasure Dolores gives me.

After we both climaxed twice, I cleaned her up and covered her, lying next to her, fitting my body to hers. I fell asleep to something she said, though I didn't remember it later because I drifted into a sweet sleep. It felt like I was dreaming. I could still smell her sweet, floral scent everywhere, but when I opened my eyes, Lola was staring at me with a little smile on her face.

"What is it?" I asked, stretching, and she smiled more.

"You!" She ran her right hand through my hair, caressing it, making me close my eyes again.

"My God, Lola. Did I say something?" I asked, worried, because I knew sometimes I'd say Mari's name while I was asleep. But since I met Lola, that hadn't happened again. Still, I wasn't sure if it would stay that way.

"You said a name, but I couldn't tell who it was. But you smiled, and it made me wonder if you were calling me in your dream. You're such a pervert, Guilhermo." She laughed loudly, but I became concerned immediately and jumped up, startling her.

"Sorry, Lola. I need a shower and to check on how the others are doing," I said, stepping away from her and heading to the bathroom. I quickly entered and closed the door behind me. I shut my eyes, trying to control my breathing. She knocked on the door, and I could tell she didn't understand my sudden bad mood and outburst. What am I doing? Damn it! I took a deep breath and washed my face, then put on the fluffy bathrobe that was there and left the bathroom, finding Dolores sitting at the edge of the bed with her head down. She didn't move to look at me, making me feel even worse for what I'd just done.

"Sorry, I don't know what got into me!" I said, my voice thick with emotion, feeling terrible.

"Guilhermo, is there another woman between us?" She finally looked at me with a lost, confused look. I closed my eyes and then met her gaze. I needed to tell her about the woman I once loved, but I didn't know how to begin that conversation.

"There's no one between us. I'm just not ready to tell you everything that really happened."

"I understand. It's complicated, I know. But there is someone else in your thoughts, at least from what I could tell. I tried to laugh it off, thinking you were talking in your sleep, but when you looked at me so frightened and rushed out, it made me think otherwise."

"There is someone in my thoughts, but not anymore between us," I said, my head down, feeling my whole body tremble. I never spoke about her like this to anyone, not even my mother or Anita.

"Oh my God!" She put her hand on her forehead and shook her head side to side. "I'm sorry. I don't want to invade your life. I'm being totally stupid with this attitude. Honestly, I don't know what happened to me."

"No, Dolores. You don't need to apologize. I'm the one who should apologize. I got confused when you said I was talking in my sleep. That happens sometimes. Actually, since I met you, it hasn't happened again. But I don't know what I said because I never remember. It was Anita who told me about it once when she had to wake me from a nightmare."

"I'm sorry. I touched on something that's too much for you right now." I moved closer to her because I needed to feel her touch, something to calm the anguish that had settled in my chest.

"Don't worry. It's something I want to talk to you about, but I'm not ready yet. I've been trying to get over it, and I'm sorry for dragging you into the mess that is my life."

"Stop. First of all, I respect you, and I care about you. Let's not let this get in the way of what we have. When you feel comfortable and ready to share that part of your life with me, I'll be here with open arms." She hugged me tightly, and as I felt her warm body against mine, I felt better immediately. Even though I was still afraid of hurting her, my desire to have her with me was stronger than anything I had realized. I couldn't stay away from her.

WE ARRIVED IN DOHA late in the afternoon, already feeling how hot it is due to its desert climate, with a long summer stretching from May to September. We discussed this in our team meetings about the *Losail International Circuit*, where the next race will take place. It's located about 30 kilometers north of downtown Doha. We always prepare according to the weather, as it influences the tires we use on the bike, which is crucial when I'm on the track.

As soon as we disembarked, we followed the signs, took the escalators down, and reached one of the immigration counters. We didn't have to fill anything out, just showed our passports, had our fingerprints taken electronically, and didn't get asked anything. They stamped our passports for a stay of up to thirty days, and that was it.

Then we walked around the airport a bit, saw the famous and enormous yellow bear in the middle of the place with a huge lamp, which impresses all the tourists passing through. We even took a

BOUND BY FIRE AND FUEL

photo with it. After that, since there was a car waiting to take us directly to the hotel that Anita had booked, we couldn't walk around the airport any longer.

This is the life of a motorcycle racer during the World Championship season, there's no time to enjoy the places we travel to. Today, I'm going to rest at the hotel, and tomorrow, I'll head to the circuit. A part of the team will go today to set up everything at the pit.

We got in the car with Anita, as Alex and Tenner went with the team. I saw Dolores admiring the places we passed by, as it's a modern capital in the Bay of Doha, a peninsular country in the Persian Gulf, near Dubai and Abu Dhabi. As we drove quickly, we noticed the city is filled with mirrored buildings and historical boats sailing in front of the Corniche. It was so surprising to our eyes. The car's air conditioning felt great because the temperature in the city was crazy. I had never seen anything like it, but it's a desert region, so it wasn't surprising.

When we arrived at the hotel, Dolores looked at me, smiling, and seemed satisfied with the place. I was happy because I had chosen it with Anita. She did the quotes and research, always managing to find amazing places with excellent locations. We chose this one because it was a bit farther from the city center, where there's a lot of hustle and bustle with cars and people. We noticed there was noise as we passed by since it's an area under constant construction. But not at the hotel we're staying at. Anita says she made sure to check those details during her research. She's amazing at everything, and I've never had any problems with accommodations.

We admired the hotel's modern decor. The impressive façade already revealed it was a beautiful hotel building with a view of the sea. As we passed through the spacious lobby, we were welcomed by two butlers, as Anita mentioned. They spoke English, which made things much easier for us. She also mentioned that some hotels don't have English as a language option, only Russian, Arabic, Filipino, and Hindi. This can even be difficult for her, even though she's a polyglot and knows many languages, but Arabic is still one she doesn't know. She said she plans to study it. Although I lived in several countries with my mom, I find Arabic the hardest. I speak many languages, but Russian is a struggle, honestly, I'm terrible at it.

Dolores seemed enchanted by everything, just like I was the first time I came to Doha. It's a different place, full of amazing attractions. It would be a shame to keep Dolores locked up in this hotel, even though it's complete and very comfortable, it wouldn't satisfy her urge to explore the capital of Qatar. That's why I turned to her in the elevator and smiled.

"You can go wherever you want, just be careful not to get lost. Anita hired a guide to help you visit some places. You'll have more free time than I will, so make the most of it."

"Oh my God! I'm so excited to explore, what a wonderful place!"

"It really is, and it's very safe, don't worry, you're not at risk of any violence here."

"Wow, that's great, I'll enjoy it to the fullest during my free time. We managed to schedule two rehearsals in the afternoon at the circuit. The others rented a hall at a hotel nearby, according to Anita."

"Great, everything is set, love!"

"You keep calling me that, but we're not dating."

"I know, it's just a way of being affectionate with you, Lola. A privilege just for you." She loved what I said last and smiled brightly.

"You have no shame, you're spoiling me, and that's not good." I silenced her mouth with a kiss, and she looked at me nervously. Then she slapped her hand on my chest, pushing me away. "Stop it, Anita is here too."

"Feel free, just like on the plane," Anita said, putting her phone to her ear, waiting for someone to pick up, leaving us both embarrassed.

After a delicious dinner where we tried typical Middle Eastern cuisine, but still with many seafood dishes, Dolores and I ate and got to know a bit more about the hotel. The capital of Qatar is beautifully lit up and stunning at night. We admired the view from our suite, seeing the other mirrored buildings illuminated. The amazing choice of room left me speechless when we saw the huge jacuzzi that offered a beautiful view. The water was at a perfect temperature, as the air inside the rooms is much cooler.

When I saw Dolores taking off her robe and stepping into the jacuzzi in a beautiful black swimsuit, I already imagined her without it and her well-defined curves. I placed the wine glass on the stone edge, which I had asked for, since I couldn't drink. She took a sip and looked at me with her eyes even more green under the yellow and white light of the lamps. I got in wearing black trunks, and Dolores looked at me with her hot, exotic gaze. I moved closer and trapped her by placing my arms on the edge of the tub. The water was warm and really comfortable.

"Did you know you look even more beautiful like this?"

"Like this how?"

"Without any makeup, with your hair wet, and those gorgeous green eyes that make me dizzy. You're a Spanish goddess who's been leaving me more and more lost."

"Are you declaring yourself to me? You know that's way too dangerous, right?"

"I should've known that I love danger." I moved closer to her, letting my lips trail along her neck, up to her ear, watching her body shiver, making me smile. She's just as affected as I am—I saw her eyes close, her mouth part slightly, and then heard her delicious moan as I nibbled her earlobe. "If the risk is with you, it's all worth it." I whispered the words into her ear, and then she grabbed me, kissing me with a passion so overwhelming and wild that, in moments, we were igniting each other in the *jacuzzi*. The warm water was nothing compared to the frenzy that overtook my body and the unstoppable desire that consumed me.

After slipping off her swimsuit and my trunks, I put on a condom and wrapped her legs around me, then sat her down on one of the steps in the *jacuzzi*. I brought my fingers to her entrance, feeling her hot and wet even submerged in the water, penetrating her with my fingers, making Dolores moan loudly and grind against my hand. *Damn* this gorgeous woman.

Not satisfied with just pleasuring her, I thrust into her with my cock, rock hard and desperate to be inside her warm, tight heat. Her inner walls clenched around me, making me groan her name in a rough, deep voice, and then I began to thrust, alternating between sucking her breasts and kissing her mouth. Lola clawed at my back; I intensified my thrusts, feeling her feverish gaze and skin, which drove me wild. I was rough, completely untamed with her that night, only stopping when we were both exhausted, the warm water mixing with our sweat. We showered together in the impressive bathroom, and then lay on the bed in a silence filled with unspoken words that meant everything and nothing all at once.

CHAPTER TWENTY-TWO

Dolores

I couldn't tell anymore if what Guilhermo and I were experiencing was an adventure. All I knew for sure was that my heart couldn't contain itself when I was with him, or even when he was away, at the circuit. We spent our first night in Doha intensely and wildly; he said he liked danger just as much as I did. I can't deny it, but nothing prepared me for everything we've experienced in the last few days.

In my free time, when I wasn't rehearsing the choreography for the Sunday race presentation before the official one, I walked around the city with the guide hired by Anita. I was bothered by it; Guilhermo wanted to cover everything, even though I hadn't asked him for anything. We had a big argument on Saturday after his fourth free practice. He set a good time, not as fast as the one he did in Jerez, but it was enough for a good spot on the starting grid.

I talked to him about the way he liked to pamper me. It wasn't a bad thing, but I was uncomfortable. After all, I have my pride, and I never depended on anyone, especially after I lost my father. I even mentioned how I supported myself and my family. Guilhermo hugged me with his heart pounding in his chest and kissed my forehead. He said he understood everything and that he would continue letting Anita find the best guides and places for me to visit in the little time we would spend in each country. That's why, soon after, I started talking even more with his assistant about everything. She's open-minded, very fun, and empowered.

We were excited for the Sunday race, especially because it would be at night. We woke up and headed to the circuit, where we would spend the day since it wasn't close to the center of Doha, being further north. Located along the coastal road of *Al Khor*, it was completely visible from the road, thanks to the floodlight system that appeared after the blue and white bulbous structure of the *Lusail Multipurpose Hall*, a sports center.

Fortunately, they found a driver who knew the area well, as there was so much construction happening around the circuit that the GPS maps were outdated, and even *Google Maps* was unreliable.

I brought my suitcase, and as soon as we arrived at the circuit, after struggling to get through the entrance gates because there were so many people wanting to see who was in the cars, Guilhermo rolled down the car window and waved to everyone, being very friendly and charismatic with his fans. Just like in Jerez, there were banners painted in red and purple, and many people wore shirts with his last name and number on the back. I found it so moving to witness this part of his intense work routine. Over three months in airports and only three months of rest when they take vacations. Still, Anita told me that Guilhermo goes to the mechanic shop he loves, currently located in Rio de Janeiro, Brazil. A country I really want to visit, as I hear and see it's full of joyful and welcoming people.

I said goodbye to Guilhermo with a kiss and went to the pit where I had to get ready. I brought all the costumes Nina made and tried my best to film everything and send real-time messages to my friend. We talked on video chat several times at the hotel, and even during my walks around Doha. She was enchanted by everything she saw, and I promised to take her next time.

After putting on the costume and slipping on a pair of sandals, I was made up by an amazing beauty team hired by the MotoGP team. The music for the night would be a mix with Arabic touches blended with a remix, and we had rehearsals with some local dancers.

BOUND BY FIRE AND FUEL

Everything was done within the venue. I thought it was amazing to explore the cultures of each place we would visit. I forgot to mention how beautiful the circuit was in the middle of that desert, at night, all lit up.

As soon as I heard the opening of Rachid Taha's song, a famous Arabic singer, we started walking and dancing to the grid with colorful scarves flowing in the air. My heart leapt, feeling the excitement of my first professional performance outside of Spain. The song *Ya Rayah* had a completely Arabic rhythm that highlighted the desert region. The costume Nina made harmonized perfectly, a long skirt full of beads that squeaked loudly with each hip swing, matching the rhythm of the song. The dance involved more hip, shoulder, and chest movements, and we followed the motions with light hand gestures above our heads, leaning back and then returning, with the scarf covering our nose.

The stands were euphoric once again, and I felt very happy knowing they were enjoying our performance, which was very representative. Everyone watched our nighttime show with total attention, the lights creating a special effect, following our steps on the track, until more girls joined and danced around me. I continued moving my hips like in a belly dance, but with my arms and head moving with the scarf, and we threw them up at the end, listening to the applause from the crowd and the pilots' fans. It was amazing what could be done when we united cultures. I had taken belly dance lessons before, but this emotion was truly unique, pure, and incredible.

We left the track in lines, bowing our bodies in thanks. The bikes had already arrived, and the riders were taking their positions on the starting grid. Hearing the roar of the engines warming up with blue and yellow flames, I smiled, feeling honored to witness the great speed show and preparing myself for the moment of great emotion.

Guilhermo was in the second row, in a good position, and as soon as the checkered flag was waved, they took off at high speed. I went to the other side of the track, where Anita, Alex, and Tenner were. When I arrived, the view was different. I was amazed by how spectacular the floodlit track in Qatar was. The teams sometimes use special paint to help the bikes stop better under the lights.

Because of the darkness, we could see things that we wouldn't normally notice in a daytime race. The bright orange glow of the carbon brake discs on the *MotoGP* bikes as they entered the first corner was fabulous. Blue and yellow flames erupted from the exhausts as the riders braked, just like when they were warming up on the starting grid. The Tron-like reflection of the lights on the riders' visors was also visible, every effect and detail was clear during the night race.

I saw Guilhermo zooming through the track at high speed, keeping his *Wacco* team in the lead. His partner was right behind him, Jacob, meaning he was slightly trapped since his teammate from *Aspire Factory* was in the last positions. By the first lap, Guilhermo secured pole position with an impressive time, and his team cheered for this milestone from a rider who was making a name for himself and leaving his mark wherever he went.

With my heart racing, I saw Guilhermo entering the tenth turn, throwing his body out of the bike, with his knees and elbows in full contact with the asphalt. The fear of him falling hit me, and I prayed to God to watch over him, knowing how fatal one mistake can be.

In reality, you really have to be a professional and love adrenaline to be a motorcycle rider and risk so much. It takes a lot of courage. After that, we saw Jacob pass Guilhermo, and they kept alternating in the first position. The tension between them for the first place was intense and was only alleviated when Jacob fell, and Guilhermo took the lead, winning the Qatar Grand Prix after completing the twelve laps of the circuit with sixteen curves.

He crossed the finish line, celebrating by popping a wheelie, balancing the bike on one wheel, and after arriving at the track, there was a massive celebration. Everyone was euphoric, seeking the rider's attention, who seemed to be looking for someone in the crowd. When he finished hugging his teammate, Tenner and Alex almost carried him. He was red from happiness, sweaty, and smiling at everyone. Then our eyes met, and it felt so right to be there for him, waiting for him so we could celebrate his second victory together.

"Congratulations, champion," I whispered in his ear, still holding onto him as tears fell from his eyes in emotion. It's so crazy, this thing we're living here, and honestly, I imagined it would be emotional. But witnessing it up close, there's no comparison to what we imagined, not even close."

"Thank you, love! You know you also deserve it for your extraordinary performance." He flashed me a warm and wide smile, and I could only return it. He then squeezed my hand.

"Go on, you still have the press conference. I'll wait for you here in the pit until you're ready."

"Grab your stuff and go find Anita. There's a celebration party, and you can come as my guest, if you want."

"I'll go with you, but are we going to walk in front of everyone like this?"

"Is there a problem with that?"

"No, it's just that..." He pulled me closer again and caressed my face after asking Tenner and Alex for a minute.

"Love, if you don't feel comfortable with this, just don't go. I don't mind showing you off, don't get me wrong, but I can't pretend there's nothing between us."

"There's no way. We could blow up this circuit just with the energy between us, it's just that I don't know how ready I am."

"I understand you, and we can go, but let's go as friends, if you want," he said, finding a way to have me with him without making me feel pressured to be by his side. I hate being so insecure and confused about this adventure we haven't labeled yet, but when I looked into his eyes, he showed me trust. I felt his hand caressing my hair, sealing our lips together, and then he smiled slightly, apologizing to me, but he had to go for the press interview.

I went to grab my things after he left me on the other side of the pit and thought a lot about how this was purely my own nonsense. Does he think I'm too silly now? Ugh, I don't want to know. A woman has the right to feel insecure sometimes, and in the middle of this adventure of ours that we haven't defined, it's normal. Especially since I'm a woman who cares about herself. But I want to surprise him at this celebration.

I went back to his pit, then headed to the press room. When I arrived, I found the place packed with journalists from the most renowned sports channels in the world. I felt proud seeing Guilhermo at that table with the giant riders from the last seasons and knowing that he was one of the greats. From where I stood, I could hear the chatter about something that was bound to explode in the media's hands sooner or later.

"Is it true that Guilhermo García is the brother of Jacob River Nolan, number 45 from the *Aspire Factory*?" Oh my god, the trouble was brewing, but I saw Anita denying everything, saying this matter wasn't up for discussion. What a bombshell, my God!

But I noticed that, despite smiling and answering the questions, Guilhermo was nervous, which wasn't good at all. He went to the podium and celebrated with the 2nd and 3rd place finishers, and when he left, Jacob made a point of congratulating him sarcastically, with a fake kindness. How can these two be brothers? They don't look alike at all. Not even in appearance. It's amazing how River Nolan loves causing drama, even outside Spain, trying to get under people's skin.

Lorenzo River Nolan arrived and began whispering in his spoiled son's ear. He smiled scornfully, not caring about what his father was saying.

I approached and went to Guilhermo's side, taking his hand even with flashes popping in our direction. I couldn't not support him if he needed it, and whatever happens after that, it's in God's hands. He turned to look at me and smiled in thanks. More questions from journalists surrounded us. I saw Anita roll her eyes and move toward us, but the rider stepped ahead, and instead of responding to his brother's mockery, he exhaled and gave Jacob a smile.

"Thank you very much, Jacob, and we'll see each other at the GP of Portugal. Good luck!" He smiled, turning his back on his brother and Lorenzo, leaving them no chance to respond.

We left together, and the paparazzi chased after us, but Guilhermo only answered questions related to his race performance and the grand prix, and so we managed to leave. There was still the celebration ahead. Surely, we'd run into Jacob and his unpleasant girlfriend again. We didn't say anything, even though our look spoke more than words ever could.

CHAPTER TWENTY-THREE

Guilhermo

"Starting over means fully surrendering to what you love to do, even if it involves risks. Flying toward what you desire, listening to your heart, and staying true to it." That was the message my mother sent me after seeing the news about my victory in Qatar and the rumors about Jacob being my brother.

Even after everything, I went to the celebration. It was pointless to hide from the situation. If there's one thing I learned from my mother, it's to face any problem with my head held high. Lorenzo kept following me with his eyes throughout the party, as if he was about to approach and say something. But he's very cowardly, I realized that back in Jerez when we met backstage before the official race. He defended Jacob and left, a man who doesn't have the courage to confront his past and come talk to me.

Dolores, who was unsure about appearing with me at the celebration, as it would make our relationship public, had a different feeling. What we had decided was to live this adventure throughout the championship season. We didn't label anything, and because of that, she was uncertain about appearing with me. Even though we had already been open about it after the first race in Jerez, when she saw the situation I was in after another victory, she didn't think twice and came to support me. That surprised me and made my heart warm and happy to have her there, holding my hand.

Later, she went to the celebration with me and met more people from within MotoGP, as well as other riders. After the party, we went back to the hotel and spent some time in the jacuzzi, enjoying some much-needed rest. After everything that had happened, I needed to relax, my body was tense, and she felt that. We talked for what felt like hours, talking about family and all the problems that surround it. Dolores is a warrior in every sense of the word. After hearing her recount everything she's been through in the last few years, I instantly tried to imagine what I would do in the place of this Spanish woman.

"You stayed strong all these years?" I asked something I had wanted to know since she started talking about how she supported her mother, took on the financial responsibility, and raised her sisters. Lola looked away and stared at another spot, and right then, I knew she was suffering from it.

"I had to be strong, Guilhermo. There was no other way. They need to see me as the person they can trust with everything, someone who won't break down at any moment. They need to feel safe."

"Lola, I understand that you wanted to be strong for them and because of them, but what happens if everything falls apart at some point?"

"I'll be standing, strong, to face whatever comes."

"You're stubborn. For some situations, that's good, but for others, it might not be. But understand that when someone forces themselves to always be strong, they hide and bottle up everything they feel, and that's not healthy. Eventually, the cup you keep filling will overflow, and it's downhill from there."

"I know that," she said, looking at me, her voice choking up, and I immediately embraced her.

"It doesn't have to be like this, love. You have the right to freak out, cry, feel your pain, or else you'll swallow up the Lola who's joyful, independent, strong, and determined, the one living inside you," I said, placing my finger on her chest, pointing at her heart. We sat in silence together, and I felt that I would have to tell her about my past with Mari soon. I can't hide something like that from her; it's clear that what we're living together isn't just an adventure, and soon enough, this will catch up to us.

WE ARRIVED IN PORTUGAL late in the afternoon after a tiring seven-hour and twenty-minute journey. We disembarked, and this time Lola and I didn't lose control. She had her period, got cramps, and I was more careful during the trip. I noticed she was more stressed and anxious, she started getting headaches and leg pain. Shortly after, she screamed in the bathroom like the beautiful and charming Spanish woman that she is. I laughed at her way, and she scolded me for being insensitive.

As soon as we arrived, we headed to my mother's house in Portugal, she arranged for us to meet again. This time, Mrs. Inês didn't come since she was in Barcelona with commitments at her catering business. My grandmother is a full-fledged entrepreneur who is very successful where she lives, organizing parties like no one else and knowing the best menu for every occasion. My mom always says that when I get married, grandma will want to take care of everything, and she'll be happy to hand the party over to her. Miss García doesn't like organizing parties, she likes to enjoy them, my mom is a woman who loves to celebrate everything, as a good Spanish woman should.

Anita arrived fixing her hair near the car, and she confessed to me that she misses the bartender, my friend Juan, who owns Navarro. They were having a somewhat heated affair while we were in Jerez, but when the season starts, we know we're stuck at airports. This made me think that Dolores and I were lucky that she's taking part in these dance performances before the races. Which makes me proud of her because with this, she's gained tremendous visibility. Anita even suggested she create a social media account to show the behind-the-scenes of being a dancer, and with my assistant's tips, she has gained excellent engagement.

Again, half the team headed to the Algarve International Circuit, better known as the Portimão Circuit, located 16 km from Portimão, in the parish of Mexilhoeira Grande. They would stay at a hotel near the circuit. My mom would only arrive on Saturday and would attend the free practice if her flight wasn't delayed.

We arrived at the house, and everything was ready and properly organized. Anita had contacted my mother, they exchanged some ideas, and they got everything ready. After talking to Alex about the track, we continued to discuss improvements for the bike. We were observing the performance to ensure that everything goes well next year.

I showed Dolores the house, and she really liked it, saying that my mom has good taste. After that, we entered my room with a beautiful view. I lay down on the bed and thought about how quickly the time we've spent together has passed. For a moment, I thought about what would come after, and Lola was right to be concerned. There was no denying it anymore, we are involved, and our bond has changed a lot. I already saw her as mine, in fact, I've seen her like that since I kissed her for the first time in Jerez. With the time we started spending together, we got to know each other more and more, and we are reaching the point where everyone thinks we are dating. This is what came out in the news with the photos of us in Qatar, right after my victory and the rumors that River Nolan is my brother.

It got so much attention that Anita had to find extreme security measures because the paparazzi have no limits when they want an exclusive. Lorenzo didn't deny anything, he simply stayed quiet, ignored all the questions asked, changing the subject. He defended Jacob when questioned about the explicit provocations he was making on the track, trying to bring me down. I just hope they realize this, because if they harm me, I don't know what I'll be capable of doing.

Anita told me something about the toxic relationship Jacob has with Lorenzo. Actually, it was Juan who told her that he is his father's dream project. Nothing is ever enough, he demands and pushes him a lot. So, I imagine that the bastard son reaching the top and dominating the championship podium must be bothering him a lot. I don't care what he thinks, I'm giving my best without harming anyone. Let his son do the same and be better to catch up to me. It's not pride, and certainly not self-conviction, it's simply the determination to be the best rider. I've always wanted this, pursued it, and fought for it.

"What's the podium favorite thinking?" Lola approached the bed, and within seconds, she was running her hands through my hair, caressing and looking at me with her bright green eyes.

"Thinking about everything, but mostly about what we are building together." She smiled slyly, but soon her lips pouted.

"What should I think about this? How to interpret what you just said?" I touched her cheek after grabbing her and lifting her onto my body.

"Think whatever you want, but know that you have me, I'm completely yours." Her pupils dilated, and I felt her mixed with concern and happiness. To calm her down, my hands covered her firm, sexy hips.

"You can't play with my heart like that." Nor could she with mine, so I had to be honest with her about what I've been feeling and everything that involves my past. Then, she decides if she wants to stay and make a home in my heart and my life.

"You know I'm not a man who plays games. I'm opening up to you, and I need to tell you something about my past that hurts a lot."

"Guilhermo, I know what happened, and I respect it if you don't want to talk." She leaned her face toward mine and sealed our lips. I pulled her closer by her hair. Dolores had no idea what she made me feel from the moment I saw her on that bike in Jerez.

"I'm ready to talk, but I need you to listen carefully and realize that nothing is as unique as what I've been feeling for you since the day I met you."

"Oh, my rider!" She sealed our lips, and I decided to let her go. We sat across from each other for that conversation. She intertwined our hands, and I felt confident enough to finally open up to her before she thought she heard Mari's name come out of my mouth while I was sleeping. I don't know how much longer I'll have nightmares about her.

"You know well what happened because Mari was a street racer, from a family with a very famous surname in Brazil. And the news about her tragic death spread even outside of there." My chest began to burn. That was a part that hurt deep in my heart. Losing her was too much for me to accept, but Dolores squeezed my hand, and I saw in her eyes that she was encouraging me. "So, I was there, and I watched the moment her life slipped away on the asphalt. She died right there. She hadn't put her helmet on correctly because while Mari was getting ready for that race, I was arguing with her. I didn't want her to participate, but one of the women from a motorcycle club provoked her and challenged her. I couldn't do anything. She was very stubborn, hard-headed, and had the courage for all the adventures she could think of."

"My God, Guilhermo." She hugged me when she saw that I was about to explode just by remembering that tragic night, the worst night of my life.

"I blamed myself for not doing anything, and for her not putting her helmet on right." Immediately, Lola silenced me with her fingers, looking at me with tear-filled eyes.

"Please, don't think you were to blame. You were warning her, the choice was hers, and like you said, she was stubborn."

"I know that, everyone tells me that, even the psychologist I went to, but I felt that weight on my shoulders."

"Losing someone you love, like that, I can't even imagine what it's like. I confess, I get tense seeing you race at that speed."

"You can imagine, yes. The pain of loss is different, but all of us who've lost special people like that feel an enormous emptiness."

"I know, I lived that with my father. It's not the same as how you lost your girlfriend, but I sympathize with your pain. And that's why you have nightmares about the accident?"

"Yes, it hasn't happened anymore, and that day we were sleeping together on the plane, I didn't have a nightmare, not like the others with Mari. But it was with someone I couldn't see, on the race track. I only heard and saw blurry shapes."

"My God, doesn't that interfere with your races? Guilhermo, are you serious about what you're telling me?" She was desperate, and I could see in her eyes that she was already involved with me.

"Don't worry, it's fine. I just remembered that nightmare a few days ago, and I talked to the team's doctor and psychologist. He knows me, and..." She cut me off and stood up from the bed.

"You can't do that, Guilhermo!" She shouted at me, her eyes filled with tears rolling down her face, and she started talking like a madwoman. "Why did I get involved with a motorcycle rider? Why did I do this to myself? Look at my state!" She turned to me with an angry expression, her face red. "Don't think for a second that you can hide things like this from me, because I can't imagine." She looked at the ceiling, put her hand on her head as if she were on the edge —

qué cabrón! — She just called me a bastard in Spanish, using one of her expressions.

I had to get up from the bed, run to her, and hold her in my arms. Her body was trembling from the intensity of her desperation. The depth of what we were feeling overwhelmed us unexpectedly. I felt like I was in a race. Where Dolores was my grand prize, and the faster I ran in her direction, the faster I felt that emotion that I thought I would only feel once in a lifetime. But fate put this beautiful woman in my way, and I was crazy thinking about what I would do if I had to live without having her with me.

"Dolores, I'm here, you have me. Remember what I told you a few minutes ago in bed? Don't torment yourself, I've been through this. I tried to deny and ignore the fact that with you, my heart beats faster, and the wild desire I feel to have you close to my body, and how much I love watching you dance. *Damn*, love!"

"So..."

"Don't deny this to me, or to yourself, don't blame yourself..." She grabbed me and kissed me passionately and wildly. Her tongue took control of my mouth in circles, and her hands took my hair. In seconds, I removed her robe and took her right there, while moaning her name repeatedly, making me dizzy with pleasure. A feeling so intense overcame me, and I couldn't control anything. I took her until she screamed my name, trembling as her body curved under the orgasm that took over her. I wouldn't let her leave my life, not when she was already mine in every sense.

CHAPTER TWENTY-FOUR

Dolores

I wasn't prepared for everything we experienced in Portugal, and I confessed everything to Nina through a video call. She jumped for joy and said that we're the most talked-about couple, and how explosive we are as a pair. The chemistry we share seemed to transcend the cameras when the paparazzi started flashing flashes in our direction.

After the honest conversation I had with Guilhermo that left me calmer, despite having lost it in front of him. But that's part of who I am; sometimes I'm sweet, other times I'm a bomb about to explode. I admit he surprised me, and since that day, we've been living every moment more fully. We still don't know how we're going to maintain the relationship after this, but he promised me that he won't let me go and will do everything to make it work.

Despite all the conversation, sometimes I still feel insecure and fearful about our future. I'm a dancer who has a family that depends entirely on my work. Guilhermo lives from airport to airport, and he only has three months of rest each year. I don't know how we'll handle this, but I can't deny what I feel for that pilot.

When his mother arrived on Saturday, we had a special dinner for her, and she was happy to see her son qualify well for the Sunday race. She told me about her medical mission in Africa, and I could see how extraordinary that woman is, a professional like no other. We talked about my performances, which are being well recognized because we bring the culture of each country into every choreography and costume.

When the time for the race arrived, I felt anxious, as we saw Jacob and Lorenzo in the paddock corridors. River Nolan's look toward his brother was deadly; he was up to something, and that made me worry. I hugged and kissed Guilhermo, wishing him luck and asking him to be careful. I then went to the locker room and makeup room to prepare myself.

We rehearsed on Friday and Saturday, and before the free practice, we managed to select a few dancers to complete the pairings for the choreography. The Portuguese music we chose had a pleasant rhythm, and Portuguese dance is characterized by traditional folk elements. I remembered my mother, as she loves Portugal, lived here during part of her adolescence, and said she'll never forget the beautiful dances and Portuguese festivals and how special the time she spent here was. That's why I made a video call with Olívia and showed them my costume. I saw my mother smile, and I was happy to see her doing so well.

Nina and Juan were taking turns staying with them, and Navarro's mother went as well. Olívia said my mom loved talking and cooking with her. It seems like she was attending Alcoholics Anonymous meetings and also seeing her therapist. I also spoke with Luna, who cheered when she saw me in that red and green skirt, the colors of the Portuguese flag. I said goodbye to them, blowing a kiss with my eyes full of tears from missing them. I missed my family.

I was called and made my way to the Starting Grid, where we would perform the famous fandango dance of Spanish origin, also called marujada, a style characterized by frenetic, lively, and flashy movements. With a touch of ribatejano style, the dancers, fully dressed, began with slow steps, moving their feet on the ground and gradually increasing speed. We entered, forming a circle of couples dancing to the rhythm of the accordion.

Spinning and moving our feet, we danced faster and then, as the music slowed down, we followed its rhythm even with our feet until we formed a line. We danced in sync, the two dancers led the way, moving as we followed behind, dancing with our hands on our waists, following the joyful rhythm. Then we slowed down, and they kept moving their feet forward and backward, crossing their feet, then standing completely upright. We returned to dancing together and ended with applause from the crowd at the Portimão racetrack.

We bowed in gratitude and left the stage. Anita managed to film part of the dance and post it on social media. She suggested showing the behind-the-scenes of my routine, and I've gained many followers from all over the world. I left the grid with chills, full of incredible energy. After I grabbed the corridor, I went straight to the locker room, wanting to change and see Guilhermo start the race.

As soon as I finished getting dressed, I went straight to where Anita and the team were. My eyes froze when I saw him on the Starting Grid, warming up his bike. The checkered flag rose, and the sound of the engines started, speeding down the small straightaway to pass the first corner of the track.

But the race didn't go as expected for Guilhermo, who had already won two Grand Prix titles. He fell on the sixth lap while leading the race and ended up compromising his chances of getting a good result, as he and his team had hoped. The victory went to Jacob River Nolan, who took first place in the race. Still, Guilhermo continued leading the World Championship for drivers, and despite the fall, he regained his time and finished in second place.

Even though he didn't take first place, Guilhermo celebrated finishing in second, which was unexpected, given that he had fallen. My heart raced in my chest until the race was over. On the podium, they climbed and celebrated. Guilhermo congratulated River Nolan out of respect, but his brother mocked him and nearly made my pilot lose his composure.

BOUND BY FIRE AND FUEL

"He's playing with fire, *fuck*!"

"You can't listen to his mocking provocations, for God's sake. Don't lose your cool," I heard Alex say as soon as I arrived. Guilhermo turned around, and our eyes met. "Help me out here, Lola."

"Right, you're not going to lose your patience with that arrogant jerk," I said, narrowing my eyes at him.

"Calm down, you two can stop. I'm in control."

"We hope so. Don't fall for River Nolan's act. Now let's go, we have a press conference. They'll definitely ask what happened for you to fall and lose your first-place position."

That day, as we were leaving the circuit, we ran into Lorenzo, and from the tension in the air, it was clear Isabel didn't like seeing him. They exchanged fierce looks, but she was polite and only greeted him. He, however, ignored her, leaving the Spanish woman talking to herself.

"Qué te den! Who does he think he is, some kind of celebrity?" she raged, her face red with anger at the man's behavior.

"Let it go, *mama*! He doesn't deserve any of your attention."

"He doesn't deserve it, but couldn't he treat me with respect? No, he's still a *canalla* of the highest order. The older he gets, the worse he becomes."

"Ah, that's true, my mom always said he was no good."

"She's right, now let's go. You need to eat and rest after so many annoying questions from those vulture-like journalists."

WE HAD A DELICIOUS dinner that Isabel had prepared for us, with one of Portugal's most famous dishes, the "cozido à portuguesa." A dish made with boiled vegetables, meats, sausages, and cabbage. It was divinely tasty, and Guilhermo remembered his grandmother and talked about our stay in Barcelona, mentioning that we'd visit her during the Catalonia GP. Isabel said that if she could, she would catch a flight there just to meet up with us.

The evening was pleasant despite the tension between Guilhermo and his mother, due to his father and brother. The Rivers Nolan leave people stressed wherever they go; it's incredible how unpleasant they are. Trying to lift everyone's spirits, I put on some music and got everyone involved, the living room in their house is huge, and we danced peacefully.

When we went to bed, Guilhermo kissed me slowly and intensely, taking me in such a way that drove me crazy. He kissed me so well that it left me craving more. I wanted him inside me like I've never wanted anyone before. It was incredible how different it was with him—new and completely unique sensations, creating such a powerful feeling inside my heart.

After a few days, we said goodbye to his mother, and she headed off to her next destination, while we caught a direct flight to France for another performance and race. Despite missing my mom and sisters so much, I still feel so free, and every new place I visit fascinates me with how rich our world is. Unfortunately, the people who inhabit it are often poor and empty. It's sad to know that many do not preserve the places and do everything to try to be bigger than God.

But that didn't take away from the beauty of all these travels, and I learned that I have to let go a little. I live for my family, and I had never allowed myself to leave like this, thinking I would get anywhere by just living in Jerez. The world is full of possibilities, and there's a place for me in it too. I just need to chase after it. After these performances, I'm going after my next show; I want to keep my light shining on the stages.

CHAPTER TWENTY-FIVE

Guilhermo

When we arrived in France, Lola immediately fell in love with the beautiful European country, brimming with happiness. Throughout our trip, she couldn't stop talking about how unique and strikingly diverse our world is. I agreed, and she shared her worry about leaving her mother with her sisters, as she had always been there since her father's death. In reality, she carried everything on her shoulders, even though she wanted so much to become one of the best dancers. She gave up what she loved to support and be with her family.

I couldn't judge her for that; in her place, I think I'd do the same. Who are we to talk about others' struggles when we've never been through anything similar? It's easy to judge from the outside. But living it firsthand is completely different. That's why I didn't lose my cool with Jacob—I tried to put myself in his shoes, imagining what it's like to have a father dictating your career path.

I didn't want to compare Lorenzo to my mother, but she never dictated what I should do with my life. On the contrary, she and my grandmother talked a lot with me, supporting me through all my wild ideas. Lorenzo seemed to treat Jacob poorly; from the little I saw behind the press conferences, he would always take over, answering for Jacob to the sports journalists. And clearly, River Nolan let some of that show. Well, he doesn't fool me, and I know it drives him crazy.

We stayed at a hotel in Le Mans, close to the French GP, Hôtel de La Pommeraie, a quiet, romantic place that Anita had found. It made me wonder, as my assistant was clearly plotting something with my Lola. I didn't ask, but I was genuinely curious to know what they were up to.

With the cloudy weather, I could already tell the race would be under rain on Sunday, possibly even during practice. Alex called me from the racetrack, saying the mechanics were already prepping the bikes for rain. According to the forecast Anita looked up, there was an eighty percent chance of rain those days in France.

I took a shower and lay down, putting on my headphones. I'd already prepared my *playlist* days before the race. I put on my large headphones and immersed myself in the guitar riffs of *Back In Black* by AC/DC. Though I'm eclectic with music, during racing season, I prefer rock. The beat of the drums combined with the violent guitar riffs filled me with adrenaline. It's truly indescribable—the mix of freedom, anticipation, and thrill as you feel yourself glide on the bike. Each corner entry, where you lean and throw your body, brings such a rush and, at times, fear. But you can't deny the pleasure in it. Being in the world of motorcycling is exhilarating and challenging. Despite what people think, each race is uniquely essential for a motorcyclist, and I believe it's the same for Formula 1 drivers.

Lost in my rock playlist, enjoying the sound of *In the End* by Linkin Park, I didn't hear Lola come in. She'd gone out with Anita, saying they were just getting some snacks for the evening.

When I opened my eyes, I was stunned by how gorgeous she looked. Lola is a storm. Her hair was loose in perfect, full curls, and her face was barely made up, as if she remembered when I told her she was beautiful without makeup. She smiled coyly, spun around, wearing long red boots, a stylish gray trench coat, and then sat in the room's armchair, crossing her legs, revealing a hint of a red garter belt.

"Damn!" I grunted, already aroused by the sight of her glowing skin, a charm of its own. I could imagine her perfume, and my mind raced as I dropped my phone and headphones on the bed, moving closer to her.

"Stay right there. We're going to have some fun, but for now, I just want you to watch me."

"Lola, you're perfect! I don't know if I can just sit here and watch, babe," I said, my voice already husky with excitement.

"Control yourself," she teased with a sensual smile, her perfume reaching me as she got up and flicked open the curtain to the room's closet, revealing a pole—"Watch, and later you can have your way with me," she said, turning her back to me. This woman was driving me insane, no doubt.

She dimmed the lights, leaving only the yellow lamps on, put on a slow, sensual song, and began moving her curvy body to the sexy beat. I shifted in my chair, already uncomfortable as I hardened just watching her dance so seductively. I swallowed hard when I saw her hold onto the pole, spinning, her green eyes full of lust locking onto mine.

Then she faced the pole, swaying down to the floor, unbuttoning her trench coat. I groaned in pleasure as she revealed herself in just red lace lingerie, a corset, and garter belt. "Holy shit!" I couldn't contain myself, running my hand roughly over my throbbing erection, desperate for my stunning dancer.

But I had to hold back, knowing she had plans for tonight, and I must admit, despite wanting to skip ahead, I was curious to see her in action. I heard the rain pour outside and smiled at my Lola, the perfection that had unexpectedly entered my life. We'd thrown ourselves into the fire together, nearly igniting Navarro along with us. Nothing compares to the feeling I get every time I see her after a race.

Then, she threw her coat in my direction, and as *Wicked Games* by The Weeknd started playing, she began dancing in such a tantalizing way. This woman was pure dynamite, wearing only red thigh-high boots and matching lingerie. She tossed her hair to one side, positioned her left foot slightly behind her right, shifted her weight, and slid her right leg around the pole. She arched her back, extending her arm downward, giving me a hell of a view of her body on that pole. All while keeping eye contact with me.

She wrapped both legs around the pole and slid effortlessly, making seductive expressions that had my hands itching, wanting to touch her skin. Then, she bent down, giving me the perfect view of her full breasts in that transparent lace lingerie.

"Hot as hell!" I said, keeping my gaze locked on her. When the music shifted to a more intense beat, I was in awe, watching Lola move her entire body, her full hips in perfect view, driving me absolutely wild. Unable to hold back, she approached, lifting my face to hers, gripping my chin—bold as only she could be.

Then she turned around, backing against the pole, positioning it perfectly between her ass, lifting one hand up and the other down as she slid down. That was my breaking point. I unzipped my shorts, sliding them and my boxers down, and began stroking myself as I watched her rhythmically bouncing, her ass dropping to the ground and rising with an impressive sway. I didn't even know she could dance like that, matching the beat of the funk tracks they played in Brazil.

Without holding back, Lola began practically bouncing and shaking her ass, driving me wild to the beat of *"Quer Mais"* by Mc Mirella and Mc Poca. Then she bent over, hands on her knees, giving me a perfect view of her ass bouncing all the way down to the floor. She came closer, laughing loudly; thank goodness we were at the hotel penthouse. My god, she sat on my lap in that tiny thong that disappeared between her delicious cheeks. Driven by insane desire, I wasted no time, palming her ass, making her arch her back. Then I moved one hand to her neck, pulling her closer to my face. Hungry for her mouth, I tugged her cherry-flavored, plump lower lip between my teeth. Then I kissed her, feeling the desire sending shivers down our bodies, heating everything around us. Her soft, warm skin made me moan with pleasure at having her like this. After that, Lola started grinding on my cock in a delightful frenzy, making us both moan into each other's mouths.

I pushed her thin thong aside, feeling her swollen, wet lips slick with arousal. Damn, this woman is hot! I massaged her clit, making her arch her body and grind deliciously against my hand. Lola is pure perfection, a complete woman who makes me lose all control. I took her mouth again after she scratched my back with her nails, wild beneath my shirt.

"Baby, I want to taste you, I can't wait anymore. I need you like this, damn it, you're so wet just for me."

"Only for you, my pilot. Speed up!" she said, and I lifted her, carried her to the bed, put her on all fours with those sexy boots still on, and lay down to devour her juicy, hot, delicious pussy. She didn't hold back, rocking against my mouth as I plunged my tongue inside her and sucked her full lips with vigor. If there's one thing I love, it's tasting this woman before entering her and fucking her hard.

"Tonight's going to be rough, Lola, no going slow; you've driven me crazy," I rasped, unable to control my voice. She just nodded, moaning my name louder as she climaxed, and I took everything she had to give. When she collapsed beside me on the bed, she looked lost in her pleasure.

I gave her just enough time to take off her shorts and shirt. When I reached for a condom, she took it from my hand, saying she trusted me. I asked her before entering if she was sure.

"I am. I'm taking care of myself, and like I said, I trust you. Now, hurry up and fuck me." Without wasting time, I ran the tip of my cock along her warm, wet entrance. She rocked against me, and then I entered her slowly, feeling a completely different, delicious pleasure. Her pussy clenched around me, driving me wild, feeling her like this without a condom. She doesn't know the trouble she's in now because I won't use a damn latex barrier keeping me from feeling her walls gripping me so intensely. The rain was torrential outside; I knew it was cold, but we were both naked and completely drenched in sweat.

Unable to hold back anymore, I started thrusting hard and deep, the bed shaking with the intensity as she pulled my hair and kissed me savagely. I sucked her luscious breasts, switching between them and her mouth. When she began convulsing and trembling, I saw her skin prickle with goosebumps as her body arched in orgasm. Watching her feel the pleasure I was giving her is breathtaking. I could spend my life doing this. I sped up my thrusts, feeling on the edge of coming inside her, completely lost in this gorgeous woman.

"Lola, you're amazing," I groaned huskily into her ear. "You're mine, and I lo..." I couldn't finish the sentence as I fell beside her, her eyes locked on mine.

"Guilhermo," she whispered, bringing her thigh over mine and looking at me with a sudden nervousness.

"Dolores, I know this might be too much, but what I feel for you is surpassing everything; it's so overwhelming it scares me," I murmured, caressing her perfect, full curls. "It's early, but I'm going to say it anyway," her pupils widened as she heard those three words. "I love you; I can't deny it, baby," I sealed our lips, and she smiled softly, kissing me slowly as we started again, making love without haste. When she climaxed, she looked at me intensely, saying those three words right back.

After the intense night Dolores and I had, we were all smiles. I have to admit she looked even more beautiful, if that were possible. Anita noticed that we'd reached a new level, and I need to talk to her about how I know she had a hand in that pole dance show by Lola. I arrived at the hotel and didn't even see a pole there, but those two pulled it off somehow, all part of their scheming.

Actually, those two are getting closer and closer; I just hope Lola's friend Nina doesn't get jealous. We've been spending so much time together that, off the track, I had to wake up early to check out the circuit and practice on it, even in the cold drizzle at Le Mans. As far as I remembered, France this time of year is nothing but rain. I trained all morning. First, I did an intense run around the circuit to get to know it better and then cycled, giving me a different view and understanding of the track.

On Saturday, after the rain let up, we managed to get some time in and complete one of the tests before free practice, giving me a sense of the wet track. This delayed practice time, but once it started, I noticed that competing with more bikes made avoiding collisions much harder. Any wrong move, and a slip was inevitable. So, I was careful, but Jacob had other plans and bumped into me, making me fall and slide off the track.

"What the hell!" I shouted, punching the first wall I saw in front of me.

"Guilhermo García, focus!" Alex urged, something he hadn't asked of me in a long time during a race.

"Did you see what he did?" I could only see red, remembering how he knocked me off the track out of pure spite. "I can't focus after that, except maybe to punch that smug face of his."

"He's getting what he wanted," Anita chimed in, and I was already trying to stop seeing red with anger. Jacob had reached a point where I could no longer ignore him; he could have done anything else, but not this.

"Yeah, because I don't know if I can get back on the track. I'm shaking with rage, and the first chance I'd get, I'd knock him out, even if it means getting disqualified."

"Do you want me to call her?" Anita grabbed me by the shoulders, looking into my eyes seriously. I knew exactly who she was talking about, but I wasn't sure if it would help. "Stop overthinking, Gui. Lola is one of the strongest women I know, brave and patient because she puts up with you." I closed my eyes, thinking only of her, how calming it would be to hold her and feel her skin. That was all I needed.

"Please, go get her now," I said, opening my eyes as Anita had already left. I started pacing, anxious and nervous, afraid she might refuse to come.

"Don't overthink, Guilhermo, for God's sake, try to calm down, breathe, and have some water." Alex handed me a water bottle, and I downed it in a minute, gazing at the track ahead. I remembered every step I took to get here; nothing should shake me like this. But ever since that clash with Jacob, he's been relentlessly messing with me. When I turned around, I saw her eyes, and in them, I found purpose. She ran to me, and we embraced. My hands tangled in her curly hair, and just feeling her warmth and scent gave me confidence. Is it strange that someone becomes your home so quickly? Your safe harbor?

"I saw what he did on the track, but please go back out there and show him what you're made of. Most importantly, be the Guilhermo who doesn't let himself get provoked. You're a champion and still leading this tournament." When I returned to the track for the second practice, after the mechanics and Tenner switched out the bike, I felt confident and secured the first position on the starting grid.

On Sunday, following Lola's beautiful Cancan performance—a traditional French dance—I had a great start, securing the lead right from the grid and effortlessly taking the pole position. The wet track required extra caution, but even so, I pressed on, doing what I truly love to the best of my ability. Feeling the adrenaline rushing through my veins, I kept my distance from Jacob, who wasn't as lucky and crashed on the tenth lap. It's worth mentioning that he went down on his own, without anyone knocking into his bike; he simply lost control.

And this happens often in such conditions, because when you accelerate too much without paying attention to braking times on a wet track, the bike completely loses control, starting to skid and lose balance. He flew off the track, and even after he recovered, he stayed close behind me. But by then, I had already found my rhythm with the bike on the wet track, celebrating as I completed the twelfth lap, crossing the checkered flag and basking in the applause from the crowd that stood to cheer.

It was exhilarating to see everyone swept up in that frenzy of victory. Winning is more than just claiming a title; at least for me, Guilhermo, the taste of victory reminds me that I've reached the place I've always dreamed of, with relentless determination, dedication, and passion. This is the life I've chosen, and no one can steer me away from this path if it's meant to be.

CHAPTER TWENTY-SIX

Dolores

Guilhermo made an excellent run even on a wet track, since it had rained a lot in France those days, which surprised everyone. Right after the race, at the press conference, all the riders were asked about what MotoGP means to them, as it has millions of fans around the world and continues to grow, being seen as one of the best competitive spectacles in motorsport.

When my rider answered, everyone got a sense of how much he loves what he does. He said that, above all, it's a lifestyle he chose to live and that it's necessary to feel passion and fire for what you do. Knowing how to test your limits to the max and exploring your best, along with the sense of freedom at all levels, gives adrenaline, and if you love what you do, it becomes even fun. Competing and winning are just a consequence of all of that. Everyone applauded and whistled his last name, agreeing with what he said. I felt proud of my rider.

We were able to perform on the wet track of the Le Mans circuit, the Cancan, a typical and delightful French dance. The spectators loved watching the dance and got into the vibe. It was touching and electrifying to feel everyone's energy. I felt so happy, free, and strong. Each choreography represented a culture; it's so much diversity for someone who lived dancing Flamenco and other types of dance. This is a unique challenge for each dancer. You gain more knowledge about each country and, beyond that, we continue perfecting our work. And as the rider says, when you do what you love, it's fun, and it gives more pleasure than anything else you could do.

In France, that hotel room was one of the most intense moments of our adventure, and we took it to the next level as we exchanged the three words that change everything in a relationship. I was scared when I saw the depth of the feeling in his eyes, but they reflected mine for him, and I couldn't avoid opening my heart to Guilhermo. We loved each other in a way that was full and delicious, like never before, and after that, I felt even more connected to him.

During the free practice, Jacob knocked down and distracted his brother, and no one has the patience to endure so much provocation and envy. He was very angry, Anita urgently called me, and I rushed over with my heart in my throat, thinking that Guilhermo had been seriously hurt. But when I got there and we looked at each other, I realized that he needed my embrace and support to continue. That gave my rider new energy, and I was happy to see him excited and determined. In the last practice, he qualified in the first position on the starting grid, leaving everyone stunned, even River Nolan.

We arrived in Mugello at night. I was tired from the travels; it's such an enriching experience to be able to visit so many countries, but I can't deny that this routine is exhausting. I imagine for Guilhermo, who is competing, even though he enjoys what he does, you can't deny that all the determination he puts into the tracks comes with a cost.

The hotel Anita had booked was pure luxury. She said it was eight kilometers from the Mugello circuit, so we are close and won't spend too much time traveling from the hotel to the racetrack. The impressive hotel *Villa Le Maschere* is located in a 16th-century village, twelve minutes on foot from the bus station and twelve kilometers from the Palazzo dei Vicari, one of the most famous buildings in the Scarperia region.

After we checked in at the grand reception hall of the classic hotel, we went to our suites. As soon as we arrived, I was enchanted by the classic and elegant décor of the suite, which includes a living room, a spacious bathroom with a hot tub, and access to a beautiful garden. I looked at Guilhermo, implicitly saying that we would enjoy this hotel a lot. He was tired and needed to relax to be ready for the adrenaline and excitement of racing on one of the most talked-about circuits in the world.

I was able to schedule my rehearsals with the MotoGP event organizer, who would always contact me to settle on the rehearsals. She had excellent dancer contacts from around the world, and I was thrilled with the Portuguese dancers she had managed to hire for the GP in Portugal. Since we arrived at the hotel at night, Guilhermo was free to rest, but I wanted to take advantage of him. So, I turned on the hot tub with his help after speaking with my sisters, mother, and Nina. Thank God, everything was fine with them in Jerez. I sent them a picture of the view of the garden from my suite. They were as impressed as I was, and I smiled, thinking about how much more of the world I still have to explore.

Although I love Spain and being with my family, I wanted the opportunity to visit many places in the world. I remembered the conversation I had with Guilhermo's mother. She had shared some details about the best places in the world she had visited and lived in. As a traveling and highly sought-after doctor, she said she loves learning new languages, cultures, and visiting new places. I was fascinated by everything she told me, and she said it was only a fraction of what she had experienced over the years.

"What are you thinking?" Guilhermo approached and hugged me from behind, starting to place delicious kisses on my neck, making me shiver.

"How good it is to travel, to know so many different places. Even though we're in a rush, I managed to explore a little, and that alone already captivated me."

"When this World Championship is over, we can plan a trip just for the two of us, take you to some wonderful beaches. Maybe the Maldives?"

"Oh my God, Guilhermo, that's too much, isn't it?"

"No, not at all. I just want to make you happy and give you the best. You can count on it; I won't let you go."

"It's good that you brought this up." I turned in his arms to face him, looking into his dark brown eyes that were serious as he listened to me speak. "I know we haven't labeled this, but after what we experienced in France, that night, what do we have?"

"Okay, Dolores López, will you be my girlfriend?" He took my hand and looked at me with loving, pleading eyes. I smiled, which made him roll his eyes and return the smile. I hadn't imagined he'd ask me to be his girlfriend like this. I thought he didn't like labels, based on what we declared at the beginning. But I can understand that we've reached a different level regarding our feelings. It was never simple, and it was never boring, or just an adventure. Since the moment we met and danced together, everything has been different from anything we had ever lived before.

"I accept, my rider, though I'm still a little unsure..." He silenced me.

"Don't say that. I have no doubts about what I feel for you. I know you might think that because I loved someone before you, I don't know what I feel. But on the contrary, Lola. Despite the pain of losing Mari, after therapy and with my friends trying to cheer me up to move on, I realized I couldn't let my life pass me by. What we're living now is a series of unique moments I will never forget, and I want to repeat them in unimaginable ways with you by my side."

"Oh my God, Guilhermo. Why do you talk so beautifully?"

"It's from the heart, Lola. Pure and simple, there's no way to lie here, love!" *Que cábron*! He's so good; how can I ignore this and everything I feel for him? Even though I'm scared of getting hurt, I want him more than I can express.

"*Guay*! How can I not love a man like you? Explain it to me!"

"If you can't deny it, just love me the way I love you," he said, his eyes shining, and I could see how sincere he was with me. I was completely wrong when I thought he could be just another one of those Rivers Nolans.

He is a García and nothing like his father or brother. My initial fear was that, but after everything I've come to know about the great man before me, I couldn't help but fall for him. That's why I pulled him closer and kissed his mouth passionately. His hands traveled all over my body, caressing fiercely. He needed to feel skin on skin. So, I took off the dress that was covering me, revealing my nakedness, and he loved me in an even more passionate and wild way. Now, we're not just an adventure; we're a couple. My goodness, I'm the girlfriend of the great rider and man that is Guilhermo García.

THE MUGELLO CIRCUIT is located in the town of the same name, in the Tuscany region, thirty kilometers northeast of Florence. It is modern and considered one of the best in the entire MotoGP calendar in terms of facilities and infrastructure, based on what I saw and heard the teams commenting. It was founded in 1945 and hosted its first MotoGP event in 1976. Since 1991, it has been a permanent fixture on the official calendar.

In 1988, the circuit was bought by Ferrari, which has since made frequent renovations, according to Alex. The track, 14 meters wide, is 5.245 kilometers long with five left-hand turns, nine right-hand turns, and a long straight of 1.141 kilometers. It is considered one of the most technical circuits in the world.

Tenner said that Guilhermo will have to be very technical and demanding with himself during the race. To achieve a fast lap, he will have to ride flawlessly, well-executed and precisely traced. But according to him, the rider will manage; they started training on the track. Guilhermo ran intensely on foot around the circuit to get to know it better. It seems he has been here before in Moto2, but he said that even so, they need to refresh their memory on the track's corners and feel it a bit before getting on the bike.

After studying the Tarantella dance, a type of dance that originated in Italy, specifically in the Campania region, back in the 11th century, I requested dancers as it is a dance performed by pairs. The name comes from an ancient belief that when peasants were bitten by tarantulas, the only way to expel the poison was by dancing. Hence, they had to dance furiously for hours, to the sound of the violin and drums, keeping the circulation alive and preventing the poison from spreading.

We rehearsed the partner swapping in the choreography on Friday and Saturday before the free practice on the starting grid. Guilhermo did a great time and secured an excellent starting position.

The Tarantella is a very lively dance, and I knew it would be no different when I entered the racetrack with the stands full. My heart raced when all the spectators started clapping along with the tune of the well-known song, the Tarantella Napoletana. In an emotional and remarkable way, feeling my body shiver, we began the intense and energetic movements, with hands on our waists, kicking our feet forward, and swapping hands with our partners, spinning around.

We changed movements to the sound of the violin and drums, switching places with the dancers and clapping. The smile was inevitable, as not only do you move your body, but you must also express yourself well as the dance requires. Italy is marked by joy, and the smile must be evident. Following the raised hands slightly when the partner touches your waist, after more repeated movements, we ended with the partner kneeling while we sat on their knees, raising our hands to the opposite side from our partner, smiling.

The round of applause we received was breathtaking; my heart could barely contain the happiness and satisfaction I felt. It is an enormous pleasure to represent cultures through dance. Despite putting on a performance that was full of joy, we had to witness a tragic and fatal accident in Moto3, which highlighted the extraordinary strength of every rider who lined up in the grid of a sport that cost one of their lives. The Italian GP entered history as one of the saddest days in Mugello and MotoGP, as it contrasts the best and worst of the sport.

My heart raced so much that I had to grab another bottle of water, so worried I was about the rider. Despite everything, I thought it was highly disrespectful for MotoGP to continue the schedule just minutes after John Huber's accident, the 19-year-old rider. He crashed in the middle of the pack and stayed on the track, which, according to Alex and Tenner, rarely has a positive outcome. The images of John lying on the track, being attended by a battalion of doctors, stayed with me, and I knew I wouldn't forget it anytime soon.

I felt terrible, tears rolled down my face without me realizing, as I was shocked by the outcome of the young Moto3 rider. Even so, it was even worse for the riders because they had to go back to the track right after for the MotoGP and Moto2 qualifying. The most impressive thing was that all of them resisted and went back to the track, whether shaken or not. Mentally capable or not. Emotionally stable or not. And I just wanted to see Guilhermo and hug him tight. Anita was shaken, as was the whole team.

Before the start of Moto3, PrüstelGP announced they would not race with Ryusei Yamanaka. Tom Lüthi, a friend and mentor of John, decided to stay at the hospital with Huber's family and did not line up on the Moto2 grid. But the smaller class of the MotoGP World Championship ran as usual, and I couldn't process what had just happened on the track, yet they kept going.

Soon after the race finished, the announcement came of the young rider's death. However, Moto2 followed the schedule as originally planned. At first, it seemed like an act of unparalleled insensitivity. After the checkered flag, it became clear that the competitors raced without knowing that Huber had succumbed to his severe injuries. They didn't know anything, and during the interviews, they declared themselves happy with their race results, sending messages of support to John's family, hoping for the young rider's recovery. Someone should have informed them before the interviews. It could have been any team member or Donna, who I always saw there. They didn't need to go through any of that.

Before MotoGP, the championship organized a tribute to the rider with a moment of silence. The grid of the premier class stood in line behind PrüstelGP members, John's bike, and Ryan, his partner, in tears. It was heart-wrenching to see that scene. Just before heading to their prototypes for the start, they went one by one to comfort the team members, wiping their tears. And then, they entered the track. To pass over 20 times at the corner that cost one of their lives. Even though Guilhermo finished in 2nd place, he didn't celebrate and was too sad. I had to give him strength because he confided in me that he didn't want to race on that track, and I was anxious seeing him suffer like that.

But we've gotten used to seeing athletes as if they had supernatural powers. As if their minds and hearts were kept in compartments with no connection. As if they could store their feelings in a drawer in the pit and only return to get them after the race. But the rider feels pain and fear, they have emotions just like anyone else. And they feel this more intensely when put to the test on the track.

What made me angry and sad was that no one asked the riders at any point if they still wanted to race. They were only asked to be professionals, and they did so very well, completing three races that horrible day. Because it's a business, right? Driven by money and speed, which, like it or not, puts the riders' lives at risk.

In the press conference interviews, all the riders reported that they didn't want to race and didn't feel good racing on the *Arrabbiatta* 2, the corner where John had his fatal accident. When Guilhermo was asked about the sad event, he replied that it was a very, very difficult race. But not for the sporting side, but for the human side, as he didn't feel very good racing on the same track where, less than 24 hours earlier, he had seen people like them die.

They were all shaken, and it was impossible to deny that and not feel sad about the loss of one of their colleagues. They revealed how hard it was to accept the decision that allowed them to race. John is the 42nd rider to die in the MotoGP World Championship. Whenever tragedy strikes the championship, there is this theory that racing is the best way to honor those who have passed. And maybe it is. But not like this, not immediately. Because those who remain, do not remain whole. They don't remain stable. They don't remain ready for what comes next.

CHAPTER TWENTY-SEVEN

Guilhermo

I didn't feel good in Mugello, at the Italian GP. It was the worst moment I've ever lived in my career as a rider, actually. Dolores was in tears when she saw me, she hugged me so tightly and for so long that I thought she wouldn't let go. What started beautifully with her performing on the starting grid, dancing joyfully and leaving the Italian spectators thrilled and emotional, ended tragically. When John crashed in the pack and ended up on the track, my God, that was violent and sad.

The circuit was filled with such tension and sadness that there wasn't a single rider who didn't say how horrible it was to race on that track. Moving forward after seeing one of ours down on that track surrounded by doctors. People are different. Everyone processes pain in their own way, we try to accept that it's a dangerous sport, but we can't trivialize death.

We can't accept as trivial that the life of a 19-year-old boy was lost this way. John accepted the risks of the sport. And? That doesn't change the fact that he still had so much life ahead of him. I couldn't stop thinking that he should have had more life experiences, like having a child, planting a tree, writing a book, and maybe even becoming a champion one day. He should have had the chance to live. And it's absolutely normal that we riders feel bad for him not having that opportunity anymore.

So, I, along with the other 104 riders who lined up on the grid on Sunday, were confronted with our own mortality. Despite that, we showed extraordinary strength in racing, even though we shouldn't have had to go through that. Above all, we are human just like anyone else and have the right to have the chance to mourn the loss of one of our own just like anyone would.

Devastated, I had to talk to my mother. She had seen the news, and sadly, they filmed everything in full. Unfortunately, everything is recorded today, a true lack of respect for human life. *Mi madre* was in tears, because she put herself in the place of that rider's mother, and I can only imagine how much she prayed for me, as she watched the race on Sunday. Dolores spoke to Juan via video call, he was at the Navarro balcony and from his expression, he was extremely worried about me.

I reassured everyone, and it was such a relief when we arrived in Barcelona. I found my grandmother and hugged her tightly. She kissed my whole face and finally gave me a slap on the head.

"You always get into trouble, boy!"

"What's this, grandma?" I smiled sideways at her, and then her eyes turned to Dolores, who had come to my side.

"You're going to give me a heart attack. Hello, young lady, welcome to my house, make yourself at home."

"Thank you, Mrs. Inês. How are you?" Lola extended her hand, and my grandmother pulled her into a hug. I was happy to see that they got along so well, as my grandmother is usually more jealous than *mi madre*.

"I'm very well, except for the worry I feel seeing this boy racing at that absurd speed."

"Oh, grandma, you worry too much." She rolled her eyes the way she always did when she couldn't hold back.

"Don't even start, we get uneasy, it's inevitable and normal." I smiled and hugged her. "Make yourselves at home, I'll just ask the boys to come help you settle in."

"That's true, if anything, we can carry our bags, Mrs. Inês!" Lola said, and she had already called the young men who help her in her big house. She bought it right after two years of opening the buffet. My grandmother has always been very determined and independent. When she saw the house, she sent us a message with pictures and then called frantically asking for our opinion. I remember at the time I had to drop everything I was doing and come help her.

"No way, you can go rest, I know you must be exhausted from the long trip. It hasn't been easy for you." She said, and the two young men grabbed our bags.

"Grandma, Anita will come tomorrow, she went to the circuit with the team, she's swamped with work and has some meetings to attend."

"She works too much, that girl, so beautiful, she needs to find a boyfriend." I laughed out loud. My grandmother is like that, she thinks people should date, get married, and have children. I confess I'm relieved I didn't have to hear her talk about me being single anymore, because now I'm with Dolores, and thank God, my grandmother likes her.

"If she's happy that way, grandma, what can I do?"

"Find a boyfriend for her, she's so beautiful and hardworking, just like your Dolores. You know I love that name."

"You can call me Lola too, Mrs. Inês," Dolores said, approaching her, who invited us to sit on the sofa in her spacious living room, full of the green plants she loves.

"Oh, Lola, I love it. You know it matches the joy you have, it's something you can feel. At least I'm like that, I like to feel the energy that comes from people. And you, my dear, are a beautiful woman because you are so enlightened."

"Don't be scared by my grandmother, love." She melted and took off her glasses to look at me, Lola kept laughing and seemed enchanted by my grandmother's lively way.

"My son, you already call her love! *Olé, Olé, qué grande eres*!" She let out the expression she loves when she's so happy about something, and I knew my grandmother felt relieved to see me loving again.

"Because I love her, and she is the woman of my life, after you and *mi madre*," I said before she could make her speech about how I'm forgetting her and my mother.

"Very well, you deserve to be happy, but for God's sake, Guilhermo, be careful in those races."

"Don't worry, grandma, I'll be very careful," I said to reassure her, and she got up, wanting to show Lola around the house. She pulled her from my side, making me furrow my brow at her. I smiled after she left, even though I had protested. A few minutes later, I called my mom on a video call to show her that we had arrived safely and were already at grandma Inês's house, which made her feel more at ease and less worried.

That night, when we settled into the room my grandmother had prepared, I felt at home. She had painted my room and made some changes to the furniture and other details, knowing that it would affect me. Even so, when I arrived, I thought I might be reminded of something I lived with Mari in that house. But no, Lola was by my side, and I'm moving forward with her. My life no longer makes sense if I don't have her with me.

LOLA SPENT TIME TOURING Catalonia with my grandmother during her free hours, while I prepared for the big race in Barcelona. The two seemed like old friends, I even believe their souls had known each other before. One would say something, and the other would complete it. They would look at each other and smile, it was so nice to see how well they matched. And I could confirm that they even shared that crazy Spanish humor, that fiery blood that takes everything by storm. Despite everything, during the time I've been with Dolores, I've realized how genuine and honest she is. Sometimes we argue because I'm a bit messy with things, and she likes everything organized like grandma Inês, because I know I took after my mom with the messiness.

"Isabel is also very messy, *Dios mio*. She drove me crazy when we lived together. Thank goodness kids grow wings, if we could, we wouldn't let them. A mother likes to suffer for her children. It's just too much love," she said in the box, and everyone was listening. She can't control herself.

"Grandma, don't let *mi madre* hear you talk like that about her."

"You defend her because you're just like her. Don't tell anyone, ah, you know what? Go ahead and tell her, she already knows about it," she said, "Now come here, let me help you with that suit. Put it on properly." I almost died of embarrassment, but I couldn't help but laugh, my grandma is a character. She still thinks I'm the boy she took care of, but I let her do everything with me. She's the woman who raised me and whom I love the most. Lola was loving it, she and Anita couldn't stop laughing at my expressions and my grandma's antics. Every moment with my grandma and me was like a flash. With this joy and energy, I was able to qualify well in the free practices for the Sunday race.

The clouds gathered in the sky over Montmeló on the eve of the race on Sunday, but we were able to find good conditions for the MotoGP event. Before the start, the temperature was around 24°C, with the asphalt reaching 41°C. We opted for a hard front tire for the race. Lola performed the Spanish dance presentation across the starting grid in a red dress, like the one she wore the first time I saw her dance at Navarro. She and the other dancers were warmly applauded by all the spectators at the end.

When the lights went out, the 19,352 spectators breaking the silence of the MotoGP stands saw Jacob get a good start to defend the lead, but he ended up getting overtaken by me and Oliveira on the first corner. On the second lap, I took advantage of a mistake by Miller on corner five and took the lead. Jacob also passed the Australian, but soon lost his position. Jacob ran off track in corner seven after braking too hard.

Wearing a pair of hard tires, I took the opportunity and pushed the pace to break the pack. At the start of lap five, I maintained a 0.8s lead over Miller. Mike was back in third, but was being pressured by Alexi, who was soon attacked by Jacob. By the way, the positions at the front kept changing. Mike took second place, with Jacob also passing Miller to take third. However, I already had a lead of more than 1s at the front.

On lap six, Daniel crashed on corner nine and ended his participation in the Catalonia GP early. On the next lap, Jacob passed Mike to take second place and began hunting me down. The race was quite different from what River Nolan expected. With Jacob in second, my lead quickly decreased. On lap ten, we were separated by just 0.362s, with Mike, Miller, and Zarco not too far behind. On the twelfth of the twenty-four laps, Jacob dove inside on corner five and took my lead.

On lap fourteen, I took advantage of the slipstream on the straight and regained the lead by diving into corner one ahead of Jacob, with Zarco passing Miller to take fourth place. I built a gap of about 0.3s, which wasn't that big, but it was enough to maintain the lead. Moreover, the two frontrunners had broken the pack, with Zarco now more than 1.1s behind.

With six laps to go, Jacob once again reduced my lead to less than 0.3s. Zarco was still a bit further back, ahead of Miller, Mike, and Victor. However, I kept controlling Jacob's approach, always maintaining the difference at around 0.3s. The frontrunners had slightly slowed down, which allowed Zarco to get closer.

With just four laps to go, I stretched my lead to 0.981s, paving the way for the fourth victory of the *Wacco Racing* team in the 2021 season. Then, Jacob gave another sign of problems by losing second place to Zarco after running off the track and crossing the long lap section. It was the chance for the *Promac* rider to cut into my rival's lead in the World Championship. Jacob seemed to have worn out the tires on his Aspire bike. I celebrated yet another victory and climbed onto the podium, emotional for realizing my great dream.

CHAPTER TWENTY-EIGHT

Dolores

I said goodbye with great sorrow to Mrs. Inês, a wonderful lady, grandmother of the man I love and who raised him. Now I understood where his incredible integrity came from, in just a few days, she taught me so much. No one stays silent around her. She is the noise of the house, the energy that flows, and joy incarnate—completely captivating and transformative.

Guilhermo had already told me about his grandmother, but even so, it was even better to get to know her a bit more. I don't even need to mention how much I loved her love for plants and for Maná, a music group known for mixing pop rock, Latin pop, calypso, reggae, and ska. I remember we danced together in her big living room to *Vivir sin aire*, and she kept up perfectly. No matter the age, what matters is the willpower and the joy for life, and Mrs. Inês, at seventy-five, is a model of life, health, and above all, joy.

When we arrived in Rimini, Italy, for the San Marino Grand Prix, Guilhermo was anxious, he and his entire team, as we were getting closer to the end of the World Championship. The Spanish rider was leading the podium as the rider who had accumulated the most points since Jerez de La Frontera.

After a few hours of disembarking, we headed straight to the hotel. I said goodbye to a tired Alex, who had been working a lot, especially when we arrived in a new country and circuit. They never left the paddock. Anita had arranged for them to stay in complete trailers with the team, so I only saw them at rehearsals, practices, and races.

We checked into another hotel Anita had booked. She always makes wonderful choices. This one was just a few steps from the beautiful beach, in the picturesque promenade of Rimini, right in the heart of Marina Centro. The neoclassical décor of the room was very tasteful and elegant, offering comfort just by looking at it, along with a private balcony overlooking the beach. After seeing the room, we discovered there was also a hot tub with an amazing view. Guilhermo and I would enjoy this room very much, even if only for a short time.

After our first night in Rimini, we headed to the San Marino Circuit. As soon as we arrived, we split up. He went to inspect the track and would train as usual. Afterward, he would test the bike, which was ready thanks to the mechanics. I could feel the competition's tension in the air flowing through the paddock. After what happened in Mugello, I realized that nothing is quite what it seems. When we watch the MotoGP World Championship, all we see is the riders putting on a show, but when we know the backstage, we can see what really happens.

Some are driven by greed, because this sport moves money that we can hardly imagine. High-level sponsors, big investments—they want to see results.

Seeing the hustle in the paddock, I reached the spot where I would meet the choreographer and the MotoGP event promoter. We gathered, and they wanted to bring Latin dance to these two races before the last one in Valencia, where we would end with *Faster* by Within Temptation right after the races. The choreography and performance would feature the bike of the World Champion to exalt the victory of the rider and the team that developed the bike.

I rehearsed with my colleagues. They revealed to me they were tired, even though they liked discovering new places, just like I do. I agreed with them, and we marked the spots on the starting grid. That afternoon, the free practices started. I decided to wait and watch for Guilhermo in his team's box, which was busy when I arrived.

Anita was already wearing her communication headset, walking back and forth, while we watched our rider take the lead right away, after managing to avoid Jacob on the first corner after a long straight. The track's corners are quite tight, except for a few wider ones, but Guilhermo was focused and persistent on his speed. On a huge TV screen in the box, I could see the throttle in the corner, reaching three hundred kilometers—such a speed that must give an immense sense of freedom.

Once again, Guilhermo secured a good position, even with Jacob trying to get closer to him to knock him down. Alex commented that if he did, he would be penalized and that they had already warned him. But River Nolan likes to push others' patience and had no limits.

On Sunday, during the official race, I was excited to dance to the Latin rhythm of *Mi gente* by J Balvin feat. Willy William. We entered the grid, moving our hands forward and swinging our hips to the sides and back, following the hot and sensual beat. The spectators cheered, and the emotion of representing through dance was always powerful. We finished by throwing the big checkered flag behind us.

After the performance, I headed to my favorite spot to watch the race. Guilhermo started strong, and with an amazing performance, he took the lead in the first few laps. When the lights went out on the Saxon track's straight, Jacob managed to overcome the strength and take the lead, but it was Alexi who dove first into the first corner. Guilhermo took second place, ahead of Zarco, Miller, Victor, and Mike. After that, my rider managed to take first place in the final lap of the thirty laps. My heart was in my throat since Mugello, I can't stop feeling anxious watching him on the track.

He celebrated on the track, standing on his bike, then popped a wheelie, making the whole grandstand cheer for his victory. Guilhermo, besides becoming the best rider, is also the most beloved by everyone. Jacob tries, but sometimes it seems forced. On the track, we can see that even though he gives his best, he doesn't truly convince us of his passion for motorsport. I suspect that his father has something to do with it. The man is always behind his son, and we hardly see Jacob's mother at the races anymore. She's a famous chef with a restaurant chain spread across Europe, always very busy. I barely saw her in Jerez.

As soon as I saw Guilhermo, even with so many people around him, wanting his attention, I could feel his gaze when he saw me and smiled to the side, that charming way he has that drives me crazy and makes me fall even more in love with him. He came up to me and hugged me. By this point, it was no longer a secret to anyone. Photos of us together would always appear on gossip sites, even talking about me. I found it strange, all that exposure, but Anita tried to remove some of the posts about our relationship.

"It's so good to see you here waiting for me, I'm getting so spoiled," he whispered in my ear. I just smiled at him and sealed our lips with a quick kiss. He intertwined our fingers and led me with him to the press room. We crossed paths with Lorenzo River Nolan, who looked at Guilhermo with his nose in the air and smiled smugly, not in a good way.

"You know you're doing too well? Let's see how long that lasts."

"I didn't ask for your opinion, and I don't owe you anything. By the way, maybe you could ask your son to avoid those shoves. That's not how you make it to the podium."

"We'll see if you'll be fast for long," he said, sounding like a threat, and I didn't like seeing how Guilhermo trembled when he saw and spoke to his father.

"Yeah, let's see. Excuse us," my rider said, pulling me with him. After that strange conversation, I had to stop him and ask him to calm down. Unfortunately, his biological father managed to destabilize him. I can't believe that one day they'll have a healthy relationship that will do any good for Guilhermo. The man is a scoundrel who sees nothing in this life, only greed, and lives for appearances.

After I helped my rider calm down, we headed back to our destination. He participated in the press conference, answering all the questions kindly. Despite listening to his team's instructions, Guilhermo also followed his instincts when participating in interviews.

When we arrived at the hotel, I prepared the hot tub, and we went in to relax a bit. We both needed this rest and each other. We stayed close, talking about the race and how much we missed being at home with the family.

"I know that strange conversation bothered you," I whispered, trying to bring up the difficult subject for him.

"It was just as I imagined, Lola. I never expected anything from him, from what my mother told me, the way he treated her. Lorenzo tried to get rid of my mom by giving her a big check, can you believe that? Where's the right in that?"

"*Qué cabrón*! What did your mom do?"

"She tore up the check and threw it in his face, just the way she does it. *Mi madre* is a wonderful woman, as long as you don't step on her toes."

"Look, I totally agree with your mom, she did what she had to do, thinking about you."

"Yes, she moved from Jerez and went after her dreams. That's when we went to Barcelona and lived there for many years with my grandmother. We left because my mom wanted to work as a doctor everywhere. Even though I miss my grandmother, I followed my mom around the world and saw her grow more and more as a surgeon."

"She's a great example of strength and determination. Even with a son, she managed to achieve her dreams. She never backed down and never needed to ask for any help from the scoundrel Lorenzo."

"Yes, she told me the whole story when I was older, in my teenage years. Before, I used to imagine my father when I was small, I idealized him in my mind, but I was disappointed. Because look, I'm a grown man, and he never even showed curiosity about getting to know me, and by pure irony of fate, we met in the World Championship."

"Fate doesn't joke around, my rider. I know it bothered you, but try to be okay, Lorenzo doesn't deserve you to be upset."

"You're right, Lola. I'll move forward with my life. I've always been grateful to God for having *mi madre*, my grandmother, and now he surprised me with you at such a grand moment in my life."

"Ah, Guilhermo." I hugged him, wanting to comfort him, because I know he feels hurt by his father, the one who only fathered him but didn't raise him. Who could say a woman needed a man to raise her son? The right thing would have been if Lorenzo had helped, even if he wasn't going to live with them. But he didn't want to, and he surely lost the chance to meet the great man his son became. He abandoned all the unique moments of his life's phase, and that's why Guilhermo doesn't deserve to suffer for a man who can't even say he's his father.

"Thank you for being here with me. You don't know how much it helps me, especially right now."

"You don't need to thank me for this. Who loves, takes care," I said, gazing into his eyes, and he kissed me slowly and passionately. His hands wrapped around me, pulling me into his lap, and the energy around us changed. The heat and desire took over our bodies, and within minutes, we were completely naked, and he penetrated me, making me moan his name loudly. Guilhermo started moaning my name too, like a mantra, repeatedly before we climaxed together.

"Lola, Lola, Lola... You're mine, love!" His hoarse voice, his dark blue eyes full of pleasure, for me the world could have ended right there, and I wouldn't have cared, I would die happy for having given myself to Guilhermo.

CHAPTER TWENTY-NINE

Guilhermo

What I feel for Dolores is so intense and genuine that it actually scares me how important she's become to me. Having her by my side has been incredible and unexpected. When did I think I could ever forget Mari? Many people believe you can't forget a great love or love deeply twice in life. But the love I felt for Mari is completely different from what I feel for Dolores. They're two different women. My ex-girlfriend lived entirely off her family's money and didn't care about anything; she was very carefree. She never appreciated the small things in life and had no respect for death, loved living on the edge. We argued a lot about it. I don't want to be a hypocrite, since my profession is filled with risks, but it's not the same. Mari never thought before making any decision.

I hate making comparisons, but I needed to understand how I could love another woman like this, two years after Mari's death, which caused me so much pain. I had the misfortune of witnessing the moment she was gone forever. Despite her impulsiveness, she was an amazing woman who helped those she loved without expecting anything in return, and she lived cheerfully and energetically. She was the kind of person who'd say yes to everything. We experienced every possible adventure together.

Now, Dolores is determined, a woman full of values. She cares for her family and guards them as her greatest treasure. She loves helping others and has always been hardworking and a dreamer. She doesn't give up easily on her ideals and seeks the best not only for herself but also for her mother and sisters. I fell in love not only with Lola's beauty but also with her simplicity, kindness, and joy. My mother and grandmother drove me crazy when they called; they wouldn't stop praising my Spanish dancer. And I understood that fate brought her to me at the right moment because I needed to move forward with my life. Mari wouldn't have wanted to see me the way I was before—sleepless nights, living only for work, and lacking enthusiasm for anything but racing.

When I saw Lorenzo in the circuit corridors at Misano, I didn't realize it would be so strange, or that hearing him speak in that threatening tone would shake me so deeply. Lola sensed this and, with all the care in the world, brought up that sensitive subject with me. I wasn't expecting praise from him, but at least a bit more respect, and he disappointed me even more. From what Lola, Anita, and I discussed, Jacob, despite being greedy and repulsive, is actually misunderstood—he's unhappy, and you can see it in his eyes. Juan said the Rivers Nolans only care about status and money; Lorenzo wants to win because there's a lot of money involved, and he pressures his son.

That's why I sometimes feel Jacob isn't racing out of passion or personal choice. I don't want anyone to think I'm going easy on him, but from what little I've seen, the father projects his dreams onto the son. This doesn't justify River Nolan's behavior, but it shows how little he's understood about life, and his provocative actions prove how little he cares.

When we landed in Buriram, Thailand, it was already late, but the sky was stunningly blue with a blazing sun between clouds. They say it's a beautiful place. After managing to get the team to the racetrack, we headed to the hotel. Anita has been amazing, and she clearly wanted to provide Lola and me with wonderful moments.

She casually mentioned that she hoped I'd be happy with Dolores because we both deserved it. I couldn't disagree with her.

Lola's smile made me smile too, seeing her eyes light up at the place we'd be staying for those four days. We arrived a day earlier than expected, as Anita decided to bring us forward because we'd never raced on this circuit and would need to prepare everything and get to know the track better. The weather's hot, and all of this affects the race.

"We'll be staying here for four days, and after the race, we'll have two nights at a resort. It's my way of giving you two some rest before the final stage of the World Championship, so enjoy!" Anita said, heading off to her room, where she had meetings and a video call with Juan Navarro. Those two are inseparable, though I know they had a period where they weren't speaking; it seems they made up.

"Thank you, you're amazing!" I called out, and she just waved, heading down the corridor to her room.

"All that's left for us is to enjoy these moments. How about we rest first and then take a walk around the hotel?"

"Sounds perfect, but I have plans to help us relax before we take a nap. So, are you excited?" Lola said, approaching my neck and nibbling at my earlobe, driving me crazy.

"What are we still doing here, love?" I replied in that seductive way, smiling sideways like she loved.

"You drive me crazy when you say that, love, *de puta madre*!" I agreed, smiling, and we went the other way, taking another corridor. Our room was at the end, perfect for our wild times; we have no limits when we're together. The sex is intense and wild, even when it's slow.

The Cresco Hotel Buriram is modern, beautifully lit at night, and comfortable. After Lola and I enjoyed our moment and took a nap, we got up and went down to find something to eat. Soon, we ran into Anita and ordered fish with sautéed vegetables and roasted potatoes. We chatted during the pleasant, warm evening, sitting at an outdoor table by the large pool lit with a blue glow, making it look even more beautiful and inviting.

"How about a swim? Is the great pilot up for a competition?" Lola looked at me, smiling provocatively, wanting a challenge. This woman is even more competitive than I am, and I absolutely love it.

"Are you challenging me?" I asked, never taking my eyes off her exotic, sexy green eyes.

"Look, you two have a vibe going on. I'm heading to my room; it's better. I don't want to be the third wheel here," Anita said, getting up and saying goodbye, telling us to lose our minds, that she would do the same. I smiled and kept my gaze on Lola. If she wanted to challenge me, well, I was ready for it.

"Well?" she asked with a daring tone, already standing up and taking off her white cover-up, revealing her tiny red bikini that had me practically salivating, wanting to *fuck her* right there at the pool's edge.

"Lola, you're playing with fire, love..."

"I love getting burned, but only with you, my pilot," she said, diving into the pool and passing right by me, forcing me to rip off my shirt and shorts and jump in after her. I managed to catch her and pull her under the water, and when we surfaced, I wrapped my arms around her and held her close. I looked into her clear, captivating green eyes above the glowing blue water.

"So beautiful, and all mine, love! You think you can beat me?"

"Not on the track, but here, I've won."

"No, we tied. I mean, I caught up with you!"

"Then I won—that's what I wanted from the start. I want to make love to you right here, love," she said "love" provocatively, and she was as crazy as I was for her. I couldn't resist her impulsive requests; they put us in a delicious kind of danger. I threw my head back, laughing loudly, and she furrowed her brow, not understanding.

"You're cheeky, defiant, and incredibly bossy."

"And the pilot loves it." She looked at me, pulling my hair in her hands, biting my lower lip, and kissing me softly while her eyes stayed locked on mine. Damn, this woman is shameless. When she wants something, nothing will stop her—not even me, who's crazy about her. With that, I took her mouth in a wild kiss, overcome by the sight of her provocative, excited eyes. I scattered kisses along her neck, moving down to her breasts. Since she was still in her bikini, I kissed over the fabric and gave a gentle bite.

"I want you to follow my lead, and please, try not to moan too loud, love," I whispered, and she nodded. I leaned her against the pool's edge, moving us into the corner. I glanced around; it was late, and there was no one around who could see anything.

Her legs wrapped around me, and she could feel how hard I was, turned on by her. She moved her hips slightly, and a low moan escaped me, and she kissed me with passion, love, and desire. I felt her shiver as my hands moved the bottom of her bikini to the side, my fingers gliding along her soft, swollen lips. As always, she was ready for me. Perfect and all mine. I slid two fingers inside, pressing and circling her clit, and Lola started moving her hips, driving my fingers deeper inside her as our tongues tangled with the urge to moan loudly from all that tension and pleasure.

Beautifully and completely surrendered, Lola climaxed around my fingers, melting into my lips, biting down hard on my lower lip, nearly making me come from the sheer intensity. Her green eyes, filled with lust, told me just how wild she was. She slid my swimsuit down, took my hard, throbbing length in her hand, running her fingers along its full length, making me groan her name, low and husky, into her mouth.

"You're so damn sexy, Guilhermo. All mine, and you drive me crazier with desire and love every time."

"Damn, Lola, you're going to make me come in your hands, but I want to do that inside you, love," I said, not breaking eye contact, holding her gaze seriously. Then she smiled like a tempting devil, licking her lips as if savoring something delicious. I felt her slide me inside her, letting her set the pace. Losing all awareness of where we were, I started thrusting deeply, while we lost ourselves in each other's mouths. She couldn't hold back and climaxed again, trembling and practically lying back on the stone edge. I wrapped myself around her, filling her, not stopping as her warmth pulsed around me, wetter from her orgasm. She rocked and clenched, sending me into an explosion of pleasure. I came inside her with such intensity that I pulled her hair, and we locked eyes, breathless, our mouths barely parted.

"Wow, Guilhermo! That was..."

"Amazing. I've never come like that before, love. You drive me insane. Now, let's get out of here as if nothing happened, take a shower, and continue everything in the room," she didn't say a word, just smiled, more relaxed from having come twice. This woman made me completely lose my mind, but I absolutely loved losing control, as long as it was with her."

THE CHANG INTERNATIONAL Circuit, also known as the Buriram International Circuit, is a racetrack located in Buriram, inaugurated in 2014. It's considered the country's premier circuit and has hosted the Grand Prix since 2018. Despite this, I hadn't had the honor of visiting before. It features twelve curves and three long straights. I took a run around the track on foot to get ready for the race. Even though we had a practice session that afternoon, I saw Dolores rehearsing on the grid and smiled at her, and she smiled back. Yesterday, we did something crazy in the hotel pool, and I hoped no one had seen or heard anything. At one point, we completely lost control and forgot where we were.

Anita and Alex spent the entire morning teasing me about it, making a joke every chance they got. She spilled the beans to that loudmouth, and while I love my friend and coach, he can be unbearable when he starts teasing someone; it gets tiresome, and I start getting annoyed with him. Anita's little laughs only made it worse.

"You two need to stop; I need to focus."

"Sure, because you're already relaxed—look what a pool can do," Alex quipped.

"Can you cut it out? This is ridiculous and childish. We need focus here." He shrugged, as if to say he didn't care.

"Relax, it'll go fine in the race. We want you on the podium, but take it at your own pace; it's a new circuit for you."

"So, you're saying second or third is acceptable?"

"We wouldn't mind if it comes to that. You're leading and are the season's favorite."

"But it would be great to take first here on this circuit. If River Nolan doesn't interfere, it might work out."

"Don't let him get to you. Forget that obnoxious driver and keep going, doing what you do best. The bike's ready. Suit up and grab your helmet," Tenner said, joining the conversation, cutting Alex off. Those two had been exchanging a few barbs lately, but they work well together, leading the team with a firm hand and plenty of skill.

I secured a good position on the starting grid, though it could've been better if I'd managed to get past Jacob, who was ahead of me. He was faster during practice, and when I tried to overtake him, he nearly clipped my bike, causing me to fall. Fortunately, I didn't get hurt, protecting myself as we always do in falls.

On Sunday, Dolores's performance was incredible. They had a beachy vibe, dancing to *Hawái* by Maluma and The Weeknd with an engaging rhythm that got everyone singing along to the chorus as the dancers swayed to the Latin beat. At the end, they waved a large checkered flag, and the crowd rose to their feet, applauding.

I admired the crowd that came to watch us and then moved to the grid. I was in the third row, and as soon as the checkered flag was raised, we took off down the circuit's short straight. Jacob took the lead initially, but I quickly claimed second, and that's how the first lap went. In the second lap, Zarco went after Mike, causing him to veer off track and drop to the back. Jacob briefly overtook me, but I reclaimed the lead on the main straight, leveraging the *Wacco* engine. He tried the same move on the fifth lap but didn't succeed.

Jacob regained the lead on the sixth lap, leaving me behind in the circuit's tight section and immediately started widening the gap. Miller crashed in the eighth lap and left the race. Meanwhile, Mike and Zarco began attacking me, and they kept swapping positions in the turns before the straight, but I managed to hold onto second place. In the end, Jacob won the Thailand GP, and I finished second. We celebrated on the podium; he kept giving me fake smiles and even hugged me for a paparazzi photo.

After the press conference, there were questions about a potential offer for Jacob and me to work together at *Wacco*, which caused quite a stir among sports reporters. I denied knowing anything about it; I didn't know where that rumor had come from. If it were true, I'd be the first to know, since it's my team. I left after taking some photos with fans and saw Lola waiting patiently. After that, I could only think about taking her to the resort Anita had booked for us to relax and enjoy a few more moments together before we head into the final stage of the world championship season.

CHAPTER THIRTY

Dolores

We lived through wonderful days at the super fancy and incredible resort Anita had booked. I made video calls every day with Nina, Olivia, Luna, and Juan. They were already looking forward to our return, but they were happy to hear that we had made the most of our time in Thailand, even though it was brief.

I can't even count the times we made love at that resort and in all sorts of places. Just remembering makes my cheeks flush and feel warm. I hardly recognize myself, I'll return to Jerez completely different from when I left for this professional and romantic adventure. I spent the entire flight to Valencia thinking about how our lives can change. For months, I had wanted to stay away from beautiful and famous men like Guilhermo. But my heart, ah! It didn't understand what my brain was trying to impose, and the moment I saw that pilot in the flesh at Navarro, everything changed.

Now, all I think about is enjoying the result of this experience. I received messages and offers from dance academies in every place I visited, even from places I had never been to. Anita recommended an excellent agent and advisor. She said that with the success and demand I'm having, I will need someone to assist me in everything. There are those who want to deceive the dancer with malicious offers, so it's better to be cautious.

After we landed, although we hadn't yet arrived in Jerez, I felt at home because we were in Spain. Valencia is a port city on the

BOUND BY FIRE AND FUEL

southeastern coast of Spain, where the Turia River meets the Mediterranean Sea. It's known as the city of arts and sciences, with futuristic structures, including a planetarium, an oceanarium, and an interactive museum. I know it has beautiful beaches, some of them in the Albufera Park, a swamp reserve near a lake with various walking trails. I like to keep track of what we have here in Spain. I already knew Valencia, so it felt like being at home.

The next morning, we had breakfast and headed to the Circuit Ricardo Tormo, located in Chester. This name was given to the track in honor of MotoGP rider Ricardo Tormo. I went to rehearse with the girls because we were going to perform right after Sunday's final race. In other words, we would close the World Championship with honors, and if God allowed it, with Guilhermo's victory, the 93 of *Wacco Racing*. Unfortunately, someone had been talking too much in the pits about Jacob River Nolan being considered to join the team and form a duo with García. But that was just speculation, and Anita took care of it as soon as we arrived. She headed to the circuit and requested a meeting with Guilhermo and the whole team.

I thought it was wise for them to speak out and put an end to the false rumors because the buzz was so intense that when we arrived at the circuit, the car that brought us nearly couldn't get through due to the commotion. If *Wacco* really had such plans, they should think it through, as they've seen how Guilhermo and Jacob don't get along. River Nolan is reckless and barely keeps himself in check, and his father, who manages him, just wants to make money off his son.

Anyway, I stopped thinking about that and continued with my rehearsal. I received the costume proof my friend had designed so perfectly and smiled. After the free practice on Saturday, I called her and showed how the outfit turned out perfect with the extra details she added. I missed her so much, along with my sisters, mother, and Juan, that I didn't even realize she wasn't in her house or mine during the video call. I ended the call wondering where my friend was, but I forgot about it when the big day of the MotoGP World Championship final arrived.

The riders were on the starting grid, and as soon as I sat in the VIP area beside the pits that Anita had reserved, I was speechless when I saw Nina, Juan, Dona Inês, and Isabel García join me. The happiness was overwhelming, and we hugged, making noise in the stands. My friend said it was Anita's idea to gather everyone for the big final, as Guilhermo would be the champion.

With our hearts racing, we watched as Guilhermo took off from the first row of the grid, picking up speed with every second. Soon they made the first turn, and Isabel cursed loudly when she saw Jacob bump into Gui on the fifth lap. After failing to unbalance the 93, he tried to overtake him and take the lead. But Guilhermo was faster, leaving me tense about what might happen.

They continued like that until Jacob managed to take the lead, but during Guilhermo's attempt to overtake him without touching the other rider, River Nolan lost control and crashed badly, leaving everyone frozen. It was the last lap, my heart raced, and I trembled when I saw him fly off and lie still outside the track. His bike fell far, thank God, as I feared it would hit him.

Within seconds, the track was filled with doctors attending to Jacob. Panic struck me, and I saw Eve crying in the stands, heading towards her boyfriend's pit. The blonde had been absent during the last few races. In fact, it seemed like they weren't doing well, as she had always been with him, but I hadn't seen her at the other circuits since Portugal.

"My God, it looks serious!" Isabel commented, standing up worried.

"I don't know," was all I could answer, and I saw Anita arrive at my side and pull me along.

"Come here, Guilhermo will need you, and so will his mother," she pulled Isabel along as well, and we headed to the *Wacco* pit.

When we arrived, we saw that the race continued, and the 93 passed the checkered flag, winning the Valencian Grand Prix and securing the World Championship podium. Although it was emotional when we reached him on the track, he was crying and asking about Jacob. Still, he celebrated with the team and took his victory lap.

We went to the *Aspire Factory* pit to find out about River Nolan, and they told us he had been taken to the city hospital, seemingly with a broken arm and unconscious. We were concerned, and before Guilhermo went up to the podium, he asked his mother to go help him. She knew the hospital and was an orthopedic and general surgeon. She agreed and told her son to celebrate his great and well-deserved victory.

After that, he calmed down, hugged and thanked everyone, happy to see his grandmother and Juan. He commented on how much Anita loved to surprise everyone. We all smiled, even though the tension lingered due to Jacob's accident. Thankfully, he was alive, and after Mugello, I started to watch MotoGP with a new perspective.

Guilhermo

I FELT HAPPY, OVERWHELMED by crazy adrenaline, when I managed to finish the last lap at over 300 km/h. The bike seemed to float with me. But seeing that Jacob went straight from the racetrack to the hospital hit me hard, it affected me more than I could imagine. I felt bad about continuing the race like that, but they always keep the show going. Unfortunately, that's the downside of being a rider—you take risks, put your life in danger. It's a choice we make, but we're human, and we get shaken when accidents like this happen on the track.

I still couldn't get out of my head what had happened in Mugello. It was one of the worst feelings I've ever had in my life. My throat was tight, feeling dirty for having to go through that turn where our fellow rider, John Huber, had just gone. When I saw my whole family there, gathered with my friends and team, I felt comforted, and they gave me the strength I needed to receive the grand prize and get on the podium to celebrate.

Alex and Tenner were overjoyed and proud, though still concerned about River Nolan. They told me he was being well cared for and had a broken arm, but was unconscious. I asked my mom that after the celebrations, we should go to the hospital. I didn't care if I had to look at Lorenzo's face. Lola came up and hugged me, never leaving my side. It felt like she knew I was on the verge of breaking down, but I needed to be strong and celebrate the prize I had worked so hard for over the months. I put my life into MotoGP, dedicated myself fully, and now I just wanted to have her by my side to enjoy these beautiful moments together.

When she let go of me, she whispered something in my ear that gave me chills.

"You're a champion, and you deserve everything you've achieved in MotoGP. Enjoy it, even though it's hard. I love you so much, and I'll be here for you whenever you need me, my rider." I pulled her close and kissed her lips, then moved forward, living my victory body and soul. Fireworks exploded in the sky, and I celebrated on the podium after drinking champagne with Miller and Zarco, who took second and third place. We threw it up into the air, creating a shower of drink, celebrating together. They congratulated me, and we headed to the press conference, where things were tense because of all the questions about River Nolan. All I could say was that he also deserved to be with us on the podium, but I wished him a speedy recovery and sent strength to the *Aspire Factory* and the River Nolan family.

Anita wanted to celebrate. She had organized a party for Jerez, and she and Navarro had arranged everything. But before that, I took my mom to the hospital with Dolores and my grandmother, who insisted on coming. When we arrived, we found Lorenzo crying, and I went straight to him, without thinking too much, asking what had happened.

"What happened? How is he?" I asked immediately, and Lorenzo turned to face me, fury in his eyes.

"What are you doing here?" He ignored my questions and grabbed the collar of my shirt, his face red with anger. My blood boiled with rage at that disgusting man who calls himself a father.

"Hey, take your dirty hands off my son, Lorenzo," *Mi madre* intervened, stepping in between and staring him down, confronting that man who had played with her and left her to raise a child on her own.

"Isabel García," he said through clenched teeth, foaming with rage. "Who do you think you are, coming here? What right do you think you have to interfere in my life and my son's?"

"First of all, I want to make it clear, Lorenzo, I'm not here for your life, I'm here for your son's. I can help if you want. However, don't even think for a second that I'm doing this for you. I decided to help because it's my mission as a doctor, and because my son, Guilhermo, asked me," she threw it back in his face. My mom is brave and faced him like a lioness. "He's worried about his brother, the one you manipulated these months to mess with my son's races."

"I don't want this woman here, this bold Spaniard, get her out of here!" He shouted, causing a scene in the hospital and attracting the attention of everyone. A doctor appeared and asked us to calm down.

Once he managed to move Lorenzo away, the doctor turned to him and said something that infuriated him even more.

"She is your son's chance of recovering well. By the way, we know Dr. Isabel García, she's a world-renowned surgeon and a specialist in arm fractures like your son's. Besides that, she'll be a huge help along with the neuro team."

"Neuro?"

"Yes, his helmet came off, and he had a small injury. We're running more tests, but we'll need to perform double surgery."

"Oh my God!" Lorenzo suddenly panicked and began to tremble.

"Look, River Nolan, I know I'm not a fan of yours, and I want to stay far away from you and your family, but we're talking about your son's health. Whether you like it or not, I'm going into this surgery to help."

"It'll be an honor to have you back in our operating room," the doctor said, excited to work with my mom, and they went down the hallway together. She winked at me and asked me to be patient.

As soon as they left, I sat down with my grandmother, Dolores, and Anita, who arrived with Juan after a few minutes. Lorenzo sat across from me, glaring at me with disdain and distrust the entire time. He didn't want me around, I knew that, but I wasn't leaving until I knew Jacob was out of danger and recovering.

Many hours passed, and when the morning came, they finished the surgery, which was a success. I was so relieved and happy that I hugged everyone. Lola hadn't slept a wink with me, and we held hands, with her stroking me every minute. She's such a great companion. The truth is, I was shaken by what happened to Jacob; after all, he's my brother. We share the same blood, even though we weren't raised together. I felt something inside me tell me to help him.

My mom said it would take over nine months for him to recover from the fracture in his arm and shoulder and that he wouldn't be able to race for a year. I was sad to hear that because I know it won't be easy for him to be without doing what he loves for a year. But the good news is it wasn't anything more serious, and he could focus on physical therapy to recover faster. According to my mom, he'll need a lot of strength, determination, and patience for his recovery treatment.

We headed back to the hotel; it was almost ten in the morning. We were all tired, and Lorenzo didn't thank my mom for her medical and surgical help. But Jacob's mother thanked her and hugged her in tears under the watchful eye of her husband. I had to hold myself back from punching that man. He couldn't be my father. How can someone be so selfish, proud, and arrogant? I didn't understand it, and it would be better for me to just move on with my life, which is complete, because I have people by my side who love me and are willing to stand with me in both the worst and best moments.

It's a shame that Jacob has the bad luck of only having his father and some selfish friends, from what Navarro told me, and his girlfriend Eve, who I can't even comment on. I'd love to get to know him better, even though he showed me his worst side. I'd like to know if he had a better side.

The End

EPILOGUE

Guilhermo

"When we accelerate too much, we don't know what will happen when we reach the end—win or lose, that's the question, but the only choice is to dare and run the risk."

Two months later...

When we returned to Jerez de La Frontera, I surprised everyone when I announced that I was moving permanently from Brazil and making my home in Spain. Dolores smiled when I told her the news, hugged me, and we were doing well in our relationship; I couldn't be away from her anymore. Not when she's going to open her own dance academy, sponsored by sneaker and sportswear brands.

She didn't close the MotoGP that day with her performance, as she chose to stay by my side and go to the hospital with me. But she gained the prestige and success of admirers from all over the world. Wanting to surprise her, I asked Anita for help with something I had been thinking about a lot in the past few days. After an interesting conversation with my grandmother, she suggested something that both surprised and excited me.

"What do you think about you two getting married?"

"Do you think she would want me as her husband?"

"Don't answer me with another question, boy. *Oh Dios mío*! You're hopeless, of course, she will say yes, that beautiful girl loves you and has been with you through the best and worst moments of your life. Do you have doubts about that?"

"I have no doubt, but sometimes I feel like she thinks I still think about Mari."

"Oh no! You lived what was already written in your destiny with Mari, that's over, and it's been three years. Now let me ask you, are you ready to be the man of Dolores's life?"

"Yes, grandma! It's all I want in this life."

"Then show her in a grand way that you love her and want to spend the rest of your life with her. A suggestion is, if she really wants, you can marry her at the Jerez Circuit, and we'll have the party at Navarro, I'll handle the buffet and everything else..."

"Grandma, you're amazing, you've already planned everything." I hugged her and carried the old woman who started kicking and screaming.

"Put me down, boy! *Qué te den*!" she cursed me and I put her down laughing loudly in the kitchen, catching the attention of everyone in the living room. I heard my mother's voice in the hallway.

"What's going on, mom?"

"*Su hijo* is going crazy because he's getting married!" she whispered and asked my mom not to tell anyone.

"I will, if she says yes!"

"Lola will say yes, she loves you, and you can see it in her sparkling eyes how crazy she is about you."

"I'll propose today, I need you to help grandma organize everything. Anita will want to help too, I'm calling Dolores's mom right now" I said, barely containing my happiness and anxiety. I grabbed the number for Dona Dulce and she picked up on the second ring. I went to the garden overlooking the pool so Lola wouldn't suspect anything.

"*Olé, olé, qué grande eres*! I expected nothing less from you, boy, since Lola met you, she's barely contained her joy. Sometimes she tries to hide it, but that's her crazy way."

"I know that, Dona Dulce, and I'm very happy to have you in my life, but I want her as my wife and I would like to invite you and your daughters to come over for dinner tonight, so I can ask your daughter for her hand."

"Let's do it, know that I'm very happy about this, and since I found out you two were dating, I've been hoping for this. My girl deserves to be happy, and she's a great woman—determined and very strong."

"She's amazing, that's why and many other things that I love her and can't live without Lola. So, we'll be waiting for you here tonight." She thanked me and we ended our call just as I saw Dolores walking to the kitchen door toward the balcony.

"Is something happening?"

"Nothing, love" I answered, trying not to make her suspicious, then I pulled her into my body and stared into her intense green eyes.

"You're acting strange, Guilhermo. What are you up to?"

"I already told you, nothing, but actually, yes, there is something. I want you to come upstairs with me right now, I need you." She smiled and then kissed me passionately, making me feel like the luckiest man in the world.

I managed with much effort to speak to Navarro and Anita, they hadn't left each other's side since we got back from Valencia. But when I told her about my plans, she got excited and helped my grandmother and mother organize the dinner. She took Dolores shopping casually, which helped us finish setting everything up. I don't know what Anita did, but she arrived at night with Lola all dressed up. My friend knows exactly how to help her lovesick friend.

Lola was a bit suspicious, and during dinner, she started asking me what was going on, since I had invited her mom and sisters to join us. I answered saying that they are part of the family too, and I wanted to celebrate that now we're all together. The woman grabbed her wine glass and drank it all at once. I smiled as I also sipped the drink. My heart started pounding as the moment to ask for her hand approached. But I held myself back, took a deep breath, and tasted the food my grandmother had prepared.

She made the most famous dish in Spanish cuisine, a perfect *paella*, made with rice, saffron, olive oil, and seafood. In this case, she made it with shrimp and mussels. She overdid it and also made *gazpacho*, a cold soup very traditional in Andalusia, but also all over Spain. The original recipe consists of tomato, garlic, cucumber, olive oil, and bread. The table was beautiful and very well set, so I tapped my glass with a spoon to get everyone's attention, making Dolores next to me squirm in her chair.

"I ask for everyone's attention, as I have something to say, or rather, a request to make, to the woman here" I kneeled beside her, making everyone sigh and watching her cover her mouth and widen her eyes, which quickly filled with tears when I took the small box with her ring from my pocket.

"You know better than anyone how much we both resisted the feeling that took us unexpectedly when we first saw each other. In fact, I was moved the moment I saw you wheelie your bike on the road when you were arriving in Jerez, that's when I fell in love with you, Dolores López" tears rolled down her face, but she was smiling, and just seeing her like this warmed my heart and gave me even more courage to go on with my request "But when I saw you dancing flamenco at Navarro, you drove me crazy, so the fiery and determined Spanish woman turned my world upside down and made me live an adventure that, even though it's only halfway through, we were already completely in love. And today, remembering our journey, I came to the conclusion that God placed you in my path for a reason, do you know why?" she shook her head, and I answered "Because you were my new beginning, the most beautiful and real thing I've ever had in my entire life. You understood me, listened to me, comforted me, smiled at me, and seduced me, my love! That's why I can't live without you by my side" she smiled and gave me the most beautiful look in the world "Dolores López, I love you, and so I ask you, will you accept to be Mrs. García, my wife, and the future mother of my children?"

"*De puta madre! Guay!* A thousand times yes!" she said through laughter and tears rolling down her face, and almost made my heart miss a beat, so anxious I was to hear this answer, which was music to my ears.

Everyone clapped and whistled at the table, and within minutes we were in the room full of red and gold balloons that Anita had prepared. We celebrated together, dancing and happy. Alex and Tenner arrived after the proposal, upset that they missed the best part. But I told them to go fuck themselves, because I had warned them about the time, but they're two slowpokes, probably slept more than they should or were with some woman.

For me, all that mattered was making my fiancée smile that night and for the rest of our lives. When we were dancing close, I told her about the wedding location to see if she would accept, it would only be there if she wanted.

"Lola, there's one more thing. I called the Jerez Circuit to see if we could get married there, but it'll only happen if you want it, my love! So, what do you think?" She stumbled on my foot and stared at me in disbelief.

"Guilhermo, I want to marry you there, my God! *Dios mío*, I must be dreaming."

"You're not, it's all real, and I'm so happy to see you as my fiancée. Who would've thought?"

"Not even I would have said that, Guilhermo. You know, I sometimes thought you hadn't forgotten, and that even when I heard you declare your love for me, it was just words. I was sure that once that adventure ended and we came out of the bubble that the World Championship had put us in, you would leave me."

"That never crossed my mind, Lola. When I told you I love you for the first time, I meant it, with all my heart. What I had before you came into my life, is in the past, and you became my present and future, my love."

"My God, Guilhermo. You make me love you more every minute. I'm sorry for thinking those foolish things, but it's just that you..."

"I know, love. But now, let's enjoy our engagement night and start planning this wedding soon, because I can't wait to call you my wife." She smiled and kissed me with desire and love. I couldn't feel more complete than after hearing her say yes.

Dolores

Two months later...

I COULDN'T BELIEVE we had come this far. I could swear and feared so much that Guilhermo wouldn't stay with me once we got to Jerez. But he surprised me two months after our arrival, first when he announced his move from Brazil to Spain, the purchase of the house, and then he left me in tears and with my heart racing when he knelt beside me at that dinner I had been so suspicious of and asked me to marry him.

Everyone already knew he was going to propose, and his grandmother helped him with everything, along with his mother and Anita. Even my mom was involved, and I was so happy when I returned from months of travel and found my mom working with sewing and helping Nina with some requests she had been receiving from abroad. With the costumes she made for me, she gained visibility and started being sought after by some famous clothing brands.

What struck me a lot was that my friend, in recent months, had been talking a lot about Jacob. She went to visit him and help with his physiotherapy, and had been hiding some things from me about it. I let it slide because she always changed the subject, and we started looking at wedding dresses. But I was curious to find out what Nina Rodriguez was doing, spending time at the Rivers Nolan's house.

Speaking of them, Guilhermo tried to visit his brother, even went to the physiotherapy clinic, but stubborn Jacob didn't receive him, and that made me furious. I didn't go there to confront him because I know he's going through a tough time and must be in a terrible mood. But I'll let it slide until after the wedding, and I'll find out what's behind this strange friendship between River Nolan and my friend.

"You look wonderful," my mom said, looking at me through the mirror. I turned around, and she smiled, looking beautiful and made up. I was so happy and proud to see her looking so well. Nina managed to convince my mom to change her life, and she has my heart forever, because it was emotional to see her with a sparkle in her eyes again.

"My God, Lola. You look stunning!" Olivia came in right behind my mom with Luna, wearing a beautiful lilac flower girl dress.

"Oh, thank you! And you both look so beautiful as well. I can't thank you enough for everything you've done for me these last few months. I love you both, and I'll always be here for you, my family, my everything!" They hugged me, and I tried not to let the tears roll down my face so as not to smudge my makeup.

"Oh, darling, don't cry, we love you so much, and we'll always be here for you," my mom said, helping me wipe my face.

"Lola, are you ready?" Anita entered the Jerez Circuit box with a gorgeous long lilac dress with a V-neck and her beautiful black hair. Guilhermo and I are really crazy to get married on the asphalt with the smell of fuel. My mom and sisters left the room after sending me air kisses.

"I'm ready, just need to grab my bouquet!" I said, looking for the pile of lilac and white flowers we chose.

"My God, Anita! I'm getting married!"

"*Guay*! As you both say, no one expected that the sad rider would find the love of his life and get married."

"It was unexpected and intense."

"Tell me about it, I've followed your story, and I'm so happy to see that I was right when I saw you two dancing together at Navarro that day. It's emotional to be here and very special."

"Ah, Anita, please don't make me cry! I can't smudge my makeup! This is crazy, guys!"

"Calm down." She smiled, and then I saw Juan enter, looking handsome in a tuxedo, his muscular body, trimmed beard, and a smile on his face.

"Ready, my friend? Because I'm prepared to take the beautiful bride to the altar. You have no idea how beautiful everything looks there, I loved the simple and elegant way they decorated it. You're arriving on the bike, right?"

"I will, it'll be perfect!" We left the room and walked through the hallways. We descended, and I saw the structure set up with some flowers, right on the starting grid. That afternoon was beautiful, the sun was shining on part of the track, but not on the altar they had set up. Then I saw him at the altar waiting for me, the bridesmaids and groomsmen entered, and soon the flower girls came in.

Juan went to the last row of seats, and then the big moment arrived, the one where I would walk down the aisle to marry at the Jerez Circuit, on the bike that Guilhermo raced and won the MotoGP World Championship, making me proud and emotional. It was a tribute to him for taking risks and simply giving himself to the adrenaline of being on so many tracks like that, pushing his limits to the max and managing to reach the podium.

The man I love, who became my life, who gave me incredible moments by his side. I got on the bike with the help of the ceremony staff, started it up, heard the engine roar, and smiled as the happiness adrenaline took over me. Then I accelerated toward the location and made a triumphant arrival to the sound of *Faster* instrumental by Within Temptation, feeling every hair on my body stand up due to the emotion. My throat was tight, and I held back tears when my eyes caught Guilhermo waiting for me, in his tuxedo and bow tie, looking so handsome and stunning, the man of my life. I made a turn and managed to create smoke in a perfect *drift*, and if I hadn't pulled it off, I wouldn't call myself Dolores López. I saw the drone passing, filming everything. Anita had hired two photographers to capture our ceremony.

Guilhermo's eyes shone as soon as he saw me stop the bike and hand it over to Alex, stepping off and receiving support from my friend Juan Navarro. He looked at me and winked, then said I nailed it. Everyone applauded, and then the tone of *Faster* shifted to something soft, played on the violin. Our choice was that song because it says everything about our story and how we feel about each other.

With every step we took, my heart felt like it would stop from the emotion, and I didn't take my eyes off Guilhermo's passionate and proud gaze. He smiled that smile that reaches his eyes, creating those charming dimples when he came closer to us. Juan handed my hand to my fiancé, and the two exchanged a few words.

"Take good care of her," Navarro said, frowning, then stood next to Anita.

"Always," Guilhermo replied, looking at me and kissing my hand. "You're amazing, you know. The perfect woman for me." After that, we turned and reached the altar, and the ceremony began. Occasionally, I felt my rider's gaze on me while Father Leo spoke. His grandmother had arranged for the smiling celebrant to officiate our wedding.

After the priest's introduction about fidelity, respect, and reciprocity, it was time for the wedding vows.

"Guilhermo García, do you take Dolores López as your wife, to love her, respect her, and honor her for the rest of your lives?"

"Yes, I do," he replied, gazing at me, making me smile at him.

"Dolores López, do you take Guilhermo García as your husband, to love him, respect him, and honor him for the rest of your life?"

"I do," I replied, letting the tears run down my face, and Guilhermo wiped them away with the back of his hand, making me smile even more at him.

"Let's receive the rings," the priest said, and we heard the violin playing as we saw Luna, our flower girl, entering. The song *La vie en Rose* by Emily Watts played delicately on the violin while my sister entered and then handed the rings to Anita.

"Very well, let's go to the most important moment of this union and love celebration," the priest asked us to take each other's hands and face one another. As soon as I felt Guilhermo's hand on mine, I saw it was sweaty too. I felt the love radiating between us, the emotion at its peak, and then I heard what Guilhermo repeated at the priest's request:

"I, Guilhermo, take you as my wife, Dolores, I promise to be faithful to you, love you, and respect you in joy and in sorrow, in health and in sickness, every day of our life."

I gazed at him with love and more tears in my eyes. He wiped them away again with tenderness and care, and I smiled at him, feeling so emotional that we were truly getting married.

"I, Dolores, take you as my husband, Guilhermo, and promise to be faithful to you, love you, and respect you in joy and in sorrow, in health and in sickness, every day of our life."

The priest continued, and the moment to exchange the rings arrived. Guilhermo took the ring and placed it on my finger, repeating the priest's words:

"Dolores, receive this ring as a sign of my love and my faithfulness. In the name of the Father, the Son, and the Holy Spirit."

He looked at my hand at the end, looking happy and proud to see that ring, a symbol of our intense and crazy love. The priest handed me the ring, and I placed it on his finger, repeating the same words Guilhermo had said:

"Guilhermo, receive this ring as a sign of my love and my faithfulness. In the name of the Father, the Son, and the Holy Spirit."

Right after, the priest made requests for us, along with everyone present, for our life, our happiness, and for everyone. Then we received the Eucharist, followed by the final blessing, and finally, the priest said:

"You may kiss the bride."

My eyes shone with happiness, and that very special afternoon would forever be marked in my life, as I became the wife of the only man I have ever loved in this life. My rider, who loves to take risks and drive me crazy and out of control, but still, I chose to live by his side. Placing a hand on each side of my face, he first sealed our lips in a soft kiss, but soon his tongue overtook me with more intensity and fire, the same fire we felt from the first moment we saw each other and our first kiss.

After our kiss, we walked down the aisle, smiling at everyone, and after receiving a shower of rice at the end. Guilhermo mounted the bike with me on the back in my white wedding dress, happy as can be to be living that moment as we deserved. This is a new beginning for both of us, and I'm sure we'll be very happy together because we feel love for each other. It's greater than adrenaline, greater than anything small that may come our way. The important thing is that we have each other, and now forever, as they say, may it be infinite while it lasts.

Did you love *Bound by Fire and Fuel*? Then you should read *Faded Colors of Us*[1] by Nora Kensington!

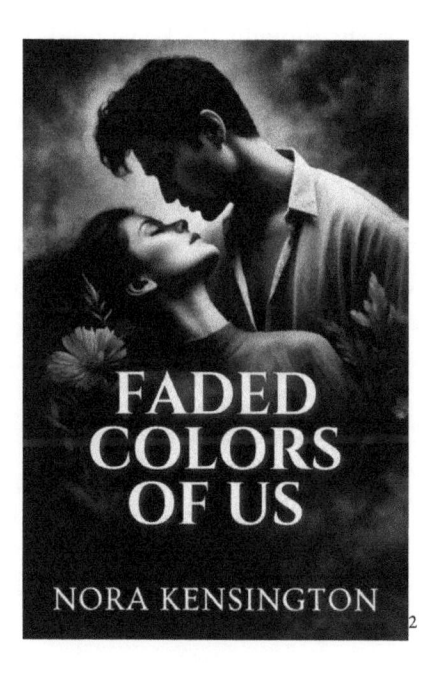

Faded Colors of Us is a gripping **second-chance romance** about heartbreak, redemption, and the lingering power of first love.

Callie and Landon were inseparable best friends, their bond forged in childhood and tested through adolescence. But one devastating event shattered everything, leaving Landon with a deep resentment that drove him out of town—and out of Callie's life. Now, years later, he's back, but the boy Callie knew is gone. In his place is a man with a reputation as **"New York's scoundrel,"** a tattoo artist adored by celebrities and notorious for his wild side.

When a twist of fate forces Callie to turn to Landon for help, she discovers just how much he's changed. Gone are the warm memories

---

1. https://books2read.com/u/4NqxDG

2. https://books2read.com/u/4NqxDG

she once cherished—replaced by shadows of the past and a man who wants nothing to do with her. But as they find themselves sharing a home, old **sparks ignite,** and buried emotions resurface. Callie soon realizes that the past she thought she knew holds **secrets** neither of them can forget.

In **Faded Colors of Us**, Callie and Landon's story explores the depths of **regret**, the struggle to **forgive,** and the undeniable pull of a love that refuses to fade. Perfect for fans of emotional, slow-burn romance with a twist of **mystery** and heartbreak, this book will take you on a journey of **lost friendship, passion,** and healing.

Will Landon finally let go of the past, or are some wounds too deep to heal? **Discover a love story that's raw, real, and unforgettable.**

Also by Nora Kensington

Rogue Negotiations
Blame It on the Boss
Secrets Beneath the Vows
Faded Colors of Us
Waiting for You to See Me
Bound by Fire and Fuel

About the Author

Nora Kensington is an author known for her captivating blend of romance, suspense, and adventure. With a flair for crafting complex characters and heart-pounding plot twists, her novels transport readers into worlds filled with passion, danger, and emotional depth. Drawing inspiration from both everyday life and her love of classic literature, Nora weaves stories that explore the intricacies of love, courage, and resilience.